THE SEIGE OF AECORATH

BOOK 1

# DAWN
# OF
# AVARICE

TABITHA MIN

RITTER HOUSE
PUBLISHING

www.tabithamin.com
Book and Cover design by Designer Eve A. Hard
eBook ISBN: 979-8-9877812-0-3
Paperback ISBN: 979-8-9877812-1-0
Hardcover ISBN: 979-8-9877812-2-7

First Edition: March 2023
10 9 8 7 6 5 4 3 2 1

*For Matthew, my fortress.*
*And for our children, our beautiful legacy.*

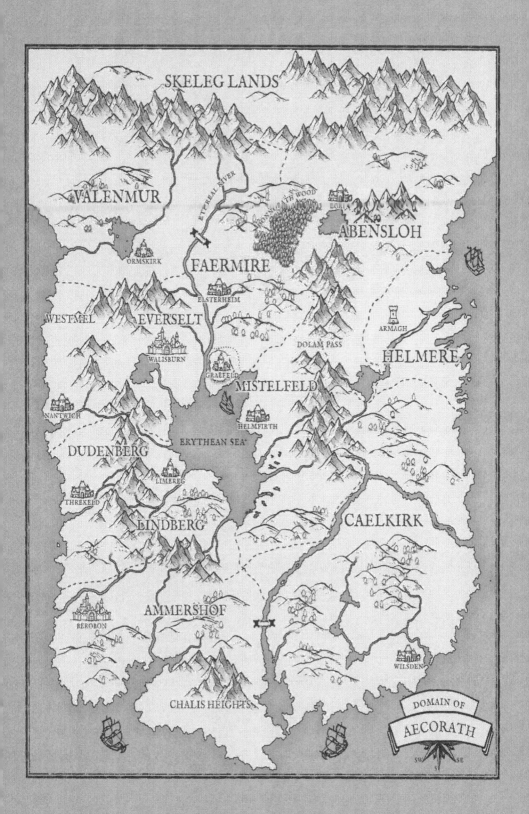

# DAWN
## OF
# AVARICE

# PROLOGUE

## KINGDOM OF MISTELFELD

AS THEY LIFTED THE BODY onto the pyre, all she could seem to feel for the man was indifference. The queen's stoic expression left little room for anyone present to guess how she had felt for the man whom she had been married to for the past fifty years. She stood tall against the bitter wind which ushered in the coming winter. And the fur which lined her emerald-green cloak gently kissed the sides of her aging face. Her silver hair hung heavily over her back in a single braid, paying tribute to the long life which she had lived, a life wrought with turmoil.

As the ritual began, she curled her arms even tighter into her body, wrapping herself deeper within her cloak. Gorhan, the seer had arrived to preside over the ceremony and entreat the gods on his behalf. It was rare for the seer to make an appearance unless the gods demanded it or perhaps his empty pockets. And her husband was certainly not known for his frugality, among other things. So, it was no surprise that Gorhan would oblige such an occasion.

The old man had covered his body with deep blue inscriptions and symbols of the old language. Like clay, the paint had begun to crack and fade against the open air. But for his eyes and for his mouth, fresh black tar seemed to drip and run together down toward his throat in one continuous stream. He shook and rattled the bones of animals he had long since sacrificed and lifted his hollow eyes toward the heavens where he uttered words unknown to those around him.

The dark skies above them gave further credence to the man's abilities as he trembled and shouted toward the churning clouds. *He is rather convincing...* she thought to herself.

After he lowered his slender arms, the local priests ushered in the two women whom the king prized most. They wrestled and screamed with their hands bound, pleading for their lives as they were each strapped down on either side of the ashen body whose eyes had been stitched shut. The drums then began to pound as a torch was lit. Gorhan then unsheathed his dagger and swiftly plunged it into the king's chest, wrenching and splitting the bones apart until he could finally reach his hand inside. Their screams grew louder along with the beating drums as he dug deeper, twisting and cutting until the king's heart was lifted into the air. He continued to chant as the dark blood spilled over and between his fingers while they squeezed tighter and tighter around the engorged organ. He then smeared his blood drenched hand across the women's faces and replaced the heart into its former place.

The women cried as they helplessly fought to pull their faces away from his hand which painted their soft porcelain skin. They struggled tirelessly until their voices were drowned into silence by the gurgling blood which filled their mouths as he drew his knife across their throats. They each grew quiet as the life left their bodies, leaving only their tear-filled eyes to watch it drift away from them. Blood dripped and rolled further down into the pyre and the seer grabbed the torch from the priest's hand, thrusting it into the pile of wood set beneath them.

The queen sighed in relief, as if by some means, her husband would find a way to cheat his death and return to her, fulfilling the dream she'd had the night before. But finally, she could see the man wasting away beneath the flame which engulfed him. She was finally rid of the bastard, and his whores.

It took everything she had to keep herself from smiling, until something suddenly caught her eye. A dark figure emerged on the ridge line just beyond the valley, looking down toward the funeral where they stood. She focused harder until she could make out the silhouette of a man seated atop his horse, watching the proceedings from afar. As time passed, she watched as the figure remained stoic in the distance, only watching, perhaps even waiting.

Until finally, just as suddenly as he appeared, the rider was gone once more. She watched as the man disappeared behind the billowing black smoke and out of sight.

She waited a moment longer, and with her eyes still fixed on the ridge, she signaled for her servant, who approached her and lowered his head with reverence. She leaned toward the man and calmly uttered,

"Send for Ludica."

# CHAPTER 1

## ELSTERHEIM, KINGDOM OF FAERMIRE

"BEOWYN, PLEASE! YOU CANNOT KEEP hiding this from Father. If you go, I will not lie for you any longer."

Estrith clung to her brother's tunic as he lifted himself onto his horse, indifferent to her pleas.

The frost still clung to the ground as the sun was still yet to peak over the horizon. Her nervous breaths left her lips in a cloud of frozen haze as she scurried to meet his eyes.

"I never asked you to lie for me, sister," he replied. "If you wish to tell him, then I will not stop you." He then kicked his heels back, forcing his horse onward toward the gate.

She watched anxiously, hoping that just maybe he would turn back around. Though the fleeting hope quickly disappeared along with her brother through the night.

Moments later, she could hear the distant bells toll as the temple signaled to the rest of Elsterheim that a new dawn was upon them. By now, her father would be on his way to pay homage to the gods, and she dare not be late.

All she could think of as she made her way to the temple was what she was going to tell him. She meant it wholeheartedly when she'd told Beowyn that she wouldn't lie for him any longer. But protecting him was simply part of her nature. They had been born together, and they had been there for each other ever since. And as much as she hated him at that moment, she loved him too much to let him face their father's wrath.

As she entered the temple, she could smell the robust incense filling the air around her. Numerous priests chanted deeply in the old language while performing the necessary rituals meant to appease the gods.

This was to be a new cycle, bringing the next full moon, which meant that Manoth was the god that they were to entreat. Outside, the commoners waited for the leaders of Faermire to finish first before they could enter and pay their respects to the highest of gods.

Ludica, their king, knelt at the foot of the statue which had been wrapped in the finest gold. It stretched to the ceiling and towered over the people who stood beneath it. Two large torches were fixed on either side of Manoth where a sacrificial table made of black granite sat between them and their god.

Estrith quickly winced and lowered her eyes as the priests then brought a young goat onto the table and slit its throat. It was a ritual that they had done time and again, but one which she could never bring herself to watch. The blood rolled into the carved gutters along the edges of the table and down into a moat at the foot of Manoth's throne.

Her younger brother Siged sat beside her and watched with eager anticipation as they then handed the severed head to their father, the king. He accepted the offering and lifted it up toward the god of death before drinking the remaining blood which dripped from the young sacrifice's lips.

As he took the final drop, all she could see was Manoth's eyes begin to glow red with fire. The god, though human in form, grew large antlers from his head, which curled and bent around the brazen halo behind him. In his right hand, he held a sphere with a serpent wrapped around his arm, where on the left, was an outstretched hand waiting for the offering to be presented.

The priests then began to chant louder as a deep groan seemed to emanate from the statue itself and faint whispers echoed through the walls. It was then that the priests signaled for everyone present to lower themselves in reverence to the power which was before them. As she bowed her head to the ground, she took notice that her brother was still watching the events in awe and was unaware of those around him. So, she quickly pulled him from his trance and forced him to lower himself to the floor along with the others.

The groan grew louder along with the whispers until a pulse of energy rippled through the congregants. Like a muted blow, she could feel the breath of Manoth flow through her chest and out of her back, spreading from one person to next. Finally, it faded away once the last of the blood had been drained from the table and she blew a stiff sigh of relief upon realizing that she had been holding her breath the entire time. Manoth's hollow eyes slowly returned to their previous form as Ludica slowly lifted his head from the ground, followed shortly by the elders of the kingdom.

She was glad it was finally over. She hated being in the presence of the great Manoth but perhaps that was the point. The god presided over those whose lives he chose to take and those he chose to spare. Fearing such a god and giving him the respect, which was due, would serve those well who chose to take heed.

After the ceremony, she made it a point to be the first out the door in hopes of avoiding her father but soon heard his call before she could make her exit. She sighed with dread and turned to see her brother pull his scrawny hand from the queen's grasp, taking her place as the first through the door. She could hear the giddish tone in his screams as he ran through the courtyard followed by his friends, wielding their wooden swords as they waged a fearsome battle.

She would give anything to be in his place at that moment...

Her father spoke briefly with the men who were present before calmly making his way toward her. The elders then made a collective push toward the court as the queen and the remaining patrons filtered out of the temple while the priests concluded the remainder of their ritual and gladly accepted the offerings presented on behalf of their god.

Ludica passively handed a by-standing priest the cloth which he had used to wipe his face and hardly made a gesture to acknowledge his daughter as he approached.

"Where is your brother?" His deep voice echoed throughout the room as the two stood alone together.

She could feel her insides begin to churn as she responded,

"I believe I just saw Siged run into the courtyard with lord Berwyn's children." She scrambled to carry on before he interjected. It was a futile attempt to redirect the conversation.

"I will not ask you again."

She couldn't help then but lower her eyes in defeat. As she opened her mouth to speak, the king's aid appeared through the door.

"My lord, the elders are waiting for you in the court."

Ludica kept his eyes fixed on her and calmly answered the man,

"Will they proceed without me?"

"W-well, no, my lord, you are the king," the man stuttered with nervousness.

"Then the elders can wait."

"Yes, my lord," the man replied as he bowed his head and slowly shut the door once again.

"I've endured your lies on Beowyn's behalf long enough, Estrith. But no longer. Why have the guards reported to me that they've seen him travel alone toward Valenmur on numerous occasions?"

"I do not know— " her words were suddenly cut short as she felt the sudden sting of his calloused hand sharply smack the side of her face. The throbbing pain was felt instantly, and she could sense the red print of his fingers emerging on her cheek. She struggled to keep the tears from erupting but knew the next time she lied to him; he would not hold back.

"He is with a woman."

"What woman?"

"He would not say." she felt the second slap reinforced over the first. Only this time, she could no longer withhold the tears as they trickled swiftly down her face.

"I swear on my life, father, he would not tell me."

Her hands clung to her cheek as she struggled to manage her composure in front of the man who towered over her. She couldn't help but see Beowyn's face through her father's own resemblance and felt as if she had been slapped by her own brother instead.

Ludica's peppered dark hair contrasted the piercing blue eyes that studied her. The man was built for war and had the scars to prove it many times over. Though years of battle and politics had proven to wear on his once young and tender good looks as well.

He relented to her answer and sighed sharply before shaking his head.

"If he refused to tell you, then it is because he needed to protect her name as well as his own... That boy has only ever chosen to think with anything other than his mind and will prove to be the demise of everything I have worked for."

He then lifted his hand towards his daughter, gently reaching his palm over her reddened cheek. She hesitated briefly before finally allowing him to touch her face. Her fair skin stood out against the auburn hair which draped gently over her narrow shoulders. Her hazel eyes flickered against the reflection of the torches around her as she wiped the tears away and struggled to meet her father's gaze once again.

The king sighed, and she could see the tension in his shoulders drop along with the sharpened tone in his voice as he studied her.

"If only you were born to me a son. Then I would delight in the day that I should relinquish my throne to you."

Her father paused a moment longer, then leaned over and gently kissed her head. The tender kiss left her in a mild daze as she then watched the man turn and head for the door, signaling toward his men.

"Find my son and bring him to me at once." His heavy footsteps echoed throughout with each passing moment, and it was a sound that she could never seem to forget. It was his steps that she could always seem find amidst a crowded sea of people. And it was always his presence that she somehow feared yet could find solace in all at once.

In all her years, she had only ever known the man to smile by the count of the fingers on one hand alone. And yet two of those times she knew to be on her account. But it only took the first, for her to know that she longed to see it even more. It was as if she had been able to unlock a hidden mystery which she had never known before, and like an unrelenting thirst, she needed to see it again, if only just once more. . .

Her father's men quickly acknowledged the king as he exited the temple, and she watched as he slowly disappeared behind the door while it slowly shut behind him.

Then all at once, she could feel the cold and hollow emptiness of the room about her. Like a stiff chill that ran down her spine, she suddenly found herself alone in the hallowed temple, watching the light from the torches bounce against the walls around her. And yet there also, was the statue of Manoth which sat before her. Its hollow eyes were all that she could seem to focus on as they peered down at her from across the room. The god of death seemed as if to contemplate her fate as his oppressive stare began to creep into her very soul.

# CHAPTER 2

## KINGDOM OF VALENMUR

BEOWYN GENTLY KISSED THE YOUNG woman who clung to his bare chest as the two lay quietly in bed together. Her soft blond hair draped gently over his arm as he caressed her naked hip repeatedly. She smiled and drew her leg slowly over his own before pressing her lips onto his neck.

The fire had begun to die, and the cold night air was beginning to break through the crackle of the burning wood.

"Aren't you cold?" he asked as he tilted his head back and closed his eyes.

"Not anymore," she replied. "You do well enough to keep me warm at night."

The inn where they frequently met was finally quiet. Not an hour earlier, the place had been filled with the loud clamor of its many guests. The ale had done its job well though, as it seemed that the pair were the only two left awake at this late hour.

It was a place of ill repute considering their class, but it was well suited for their needs. Beowyn had dealt with the owner on numerous occasions and found that he was a man which cared little to know about his guests, so long as they paid their bill. And considering that he was a patron who frequently paid for a room in advance, it was reason enough for the inn keeper not to ask any questions.

As they lay together, he couldn't help but recall a man who had sat across from the door as he'd entered the inn earlier that night. Normally, most of the inn's patrons were too involved in their own affairs to notice when another came or went, but on this occasion, it wasn't hard to miss the stranger's frequented glance.

Beowyn usually made it a point to limit his time downstairs and would make his way to the room where Tanica would be waiting for him. He would often find himself weaving through the crowd and sifting through the chairs as the thick air permeated with the smell of stale bread and men alike. The only thing which seemed to add a bit of class were the musicians who played by the hearth, albeit slightly out of tune.

It wasn't long before he disappeared up the stairs, but he could still feel the stranger's gaze upon his back. Then, as he made his way up, he noticed the man stand in his periphery and casually leave the tavern.

Perhaps it was nothing. And perhaps, he was simply over thinking the mundane. It had left his mind entirely until he found his thoughts drifting later in the night. One thought led to the next, reminding him of his sister's words before he left their lands. He knew her warning rang with truth, as it was only a matter of time before his father would find out, with or without her help.

Though seeing the woman he held in his arms made it worth the risk, even if it was just for another night. He loved her and she loved him equally. Of course, he had considered countless times the repercussions of their relationship but couldn't bring himself to end their bond. Tanica was reason enough to forget everything when they were together, but on this night, he couldn't help but be reminded of it all.

Finally, he sat up from the bed and pulled the blankets of fur away, resting them on her supple skin.

"What troubles you?" she asked.

"I grow weary of hiding," he replied.

"Beowyn—"

"We've carried on like this for far too long, and for what? Our fathers' feud is their own, not ours." He carried on, audibly reasoning to himself as to why their union was justified. But the longer he continued, the more he found it somehow difficult to believe the reasons which he had devised himself.

But finally, the sound of Tanica's voice cut through the noise of it all in his head. Though the reprieve was less than comforting as he soon discovered.

"My father would gladly kill you if it meant simply to spite Ludica. I could never bear the thought Beowyn..." She pulled herself close to him, resting her head against his back. After some time, he heard her hesitantly say the words...

"He plans to give me away in marriage by the first of spring."

In that moment, he could feel everything within him wrenched with pain. His heart sank just as quickly as it flooded with shock to hear the words spill over her lips.

"To whom?!"

"Beowyn..."

"Tell me." It took all that he had to hide the anguish in his eyes but to no avail. He watched as she lowered her head to avoid meeting his gaze and took the moment of the piercing silence between them to gather her words.

"There is talk that I am to wed Nothelm, the high councilor's son..." She waited briefly for a response but was met instead with a silent disbelief.

"I did not wish to tell you for exactly this reason. I'm sorry—"

"Come away with me."

"What?"

He was growing desperate. And with all logic and reason cast from his mind, it was all he could think to keep himself from losing her. It even seemed like perhaps he could see that she was considering the notion, if not just for a fleeting moment.

The dying light from the fire clung to her golden hair like an anchor in a blackened sea. The hazel color in her tender eyes disappeared amidst the darkness in the room, but he could still see the worried expression upon her face.

"But where would we go? If my father ever needed a reason for war, Beowyn, that would be it."

"I don't care."

"Stop it! If you truly don't, then you are fool. Think of what you are saying!"

"Tanica, please..."

"You are to be king, Beowyn. Do you not think that I would give up everything to spend my life with you? I have spent every waking day trying to think of any possible way this could work, but the truth of the matter is that it cannot..." Tears began to flood her eyes and drip from her cheeks as she turned herself away from him.

"I love you, Beowyn, with every fiber of who I am... but our love was doomed even before it began."

In that moment, all he could seem to feel was utter despair. She spoke the very words that he tried desperately to suppress within himself, and it cut him even deeper when it was spoken aloud. But even when it was said, he still could not bring himself to find the right response.

And whether it was the cold seeping in, or the sadness that so quickly overcame her, Tanica began to shiver and pulled her arms closer to her body. The very image of what sat before him was far too much to bear. For she was the one thing in his life that he knew to be right. From the moment he first laid eyes on her, it was as if a new life had taken hold of him. One which brought him happiness for once. And so how could one relinquish such a gift when it was all that he was truly able to cherish.

It was her love that he longed for, and she freely offered it to him alone. She was everything to him and for that, he was willing to risk it all. But if such a risk also meant the possibility of losing her forever, then he found himself to be at a crossroads. By all accounts, it seemed that he would lose her one way or another, and so it was left to him to decide if one decision posed a lesser risk than the other.

But all the while, there she remained before him. And even as the reality of all that they faced grew ever more oppressive, her soft and trembling body called out to him. He could do nothing at that moment but pull her deep into his arms and kiss her. He brushed her golden curls aside and caressed her cheeks as she looked to him for comfort. The two lovers embraced each other as she cried, and he gently wiped the tears from her face. Even as she was overtaken with such sadness, the man could not keep from being lost in her beauty.

Whatever the future held, they still had each other in that moment and for them, it was enough.

Then, suddenly, the door flung open as a man kicked his way into the room. Several others followed closely behind with their knives drawn as they rushed toward the couple.

Beowyn reached for Tanica as they pulled her from his arms while she screamed.

"Tanica!" he shouted as he flung his fist at the first man he could find and then another. The small room grew even more crowded with each passing moment, but if he retained anything meaningful from his father, it was how to fight, even in such a circumstance as this. He fought desperately against the four men which surrounded him and nearly succeeding in breaking free of their grasp. But like cornered prey, they soon overran the young prince, beating him into submission and forcing him to the ground. By the end, he quickly found himself beneath the sharp tip of a blade being pressed further into the skin of his neck. The man at the other end of the blade, pushed it further, forcing him down to the ground as he winced in pain. The others quickly pinned him down so that he could no longer resist the inevitable and he slowly relinquished his grip as he finally surrendered.

"Get him up," one promptly ordered, and they quickly pulled the man up from the ground before leading him back down the stairs.

Outside the tavern, the men threw him into the frozen mud, with his nakedness exposed for all to see. Several torches lit the night around him as he lifted his bloodied face from the ground. His sight was blurred and a mixture of both blood and sweat slowly seeped into his eyes.

He was surrounded and felt like little more than the dogs which barked from beyond the circle. All eyes were fixed on him and the men who sat atop their horses watched with a collective amusement at his humiliation.

After pulling himself up, he wiped his face and spat at the mud beneath him. He fought against the instinct to shiver amidst the bitter cold and took a moment to calm his labored breaths.

Before the prince, stood a man who towered over him while gently tapping his finger against the pommel of his sword. And before long, the man slowly began to remove his gloves as if contemplating the young prince's fate. He remained silent and unrelenting as Tanica threw herself at the man's feet, pleading for Beowyn's life to no avail. Instead, he gestured toward his men, who then yanked her from the ground. She cried aloud and wrestled against their grasp, and she reached back toward them as his men forced her onto a horse nearby.

"Father please! I beg of you!" she cried.

Beowyn helplessly watched as the rider seated behind her turned the horse away and kicked his heels back, urging the horse on and into the night. In a single moment the woman whom he loved disappeared into the darkness beyond the torches' light. All that remained of her were the distant screams that soon faded just as quickly.

The prince soon found that the moments of contemplation he had earlier in the room were all for naught. For whatever choices he felt lay ahead for him and Tanica were quickly made on their behalf. No sooner did he have her in his arms, when she was just as quickly ripped away from him. He hadn't even the ability to process the loss of the woman he loved when there before him stood the very man who would seal his own fate that night.

He was alone and at the mercy of the king who had yet to even speak a single word. The man just stood there waiting, and patiently formulating his thoughts as his men took their cue from their leader.

The prince had nothing to grant him solace and knelt alone in the mud. Then finally, the man before him opened his mouth to speak.

"Beowyn, son of Ludica. What am I to do with you?"

## Elsterheim, Kingdom of Faermire

The king gently rubbed his brow as he listened to the elders bicker amongst each other within the court. Word had spread that Graefeld had begun attacking villages to the south, breeding talk of yet another conflict.

"We should have taken the city when we had the chance!" cried an elder from the northern hills.

"And risk losing half our army to their stronghold? Your madness rivals only your stupidity. The reason Graefeld remains is because it stands atop the Golis bluff," another argued.

The city remained a barbaric fortress between the two kingdoms of Faermire and Mistelfeld. Its borders once expanded well throughout the land for over a century, until Ludica's armies had driven them back in the years that followed. He had considered an attempt to take the city but couldn't risk further losses with Ascferth waiting to seize a welcome opportunity against Faermire.

Ludica had known that one day, the consequences of his decision would come to face him, but what he couldn't understand was, why now? Something had changed.

Graefeld, he feared, was trying to lure them into a trap.

Perhaps they were in league now with Ascferth's army or that of another.

The men seated around him argued further, raising their voices in an attempt to speak over one another. An elderly man rose to his feet to silence the court as he directed his address toward the king.

"My Lord, my people have not the numbers nor the resources to withstand an attack should they make their way further into our lands."

"That's because your gluttony has consumed everything within your villages!" an elder interrupted. "If there is to be war in Elsterheim, it is because you will have squandered your ability to protect the king's road!"

"How dare you!" The elderly Rodmar's rotund belly jumped with each word that left his mouth, giving further credence to the accusation against him. He threw his finger at the man and the two began arguing once more, inciting the others to join them.

Finally, the king spoke in the midst of them, invoking silence from all who were present.

"I am well aware, gentlemen, of the implications regarding these attacks from Graefeld." His deep voice reverberated through the court, commanding respect with his tone.

"Such action implies that they have lost all sense of reason, or more else, they have found an ally."

"With Mistelfeld perhaps?" one of the men asked.

"The scouts report no sign of movement with Ascferth's army. If they were, we would've seen them mobilizing by now. Which we have not," one man replied.

"Then who?" another asked.

Ludica could hear the men begin to murmur amongst themselves yet again and found himself contemplating the barbarian motive just the same.

As the elders carried on with their debate once more, the door to the court groaned open with a lamented drone as though it ached with displeasure. Behind it, emerged the only man who could actually give account for the barbarian presence to the south.

"Pardon the intrusion..." he uttered. "Though it seems you have already begun without me." The man casually walked to his empty seat as everyone watched him, unamused by their silence. Then, as if the thought had nearly left his mind, he nodded toward the king with a passive sense of veneration.

"My Lord," he said.

"Brother..." Ludica replied. "What news do you bring of the south?"

"My forces have met the barbarians with little resistance along the border. They have seized Taernsby and ransacked the local temple of Shea. But we shall overtake them within a matter of days."

"Is that all?" An elder asked, discontented with his response.

"Would you prefer they'd have taken Oderburg? Or perhaps Narfolk even?"

"That's enough, Sidonis," the king interjected. "Their attacks are reason enough to consider the notion of an alliance with someone else."

"Well then, you overestimate them, my King. They are brutes. Nothing more than thieves and pillagers. Chicken snatchers..." The king's brother made little effort to conceal the sarcasm in his voice as he eased himself deeper into his chair.

Each seat was ornately carved from a single block of stone, with eight chairs that lined the court on either side of the throne where the king sat elevated before them.

Sidonis waved his hand at a servant who stood nearby and grabbed a chalice of wine as he began picking through the varied fruits on the young man's tray.

"The inclination, my Lord, that Graefeld has somehow managed to forge an alliance with anyone is nothing short of nonsense. They cannot maintain a solid governance amongst themselves, let alone an army," he continued. Further information regarding the ongoing feuds amongst those even worth mentioning made it seem as though the barbarians would just as rather wipe themselves from the face of the earth.

"You seem to have an intimate knowledge of the savages, Lord Sidonis..." an elder quipped.

"Better to know your enemies well, Lord Haemund, than to know your servants' beds," he replied as the man promptly slammed his fist down, his outburst quelled only by the king who rose casually to his feet.

"If it is as my brother says, then the barbarians shall be driven back to their lands and our borders reinforced. I will not provoke a war if there is none to be fought. Each of you will secure your lands as necessary until I call for you once more."

Ludica could sense the disapproval from some of the elders while the others approved merely with their silence. It had been some time since all the leaders from the kingdom had gathered together at the King's court, but the conference proved no different than any time before. Only this time, some arrived more aged and corpulent than ever before.

As he stepped down from his throne, the elders all rose to their feet and bowed toward the king. Sidonis, however, remained seated and downed the remaining wine in his cup before eventually joining the others. Once Ludica had left the court, the men also made their way toward the door, trickling out into the cold as they carried on with the subject at hand.

From the balcony, Estrith watched her father emerge from the court, brows furrowed, and his jaw clenched. He quickly disappeared through the stone pillars, as though he were trying to evade a hunting party, one out for blood. It was not her place to know of such things spoken of in the king's court, but it wasn't hard for her to find a means to participate by way of a covered space between the walls. One hidden enough to have gone unnoticed for as long as she could remember.

It was her only way of gleaning any sort of meaningful information about the kingdom, her home. Each of the elders gradually left the yard before her as they prepared for their journey back home. Sidonis, however, lingered behind, waiting as the last man disappeared.

Curious, Estrith watched as her uncle searched the yard for any stragglers and peering eyes, prompting her to pull deeper into the shadows which cloaked her. After a moment longer, he made his way toward a figure hiding in the corner. He then yanked a woman into the light and kissed her. The two joined eagerly in a passionate embrace before the woman pulled herself away and smiled.

In that moment, Estrith watched in disbelief as Richessa, the queen, stared seductively into her uncle's eyes. She then glanced around the corner and led him by the hand as the two made their way to find their privacy, leaving her alone, still yet in the shadows.

She was quick to cover the gasp that nearly left her mouth. As shocked as she was though, it should've come as no surprise to her that the queen was capable of something like this. Though together with her uncle, this proved to be something else entirely.

The woman was cold, and equally abhorrent of anything that she deemed to be beneath her. She hardly so much as ever granted a passing glance or word at Estrith unless it was motivated by her own self-gain. The equally requited distance between the two women was a precedent which had long been established. And she was more than satisfied with it.

As for her uncle however, the man came and went from Elster-heim whenever he saw fit. His meetings with her father had become less in number over recent years, and his business within the capital was known to only those involved. He was charming indeed, and she admired his ability to gather information, no matter how insignificant it seemed to be. He always managed to know just how to use it when the time came. But also, much like her father, the man was a vault, albeit more charismatic. And what little times he did converse with her, she always found herself captivated by the stories he told whether true, or not.

But seeing the queen with her uncle stirred countless thoughts within her mind, none of which she could seem to make any sense of. Seconds felt like hours as she stood there pondering her next move and when the thoughts eventually found their way toward logical sense, she emerged from her cover and walked confidently through the corridor once more.

# CHAPTER 3

THE PAIR HAD HIDDEN THEMSELVES away in a secluded spot at the furthest end of the western wing, safe from prying eyes. Neither of them said a word, but the faint echoes of their tryst could be heard through the door if one listened close enough.

It had become the place where Sidonis and his lover, Richessa would often meet whenever he found himself in Elsterheim. The two would steal away to the room and there, they would indulge themselves in an ongoing passion which had lasted for several years. Though, as of late, their meetings had become less frequent, as did his visits to the capital.

As they finished, Sidonis was quick to pull himself away and gather his belongings as Richessa studied him. He could feel her eyes glued upon his back as he fastened his belt and carried on with a casual, and somewhat distant disposition.

"Have I displeased my lord? Or is there perhaps another, with whom you have found favor?" Richessa tugged gently at her dress and smoothed it over with the palm of her hand.

He scoffed at the notion and turned to face her.

"None can please me the way you do, my love. At least not yet..." he chuckled softly but noted the rapid shift in her expression. He had apparently struck a nerve.

"I have not seen you in months, and when you finally come to me, there is hardly any word spoken between us."

"If it is idle talk you desire, then perhaps lord Edric's wife would be better suited for the task."

"The woman is no better than a boorish hen, and yet, even she knows more about the affairs of our land than I."

It was clear to him that she had learned of Graefeld's movements from talk amongst the elder's wives. A most abhorrent revelation for the queen to be robbed of such first-hand knowledge. Sidonis looked at her as a smirk emerged on his face.

"So, then it is more than just talk you seek. And just when I thought you only wanted me for my body."

"I want more, my love," she replied as she slowly approached the man. "I want to be more than just a shadow of an existence. I want more than our childish affair, always hiding ourselves away in secret. I want to be *your* queen, Sidonis, truly. To rule as a queen should rule by her husband's side, and I want that husband to be you. As it always should have been. . ."

He couldn't help but find himself somewhat taken aback by her words, but they spoke to him in a way that he found enticing. In all their time together, the woman had only ever offered herself to him in a way which satisfied the burning lust he felt for her. But now he grew fonder of her in a new and somewhat endearing light.

"And what is it I am to do about your plight, Richessa? As I last recall, you are married to my brother, the king. Am I to commit treason on your behalf?"

"To commit treason, would imply that you're positioned on the wrong side. What I am merely suggesting my love, is that you be the man I know you to be and take your rightful place. You are no less a shadow in this world than I, Sidonis. Only I am the one who has no say in the matter."

"You have the one thing in this life Richessa, that a woman like you has ever needed or wanted for that matter. You have your throne, your 'king', your power, and your heir. Do not think for a moment, that we were ever alike, 'shadow' or otherwise. Your only fault in all of this is that you still play yourself as the desperate whore—"

He could feel the sudden sting of her hand smacking the side of his face. Her cheeks grew as red as the fiery hair which draped down her back and her lips pursed tightly together.

He had struck the final blow.

He merely chuckled aloud as she stood there watching, overwhelmed by the apathetic insult he threw in her face.

"Do not speak to me of what you do not know, Sidonis. My throne and power are both meaningless to a man who sees me as little more than something he can hump. And my son is all that keeps me from being cast aside like the slop they use for pigs.

"You actually stand a chance to be more than what you are, and yet you have only ever squandered the opportunity. For a man who sees himself as larger than life, you have left little to mark your legacy by. And if you wish to know what others truly see of you, then you have but to merely look at their faces when you enter a room. . ."

Whatever motivation she had to speak to him in such a way came from a place he had never known of her. Be it that she saw him as lesser man for the role he played in this life or merely a pawn in her scheme, he wasn't sure. And truth be told, she saw in him the one thing he hated most about himself, and it vexed him.

But, at that moment she had proven herself to be more useful to him than what he had previously thought all these years. Though, what he could not decide was whether he should subject himself to the defensive barrage of insults, no matter how much they rang with truth.

The pair stood together in silence before he finally broke the tension.

"Legacy..." Sidonis chuckled, as he said the word aloud. Somehow repeating it made seem even more imperious. The lingering sting from her slap nearly had him consider returning the favor. Instead, he took a step closer and gently stroked his finger down her cheek, tracing the sharp line of her jaw. Her pale, green eyes studied him with apprehension as she waited for him to speak. The man drew himself closer and began to lift a loosened lock of her hair toward his face.

"Shadow or not, Richessa, yours is a legacy that will be forever tied to that of my brother's. His triumphs, his power, and everything in between, are what shall be written down for the ages to come. And by his name, there yours will be also; marked forever as the wife of the man whose illustrious reign would stand the test of time. Yet even now you say that it is not enough?"

He waited as she looked to him, seemingly searching for the one thing she longed for. She peered deeply into his eyes before finally leaning in for one final kiss and whispered into his ear,

"Make me your queen, Sidonis. And you shall want for nothing."

Days later, the king paced throughout the castle grounds, sifting quietly through each of the problems that were added daily to his

list. First, granting priority to the most pressing issues at hand, and then to the rest. One by one, he created the list in his mind, but the foremost being that of his son.

His men had yet to return with Beowyn, and it festered within him each passing hour. The heir to his throne was the last of those he would have chosen to rule, but he was his son, nonetheless. Reckless in every sense of the word, and yet, he was the very image of his father.

He could not fault the boy for inheriting his own foolishness in youth, but if the years of hardship had taught him anything, the throne did not care for reasons or excuses... it demanded responsibility. And that was nowhere to be found in young Beowyn.

He paced through the halls and into the courtyard, where he suddenly found himself standing before his brother, who had just entered the grounds from within the city.

"I thought you had left," he uttered.

"Apologies, dear brother, I was unaware my presence here would prove such a burden," Sidonis replied. "My men are in need of supplies and ale. So, I took it upon myself to grant them leave. Though we shall be gone by morning if it pleases the king." He bowed his head in an over exaggerated manner before taking a large bite from the apple in his hand. He took a moment and studied the king before continuing,

"You are troubled, Ludica, I can see it in your eyes."

"I am always troubled, Sidonis," he replied.

"Indeed. I suppose the burden of kingship weighs heavily on those who care enough to be a good king. And a good king you truly are, Brother... Far better than I could ever be, but I suppose that is why the gods chose you to rule and not I," he uttered as he lowered his eyes toward the ground.

Ludica paused and cautiously looked to his brother. The two men stood in contrast of one another. Sidonis was tall, yet slender. His hair dark like that of obsidian and his eyes a pale and sharpened green. Though he did not match the brute strength of his elder brother, Sidonis was cunning and often found the advantage through his wit. He longed for the throne and Ludica would be a fool to think otherwise. Everyone longed for it just the same and the decades of political games grew heavily on the aging king. He was tired.

Ludica could sense his brother's attention drawn to the parchment in his hand. The man's eyes briefly scanned the paper as if hoping to read the contents marked within it, so the king gently rolled it back and carefully placed it at his side. Sidonis softly chuckled at the gesture, noting the somewhat defensive posture Ludica held against his presence.

"Whatever vexes you brother, I am sure it is of little consequence. You always seem to know just to how to make it right in the end. Though perhaps it is something more which brings such plight to your eyes. If that is the case then, perhaps I can—"

"I have little time to waste, so tell me what it is you want, Sidonis?" Ludica asked. If there was anything the man grew more weary of, it was it his own brother's endless schemes. Though his words were curt, he could see the mood quickly shift in his brother's face as he abandoned the humble facade and returned a stern look into his eyes.

"I want nothing, Ludica, not from you. This land, the home of our father, our ancestors, is everything to me. I would gladly give my life to protect this kingdom as I have so willingly offered many times over. Do not forget that!" The soft expression on his face suddenly formed a sour and embittered one as he lowered all but his eyes before the king. His words became sharp and any attempts at civility swiftly fell apart.

"If it is my loyalty you question, then you have truly lost touch with all sense of logic. You may be the king, Brother, but do not forget that it is I who protects the throne on which you sit. It is I, who safeguards our borders, and it is I, that knows all within our walls!"

Ludica felt the rage boiling within his veins as he fought with every fiber to contain it.

"Mind your tongue, Brother, lest you lose it!" The two men inched closer to one another with hardened fists and unwavering glares.

The tension between them was broken only by the sound of tolling bells in the distance. They could hear the guards shouting from the gates as they scrambled to alert those around them.

Sgell suddenly appeared from around the corner and approached the men as he lowered his head in reverence toward the king.

"What is it?" he urged.

"My Lord, Elwin rides from Valenmur to our gates. . ."

The two brothers glanced at one another before Sidonis tightened his hand around the sword fixed at his side and made his way toward the city's gate.

"He rides with his army and. . . and Beowyn stands among them," the servant continued. Eorhic, captain of the guard soon arrived at the king's side also, to give account of their defenses.

"Bring me my sword," the king demanded.

Panic filled the air in the city as the king and his party made their way toward the outer wall which overlooked the palisades. People scrambled to secure their carts in the market and mothers led their children inside as others took advantage of the chaos at hand, stealing what they could before scurrying off through the alley. All the while, Ludica's men forced their way through the turbulent frenzy as they cleared a path for his company.

At the gate, the archers stood ready for their order to fire, and the soldiers prepared themselves down below. Ludica climbed the steps through the tower and onto the wall where he could see the numerous orange flags of Valenmur waving in the wind. A large army stood before them, with his son at the forefront. He was their trophy, displayed for all to see. Elwin's own two sons sat atop their horses on either side of him as they held the reins of his horse close to theirs. Hundreds of painted shields formed a blockade of soldiers behind their king as he proudly approached the city with an air of victory painted upon his face.

"Ludica!" the man shouted. "Send me Ludica!"

# CHAPTER 4

THE MEN WAITED IN SILENCE AS their king contemplated his next move. He couldn't help but keep his eyes fixed on his son tied to a horse, bloodied and bruised. A sense of desperation began to cloud his thoughts as he struggled to maintain a sound judgment through it all.

The bitter winds pierced through his skin like knives, driven further with each passing blow. Ludica's army stood with the physical advantage over the men of Valenmur, though he knew that Elwin held favor in his own hands by means of leverage over the life of his son.

He considered Elwin's move, like he would his own, had he stood in his Enemy's place. Elsterheim held the advantage over the land which the city presided. Behind it, however, the river stood at the city's back, giving way to a potential trap. Elwin could attempt an attack from the waters, but that meant exposure for his ships.

"Have their ships yet landed onto our shores?" he asked calmly.

"They have not, my Lord. Neither have our scouts found any remnants of his armies ready to make flank. It seems that they have taken the bridge at Saeragoth," Eohric replied.

"Then it is not a war he seeks..." He ordered his horse to be brought and gathered a party to ride out and meet Elwin in the field. Ludica looked at his brother, Sidonis, as he remained at the wall and watched with cautious amusement at all that was unfolding before him. Whether it be a sword, or a drink that Elwin sought, Sidonis would be sure to eagerly partake in either affair.

The large wooden gates moaned as the iron chains pulled them open before the king. He glared unwaveringly at the man before him and kicked his heels back, urging his horse out into the open terrain. Beyond the walls, they were alone, caught in the vast expanse of nature and isolation. The multitude of beating hooves on the ground beneath them rumbled along to the beat of his racing heart.

Elwin too, gathered a small party to meet them in truce, further away from his army. As their horses slowed to a stop he smiled and loosened his grip on the reigns.

"The gods continue to smile down on you, Ludica. Such a vast city you've grown since last I've seen you, old friend." Ludica remained silent as he studied the arrogant man before him. "But, alas, it seems that it is not for pleasant formalities which fate has brought us together again after such a time."

"I can see the blood upon my son's face even here, and yet you dare speak of formalities to me?"

Elwin chuckled and glanced over his shoulder toward the young prince, whose eyes looked eagerly at his father.

"With good reason, I can assure you," the man replied. "You see, it was in my own daughter's bed where I found that he had defiled her. And I admit that in my rage, I allowed my sons to beat him nearly to the end of his days. But by the gods, I have found it most favorable to both you and I, to spare his wretch of a life and return him to you."

Ludica's grip tightened around the leather reins which cracked and turned within his hands.

"What are your terms?" he demanded, and watched in disdain as Elwin leaned back in his saddle, tilting his head toward the gray skies above. The copper braids within his beard slid along his armor as he carefully gathered his words with delight.

"It has been an arduous journey, Ludica," he replied. "Perhaps this would be better settled over a drink and away from prying eyes. After all, my daughter's virtue and your son's dignity lie in the balance."

Ludica's men looked to the king in disbelief as he promptly agreed, but only on the grounds that Beowyn be released to them.

"Well, it's an issue of safety you see.... What assurances do I have for my men if your son is not there to ensure it for them? I have no guarantee that they will not be fired upon the moment he is released. So, no," he continued, "this, my friend, is non-negotiable."

Far be it that Ludica would dispute such a notion but considering the rage he felt for the man before him, he could not guarantee it either. He sighed aloud but nodded his head in agreement before turning his horse back toward the city. As they prepared to usher their horses onward, Elwin called out to his sons, who handed Beowyn's reins off to another, before riding toward their father. With his eyes fixed upon Ludica, he then leaned over to one of his men and gave the order,

"Secure the boy," he commanded. "Post scouts along the border should they try to seize him from us. If they should try, kill him." The soldier acknowledged the order and made his way back to the army. Ludica fought to hide his enraged expression as Elwin sneered and gestured for the king to lead them on.

Within the walls, Elwin and his men joined Ludica at the gate where a heavily armed escort awaited their arrival. The air was thick with the strain of their disdain for one another, but both men held their head high as they crossed the threshold of the city's walls. Soldiers whispered amongst themselves as Elwin's sons goaded them on. Both men looked nothing like their father, but perhaps that was to their benefit. The only resemblance they held was the arrogance that so readily emanated from their smug faces. They reveled in the moment and needed only the opportunity to strike the first blow.

Sidonis, however, broke through the silence as he approached the party.

"By the gods, Elwin, you've gotten ugly," he uttered with a pompous grin upon his face.

The man returned a slight chuckle as he replied with confidence,

"I thought I killed you, Sidonis. Pity. . ."

Ludica's expression remained stoic as he led them toward the castle.

He whispered an order to one of his men, who then scurried off to fulfill the king's command. Each step that brought them further into the city brought more curious eyes to the streets, as the commoners were eager to have their fill of theatrics. When only moments earlier, the same onlookers ran for their lives into any safe space that they could find within the city's walls, they now found themselves at the forefront of the streets to merely catch a glimpse of what was unfolding before them. The citizens bowed themselves before their king, yet kept their eyes fixed upon the man who once charged their very defenses.

Elwin's eldest son, Alfric, spat at the ground with disdain as the younger, Ealric, studied the city before him. He carefully observed Elsterheim's vast expanse of buildings which packed the endless web of streets around them and appeared to take mental notes of it all.

In that moment, Ludica found himself questioning whether he had made the right decision. He knew very well the nature of Elwin of Valenmur, and yet, here he stood, leading them beyond the gates and into his streets. There was a price to be paid, of that he had no doubt, but now he wondered if he made the mistake of becoming the one to pay it. The streets now appeared even more narrow than before, and the steps which led them toward the castle emerged as steep obstacles in his path.

As they reached the steps, Estrith, along with her brother stood next to Richessa as they awaited the king's arrival. The queen stood tall and proud as she held her head high while her hands remained loose and free down at her waist. Estrith, however, couldn't seem to stifle her nervousness as she tightly clasped her hands in front of her, knuckles white and breaths hastened with each passing moment. Siged stood curiously watching the men as they approached. His eyes widened with anticipation at the sight of the fearsome foreigners before him, but quickly turned to his sister and reached for her hand as she eagerly obliged.

Ludica rose up the steps to where his family greeted him with a bow. The king's council, however, stood in shock as they watched the very man whom they once waged war against, entering the king's court.

The group was led to the dining hall where Elwin and his sons eagerly took their place in their respective chairs. Those present remained silent as they watched the men happily glean from the king's reserves. Estrith looked to her father, whose eyes remained fixed on Elwin and waved the servants away as they tried to serve him. Richessa also watched in disgust as they ate and drank amongst themselves. Like watching pigs fight for the scraps and the sludge tossed out to them in the mud, she curled her nose, as if there was a stench too unbearable to withstand. Her furrowed brow then turned to Ludica with contempt for his role in their presence but seemed to go unnoticed by her husband.

Sidonis quietly sipped the wine from his chalice before raising his cup toward the burley king of Valenmur, who then wiped the food and wine from his thick beard. With a satisfied burp, he leaned back in his chair and smiled at the Ludica.

"Many thanks to you! We are grateful for such a welcome hospitality." His son Alfric continued his feasting, unamused by those around him, though Ealric soon eased himself also into his chair. Beyond the food and drink, he soon found his attention captivated by the sight of the king's daughter, who sat opposite him across the hall.

She could feel his eyes creeping over every inch of her body as she tried desperately to avoid his gaze. Thankfully, her father's resonating voice echoed throughout the room, commanding everyone's attention.

"In my old age, I grow weary of politics and formalities. So, tell me, Elwin, what is it that you want?"

The King of Valenmur hesitated briefly as he finished chewing the meat in his mouth. Small chunks tumbled over his lips as the grease trickled down his chin, and into his beard. The two men looked only at one another as if the room aside from them were empty. Each man studied the other, calculating and strategizing their next move.

"My daughter was arranged to be married by the first of spring. Though with her virtue no longer intact, Nothelm has refused Tanica's hand and therefore, a promising alliance. Such circumstances do not bode well for either myself nor my daughter. And all, mind you, at the hand of none other than your own son." He paused a moment longer before continuing, "So, I demand retribution. Recompense."

"What sort of recompense?" Ludica already knew Elwin's scheme but could not bring himself to say it aloud.

A smirk emerged on the other's face as he took another sip of wine.

"I had considered pulling the flesh from young's Beowyn's bones and my sons would have gladly obliged. But with such an opportunity, I found myself at odds.

Should I rather go to war once more with the great king of Faermire? Or forge a permanent alliance between my kingdom and yours through a marriage?"

"Your alliances, Elwin, are as thin as the edge of your dagger."

"And thus, such an agreement would forge a greater bond for us as brothers, Ludica. Brothers once more... My daughter will have her virtue restored and your son, his cock." Alfric chuckled as his eyes peered up from his plate to see the king's response. The others present remained quiet as they also awaited his answer, each with their attention fixed upon him.

An adviser stood to voice his response but was quickly waved to silence by the king.

"You shall have it," he responded. "If your daughter was to be wed by spring, then we shall keep the arrangement and will send for her upon the new cycle."

"Done!" Elwin promptly replied. The tone in his voice was suddenly appeased by the welcome, yet somewhat unexpected response. Alfric's expression, however, shifted quickly to that of disapproval and looked to his father, who ignored his sharp glances. All the while Ealric, kept his focus deeply fixed on the young princess across the way.

Though she had long been of age to be married, her father had yet to find a suitor worthy of his approval. And for that, she was thankful. Marriage would bring an end to her very existence as she knew it. The only respite would perhaps be to forge it in love, but the concept itself was foreign to her. Only through futile hope did she ever dare to dream of such a gift. Though many had sought to take her hand, none had even been granted so much as an audience with the young princess, let alone, the opportunity to gawk at her in such a manner. Ealric's glances only seemed to bring an overwhelming sense of dread which she couldn't seem to overcome.

The man, though admittedly rather handsome, presented a certain sense of foreboding that he carried with him. The way he peered through her as if he had already undressed her a thousand times over, sent a chill throughout her body, and she could feel the hair rise at the nape of her neck. His sharp features only accentuated the fierceness in his eyes, and it was those dark brown eyes that never left her while he remained. Unlike his brutish older brother, Ealric remained quiet and focused throughout the encounter and merely listened, while the others made a show for all to see.

Though finally, his fixation came to an end as both kings rose to finish their terms of agreement in private. Alfric's large stature demanded more food to fill his belly and so he chose instead to continue in his self-indulgence, ignoring all those who remained in the hall.

Richessa signaled for the maid to remove her son as she then rose to leave the hall as well. Sidonis gathered himself among the advisers while they whispered amongst themselves, then left on his own through the door, leaving Estrith alone at the table. During the brief distraction, she had found that Ealric was suddenly gone as well. Amidst the transitory commotion, the man had disappeared and was nowhere to be found, which she found to be a welcome opportunity. She then took the moment to quickly recuse herself to her own quarters.

Outside the hall, Estrith embraced the solitude and made her way down the corridor. The event would have normally garnered her undivided attention, and she would have made sure to be within earshot of her father's conversation with the king of Valenmur. Though, the unwelcome infatuation from his son soured any desire she once held to be captivated by it.

She had only ever heard stories of Elwin and his kingdom, but from what little interaction she had with the man and his offspring, she'd had enough for one day. Now, the further away she was from that place, the better.

As she rounded the corner, however, she suddenly found her path blocked by the very man she had hoped to escape. His height overshadowed her by a full head and the broad width of his shoulders obscured her view beyond his stance. The dark braided leather of his armor covered his chest beneath the cloak of fur which rested heavily on his shoulders. Metal gauntlets were all that stood in contrast to his harsh appearance and the dreaded yellow braid upon his head only added to the scabrous demeanor that he presented.

His outstretched arm blocked the way ahead for her, striking a resounding fear deep within. She couldn't bring herself to look him in the eye and risk meeting his gaze once more. It was far too much to bear the first time around. So, she turned to retrace her steps as she passively mumbled to excuse herself. Only once more, she found herself trapped by the lout.

"If I had known such beauty existed in all the realm milady, I would not have tarried so long to meet you." He vied to meet her gaze just as she eagerly fought to avoid it. She could feel the man inching closer toward her and if ever there were a time when she needed a guard nearby, there was none to be found.

"Let me pass," she demanded, hoping that he somehow missed the soft tremor in her voice.

"Would you rob an honored guest the mere pleasure of knowing the lady's name?" His playful smile only fueled his pressing more.

Honor. . .

"There is no honor here." His remark ignited something within her that began to squelch the anxiety which once gripped her. "You hold my brother for ransom, and yet you demand we honor you? Your hubris is as fruitless as your delusions. Now let me pass."

"Or what?" The man remained unmoved by her words. "Shall you scream? Or perhaps fend me off with those delicate hands of yours?"

Ealric reached over, gently clasping her hand just as she ripped it away. Overcome in the moment, she used the same hand to smack him as hard as she possibly could. His face jerked to the side, though not without returning a surge of pain throughout her palm. It was like hitting a wall, but more than worth it in the moment.

She watched as he rubbed the side of his cheek and looked to her once more.

"Not so delicate I see," he said, before he forcefully grabbed both of her arms and pulled her into his chest. She wrestled as hard as she could to pull herself free, demanding that he let her go.

Moments later, she could hear the call of her name from beyond the corridor by the guards.

"Lady Estrith!" The two men ran to where the pair stood, prompting Ealric to release his hold on her. He smiled as they approached and casually raised his hands in the air only after audibly sniffing her hair.

"Just in time gentlemen, the lady nearly had her way with me." Both guards held their swords toward the man as Estrith took her place behind them. Her father's servant, Sgell then appeared from around the corner with two more guards in tow. She had never known relief like she did in that moment to see the man and nearly cried at the sight of him. As they circled Elwin's son, Sgell prompted the princess to find her father.

"The King has called for you, lady Estrith, I suggest you find him at once."

"Yes, of course," she quickly replied. As she turned toward her exit, she could hear the deep tone in Ealric's voice echo through the hall.

"Estrith... A fitting name," he uttered. "I won't forget it."

She hesitated briefly at his response, but quickly took her leave and disappeared around the corner where Sgell and the others had arrived. The moment Ealric was gone from her sight, she rested her back against the wall to steady her trembling legs. As she stood there, she could still hear him talking amongst his captors. Though it was Sgell's response which drew her in once more.

"Consider this a gesture of Faermire's good will toward Valenmur. One son for another, young Ealric." She could hear the man scoff at the notion. "Return the prince to his father. We wouldn't want to escalate things any further than they already have today."

"And what a pity that would be..." Ealric replied. Soon, she could hear their footsteps heading further down the corridor and she too carried on, turning back to look for her father.

She later found him in the courtyard as the others gathered around him. He spoke amongst his advisers, presumably regarding the situation at hand and remained oblivious to her presence as she arrived.

"I am here, Father," she said as she approached the man, drawing him away from his conversation. He briefly glanced at her before responding with a slight sense of irritation in his tone.

"Very well, Estrith," he replied, and quickly returned his attention toward the men before him. It was clear to her at that moment, that Sgell's direction was merely a ruse, prompting her to leave the scene, which had indeed worked. Though not long after she had arrived, Ealric followed shortly after, along with his escorts to join his father.

Upon their arrival, Elwin and his sons were immediately escorted back to the gates. In a fleeting moment, she caught a glimpse of Ealric once again smiling over at her before offering a single wink and turned to join his family. Never, had she felt such contempt for a man she had only just met, but felt utter relief in seeing him leave once more.

At the entrance to the city, they casually mounted their horses before riding off toward the distant lights which were scattered throughout their encampment in the fields.

As they rode off, Estrith drew herself away from the party and climbed the stairs, up the tower, where young Siged had already nestled himself against the over-watch, eager to see the events at play.

"Siged! What are you doing? You shouldn't be here."

"Neither should you!" He quickly turned himself back toward the scene, for fear he that might have missed something during the brief distraction. Of course, he wasn't wrong. And so, she pulled herself up beside her younger brother as the two peered through the opening, waiting to see what would happen next.

She could see her father, Ludica, standing alone at the entrance to the city, as he waited for Beowyn's return. They all waited and waited through the silence of the night but heard nothing. However, the king remained still and unwavering in his stance, as though he were made of stone.

"Where is he, Estrith?" the young boy asked his sister.

"He is coming, Siged. Be patient." She feigned a calming smile at her brother but quickly turned her head back toward the field. She would've asked the same question had he not done so first. It had been far too long, or so it felt.

Still, they neither heard, nor saw anything.

"Estrith—"

"Shh!" She cut him off before he could finish the thought as she clung to the sound of what she hoped was that of a horse's hooves.

"There!" Siged shouted as he pointed into the darkness. "I see him!"

She squinted her eyes, hoping to pierce the veil and see where he had pointed, searching desperately, until finally the horse appeared into the light. She sighed in sheer relief and smiled as Beowyn's face emerged from the darkness.

But his head hung low as he approached his father as he stood at the gate to greet him. Both Estrith and Siged ran down the steps to greet their brother but were stopped short by Sgell's outstretched hand holding them back.

Beowyn slowly dismounted the horse and approached his father who remained silent. Estrith gasped at the sight of her brother's bloodied face, the blood dried and cracked around his nose and mouth. His eyes were swollen, and his hair matted from the mud which caked against his cheeks. He wore tattered clothes which were far too big for his size and his feet were bare, exposed to the harshness of the frigid air.

Ludica remained silent as he watched his son. His lips were tight, and his jaw clenched sharply together before he finally spoke, turning his head to the side.

"Have a healer tend to his wounds. And take him back to his quarters at once," the king curtly ordered.

"Yes, my Lord," Sgell replied with a bow as he ushered Beowyn along and signaled for the other servants to tend to their wounded prince.

# CHAPTER 5

BEOWYN COULDN'T BRING HIMSELF TO see his father again after what had happened the night before. Nor did he think that his father would even wish to lay his eyes upon him again. When they met at the gate, there was nothing but rage and utter disappointment in his father's gaze, and it cut him deeper than any of the wounds which he had already endured.

The new dawn brought only a fresh reminder of the night before as he stood atop the city's wall.

It shouldn't have come as any surprise to him that they would eventually be found out, but not this way. This way had never crossed his mind, and he paid dearly for it. As had Tanica, he presumed. He could still hear her screams as her father's men rode off with her, away from him. She called out to him and there hadn't been a damn thing that he could do about it. He longed for her now more than ever, to hold her in his arms and smell the sweet scent of lilacs in her hair. It was something which calmed him in a way that most things never could, and in that moment, he was unsure if he would ever get to see her again.

Elwin's men had only scoffed and prodded at him while he'd waited alone for word of his release. All he could remember was the sight of his father riding toward him and then off again only moments later with the very man he hated most. It had crushed him.

Beowyn had cycled through countless scenarios in his mind about how it all might play out within the city walls.

What sort of talks would bring about his release?

Clothed with merely a light tunic and worn trousers, he shivered as the cold winds engulfed him that day. Too cold to even move, all he could do to keep himself warm was to ensure his mind stayed busy.

But soon, moments turned to hours, and there was still no news of his release. Elwin's army ate and drank within the camp, encouraging one another with stories of battles they had once fought, all the while trying to outdo the latter with each story more gruesome and braver than the next. They had come ready for a fight, and it was all at his own expense.

Finally, there was a glimmer of hope through the darkness of night which had fallen over them. The light of their torches emerged, growing closer and closer along with the hope of his freedom. He could see Elwin first, followed closely by his sons and the rest of his party. Their king was brooding with a look of satisfaction on his face as he approached the camp.

He casually dismounted his horse and nudged his head toward the prince, who then rose eagerly to his feet. Alfric took the lead, pulling his knife from its sheath as he approached the prince. The battered man drew back at the possibility of his demise, only to have his ropes cut from his blistering wrists.

"Your life has been spared this day, wretch. Next time, I will ensure that it is not." Alfric uttered as he shoved the prince toward his horse.

The words continued to ring out to him as he stood atop the castle walls, surveying the land before him.

The morning fog had settled along the fields as Elwin gathered up his army to depart back toward their lands.

Estrith casually approached her brother, as they remained together in silence. She glanced up at him from time to time, catching glimpses of the deep wounds upon his face. The light of day brought a devastating appearance to his broken figure, and her soul sunk at his sight.

"You should be resting."

"How could I?" he replied. "I nearly brought our kingdom to its knees."

"Nearly, yes," she uttered. "But it is not, and you are alive... You should be resting."

Her brother remained quiet as he continued to look out at Elwin's army, replaying the events over in his mind again. She could see the shame which weighed heavily over him and turned herself toward a possible distraction.

"I've heard news that Graefeld has been spotted along our southern border. Uncle and his men have scattered the raiders with little resistance. Though I believe the elders were dissatisfied with his response. Lord Aethelwyn, more so than the others," she added.

Beowyn glanced down at her through his periphery before returning his gaze out beyond the wall.

"You've been sneaking into the council again..."

"What choice do I have? Only because I am a woman? Pff!" she scoffed. "Half the men in that room spend more time wetting their cocks than making themselves of any actual use to their people."

Beowyn, taken aback by her crass remarks, chuckled aloud only to wince in pain and reach for his ribs.

"Where did you learn that from? Certainly not within these walls..." he alluded.

"There are other passageways out of the castle you know."

"So, you fancy yourself an ale or two at the tavern, do you? Become one of the common folk..."

"Sometimes," she replied.

"Then it seems I am not the only one with secrets," he uttered with a gentle smile on his face.

"It would seem that way, yes." The two siblings looked at one another with amusement for a moment before they heard the sound of bellowing horns in the distance.

Elwin's army began their march back along the king's road toward the river Ethreal. His smile quickly disappeared however, as he then turned toward the steps. The brief distraction left him once more as he pulled himself back into the reality that stood before him.

"Where is father?" he asked.

"He remains at the gate," she replied as her eyes followed his every move.

Ludica watched from the city's gate as the men of Valenmur departed through the thickening fog. Their ranks disappeared into the haze like spirits passing through to the underworld. The sound of their feet marching through the field rumbled in the distance, as did the clamoring of their armor and weapons. And though they were no longer in his sight, the weight of their presence remained just as heavy as ever before. It clung to him like chains around his neck.

"What an interesting turn of events!" his brother suddenly quipped. Ludica glanced over his shoulder to see Sidonis standing with his hands clasped behind his back.

"And here I was ready to depart when suddenly an army stands at your gates. Never a day without turmoil is there? Truly inspiring, Brother..."

Ludica ignored the man, only responding with little more than a subtle sigh. As he turned to leave the wall, a soldier alerted the men to a distant rider approaching the city from the king's road to the south.

As he emerged from the fog, he raised a green pennant in the air and slowed his horse nearly to a halt.

"Mistelfeld, my lord!" a soldier shouted.

The two brothers looked at one another with surprise as they made their way down the steps to greet the messenger.

"Raise the gates!" Eohric commanded. The rider quickened his pace and brought his horse into the city.

As his servant greeted the man, he received a sealed parchment meant only for the eyes of the king and presented it before him.

Ludica broke the waxen seal and read the contents inscribed by the queen. The words on the page were many, but the king lifted his head and looked to his men, citing only a single line from it which read; *Ascferth is dead.*

"Well then, it seems that Gwenora seeks to make an alliance with you now that the king is dead." Sidonis was quick to piece together what little information was presented. "Will you?"

Ludica ignored the man, turning instead, to Sgell, ordering that the provisions be made ready for his departure the next morning. His brother further pressed him on the contents of the letter, only to be stifled by his silence.

"See to it the rider and his horse are fed and well rested. Ready my ship as well, we shall set sail at dawn." The messenger of Mistelfeld, bowed his head in thanks to the king as he guided his horse toward the stalls, while his men worked to fulfill his order.

"Do not think that I have forgotten our conversation yesterday, Sidonis. You will ride south again and meet your men at Taernsby. There, you will remain until I send further orders," Sidonis sneered at his brother's command, though he nodded his head in acknowledgment.

"As you wish," he replied curtly.

He turned to make his way toward the tavern as the king and his party left through the city. His men greeted him with merely a nod as they returned to their food while seated at a table near the back. It was quiet in the early morning hours. The keepers were still tending to their chores around them from the night before as the local minstrels would not return until the coming night. The air was stale, and the fires had burned until only the coals remained.

"What next Lord?" one asked.

"Quiet," he interjected. "I need to think." The others continued in their conversation as the man pondered silently amongst them. Several minutes later, he lifted his head with a smile on his face. He grabbed a cup from one of the men and took a sip.

"We shall return to Taernsby as the king commands. Though, there is someone whom I should like to meet."

As Ludica entered the court, he hesitated briefly at the sight of his son who had been waiting for him near the empty throne. Beowyn quickly straightened his posture and watched his father approach the seat. He held out his hand toward Sgell, who then passed several documents to the king.

"There are several matters I must tend to, Beowyn. So, if there is something on your mind, I suggest you say it quickly." He hardly lifted his eyes from the papers he held while carefully sifting through them.

"I-I've come to apologize, father. For all that I have caused you with my recklessness."

"And what would you have me do then, my son? You have chosen not just any women in the land to bed, but the very daughter of Elwin, the King of Valenmur. It was not recklessness Beowyn, but more akin to treason in my eyes."

"Treason?" The word took the prince aback as he stood alone before the king.

"Father, I did not seek her out. It was merely by happenstance when I met her, I did not know who she was."

"And it was by happenstance that you fell into her bed no less! You were to be king Beowyn!" The rage in his voice erupted from the depths which he could no longer contain. His hands tightened into fists, knuckles white with strain as the papers crumbled beneath his strength.

"Were? Father, what are saying?"

"Leave us. . ." Ludica waived his servant out of the court so that they alone remained.

"What were the terms of my release?"

"Marriage." His father promptly replied.

The young prince could not find the ability in that moment to piece together all that was unfolding before him. The idea of marriage to his beloved Tanica was welcome news but stifled at the potential loss of his inheritance.

"You were reckless enough to risk your kingdom for your lust, that much is certain. And if it is that woman you wish to marry then she is yours." Ludica lifted his head and his eyes to meet his son's directly so that he knew the words spoken were to be heard.

"Elwin desires to fight a war with Everselt but has always lacked the numbers to do so. You, however, provide the means and the numbers for him to wage his war, and it was a welcome opportunity by the gods as he sees it.

"What better way for him to rule both Valenmur and Faermire than through the very man who is set to inherit my throne? Under the guise of marriage, he seeks to usurp my power, and that of yours as well."

"Tha-that cannot be."

"If you cannot see it as plainly as I, boy, then you are no more fit to rule this land than your brother who has yet to reach his tenth year. You are a fool, Beowyn!" The king tossed the papers at the prince's feet and rose from his throne.

"His terms demand that we forge an alliance between our lands through your marriage to Tanica, and I have agreed to that as such. You will marry the girl, but you will no longer inherit my throne."

"What?"

"When Siged is of age, he will take your place as king, and you shall dwell in Valenmur with your wife."

"You would damn me to be Elwin's jester in his courts, and disown me as your son for the sake your pride?" Beowyn's face grew red with anger as he quickly abandoned his submissive tone.

"Not mine, Beowyn. But yours."

"You cannot do this!"

"I can. And it is already decided. Come spring, you will have your wife and you shall go with her back to her father's lands. What you do once you get there is no longer of any consequence to me."

The prince stood quietly, defeated by the shock which overwhelmed him. Whether it was rage or despair he felt most in that moment, he couldn't tell. Only the silence which filled the air around him remained to give him little solace. His father's footsteps soon faded in the distance and eventually disappeared behind the door as it closed shut.

Left alone to face the reality of his father's words, he nearly crumbled to his knees. In a single moment, everything he once held; his birthright, his people, and his dignity were ripped from his very hands that day, and there was nothing he could do to stop it. The woman whom he loved also was to be used as a weapon against him, and the only person he could bring himself to hate in that moment was his father. That much was certain to him.

As he pulled the doors open to the courtyard, two soldiers met him at the threshold. He looked to each man, who were careful to avoid his gaze. They tightened their stance and acknowledged the prince as he emerged.

Beowyn shook his head with disdain as spoke aloud,

"Am I to be a prisoner within my own home?"

"The king has ordered us to remain at your side, my Lord. For your protection."

He scoffed at the notion and pushed his way past them. Out in the yard, he could see his brother Siged playing amongst his toys which had been carved from wood. And there he stood, watching the boy creating a world within his own mind, unaware of the world around him. One toy slammed into the next between his hands as he mimicked the sounds of a gruesome battle and the dying soldiers as each were slain by a fearsome warrior.

Raising his head to further his game, he suddenly noticed Beowyn standing opposite him by the court. The young boy was filled with delight at the sight of his brother and jumped into the air, leading a sprint toward the man.

"Brother!" he shouted, raising an object in the air as he approached. Words then began to spew from the boy's mouth in an endless stream which he could not seem to contain. The excitement at all the useless news he had gleaned since last they saw each other was too overwhelming to form into coherent and meaningful phrases.

Beowyn, however, remained silent as he watched Siged ramble on and lift his head up at him more times than he could count.

"And, and Eohric showed me how to carve this snake. You see?!" He raised the wooden object up toward his face which he noted to be crude at best but promising.

"I made it for you," he uttered as he waited for his brother to accept the gift. With all that he tried, Beowyn could not bring himself to hate the boy who was set to take his place. And what anger he had garnered before that moment had been wiped clean by the sight of a poorly carved serpent at his chest.

He slowly clasped the object in his hand to his young brother's delight as a grin, wider than the breadth of his cheeks, emerged upon his face.

"You have quite the gift, Siged," he uttered with a slight grin. "Thank you." He gently clasped the side of his brother's head and ushered him along to play once more. In all of his days, that boy could only ever bring a smile or chuckle for Beowyn, and perhaps one day when the time drew near, he could bring himself to hate him, but in that moment, all he could seem to feel was sadness.

He brushed the thoughts from his mind as he felt the words of his father creeping up within him again, but the more he tried to forget them, the more suffocated he began to feel. Suddenly, he could feel the world around him beginning to shrink and his breaths grew shorter. He meant the words he spoke to Tanica that night in the tavern; that he would leave it all behind so long as they could be together. But not like this. His father meant to spite him for the sake of their love, and he meant to discard his own son merely out of convenience. For in the end, Beowyn would be nothing more than a pawn in the schemes of his father and Elwin. And he wanted no part of it.

What should have been a joyous occasion for him, was turned bitter by the callousness of his own father, as it seemed to be nothing more than a game to him. But as much as he longed with be with his beloved again, he couldn't stay in that place a moment longer. Not to be played for a fool. So, he had to do something, anything. But it wouldn't be in the palace, that much was certain. He would find a way to be reunited with Tanica once more, and it would be the right way. But until then, he needed to escape. So, he turned to search for his sister; the one person who could help him in his time of need.

He scoured the castle grounds, eventually finding her in their father's library.

She rose from her seat, surprised by his abrupt arrival. And as his guards remained at the door, he swiftly shut the door behind him.

"Beowyn..." she muttered; eyes widened with bewilderment. He lifted his finger to his lips and quickly searched the room.

"Is there anyone else here with you?" he asked as he subdued his tone.

"No," she replied, "I am alone. What is going on?"

"You said there was more than one way to get through the city. If that is so, then there must also be a way to escape unseen."

"Escape? Beowyn what are you saying? What is going on?"

"You read all of these books, you know these walls inside and out, surely you must know of another way!" He was careful to lower his tone again as he looked toward the door.

"I will not help you unless you tell me... now."

He sighed as he lowered his head but nodded in agreement. The words slowly poured from his mouth as he recounted the conversation and the words spoken to him by their father. First, there was the deal with Elwin. Followed then, by his own disinheritance of the throne and subsequent banishment from the land, come spring.

As Beowyn spoke on, Estrith could do nothing but listen. The shock of it all overwhelmed her just the same as it did for him, and she slowly lowered herself back into her chair. He continued for some time before finally dropping his head in defeat as he leaned onto the table between them.

"I cannot stay here. I cannot be a prisoner here and do nothing as my life is stripped away from me..."

"What will you do then? Where will you go?" she asked with a sense of hopelessness in her voice.

"I shall find Qereth, and perhaps then I will know." He looked to her with desperation in his eyes as he pleaded for her help once again.

"Please, Sister, surely you must know of another way."

She hesitated and shook her head in disbelief, mumbling words quietly to herself. Finally, she raised her eyes to meet his gaze and opened her mouth to speak.

"I know of only one..."

# CHAPTER 6

THE PLAN WAS QUESTIONABLE AT BEST, but he was desperate enough to try anything. She informed him of a passageway which supposedly led out of the city through an old sewage tunnel beneath the castle.

It was meant to act as an escape for members of the royal party should the city ever come under siege but had never needed to be used. She directed him to the cellar where he could find the hatch, most likely buried beneath a pile of goods.

"You've not seen it?" He stopped her as she spoke.

"Well, no," she answered.

He dropped his head as it shook from side to side.

"Then how do you know it actually exists?"

"I told you that I know of it Beowyn, not that I've had the occasion to use it! Pardon me, if I've not had the desire to casually stroll around in excrement with the rats, just so that I could see our city from a different perspective!" She rolled her eyes and sneered at him. "I'm not the one who's trying to escape you know," she then added.

"Fine. Alright, I'm sorry. Carry on," he relented.

"That's it."

"What do you mean, that's it."

"I mean, that is all I know. It is supposed to lead you out of the city, but to where I cannot say. That is up to you to discover for yourself."

He sighed aloud, dissatisfied with her response but carried on with his need to distract his newly acquired entourage.

"Well, it's the only option, so then I suppose I must. But I'll need a favor from you first."

"What is it?" she asked.

"Have a rope brought to my room."

"A rope? What for?"

"To hang myself with..." he muttered sarcastically. "To escape, you dunce!"

"Watch your tone with me Beowyn. I am after all, the only person who can help you and I will not be treated as such."

"My apologies, Sister. You're right. Now please, go and fetch me a rope."

She finally agreed and rose from the table before making her exit through the door. He followed shortly after and emerged from the room as the two men took their place behind him. He then led them on a leisurely walk through the castle grounds before eventually making his way back towards his room.

"I think I shall rest a bit," he noted to them before entering the room where he spotted the rope his sister acquired at the foot of his bed.

In his desperation, he quickly gathered his belongings and secured his weapon to his hip. With all that he could hold on to his person, he then lifted the rope and wrapped it around the leg of his bed, tugging on the knot to ensure it's hold.

As he peered out through the window, the cold winter air pierced his cheeks, sending a chill down into his spine. No guards could be seen in the vicinity, so he tossed the rope out as it clacked against the stone wall. One more search for guards to reassure him, before he leapt over the edge and repelled down towards the window below.

Estrith poked her head out and looked up, surprised by the sight of her brother's boot nearly missing her face. He scurried down carefully as she then reached out, helping him into the room.

He quickly thanked her and readjusted his belt before making his way to the door.

"Wait!" She caught his arm in her hands as she drew herself into his chest, tightly wrapping herself against him. He winced from the pain shooting through his tender ribs, but eventually joined her in the embrace as they stood before warmth of the fireplace.

"Don't do anything foolish Beowyn please. I cannot lose you."

"You won't." He calmly replied as he smiled down at her. "I swear." After a gentle kiss on her forehead, he swiftly disappeared through the door, leaving her behind.

Outside, Beowyn quickly made his way through the halls and down the steps to the cellar, being sure to avoid anyone he could see. His heart raced as he looked in every direction, hoping to avoid his detection by any guards that might spot him. And it seemed that perhaps, the gods found favor in him that day.

Upon reaching his destination, he searched the room and displaced whatever barrel, crate, or sack he could find which might have hidden the door. Finally, he spotted an iron latch on the floor beneath a collection of large barrels in the corner by the grain. He nearly missed it but noticed the large wooden container he was moving caught on the handle has he slid it aside.

He smiled with delight at the confirmation of his sister's well-found knowledge and began shoving each of the barrels aside to finally gain access to his means of escape. Being careful not to expose the door, he placed the barrels and remaining supplies strategically in front and around the area, so that none would find it.

One item after the next, he lit a torch and made his way through the hatch and dropped down into the tunnel. The putrid smell of feces pierced his nose as he coughed and gagged, nearly vomiting at his feet. There, he could see the dark waters flowing nearly to his ankles as the rats scurried from the light of his torch. He then wiped the liquid which had splashed onto his face as he fell before taking his first steps through the darkness.

The trail was straight enough but felt longer than the days as he slowly trudged through the filth and the stench. Distant squeals of the rats echoed through the tunnel in front and behind him as he carried on. One would scurry past his feet as others seemed brave enough to run between them. Some were too large to even be called a rat and he cursed heavily as they appeared before him.

Finally, he spotted what looked to be light breaking through from further down the way. He quickened his steps and found himself looking through a heavy grate which continued further down the path. He then looked up toward the light where a long, skinny shaft stretched toward the sky. Several wooden boards barred the opening overhead, but it seemed weak enough for him to force his way through.

And with no ladder in sight, he reached for his knife, taking note of an oddly shaped stone in his periphery. He paused, and pulled the torch over the wall, revealing a deeply carved symbol which had been engraved within the rock. It appeared as though it was a letter, or perhaps a word in some foreign language which he had never known.

Curious, he gently traced the markings with his hand and briefly pondered its origin. If this passage was meant for the royals, then why had he never seen this symbol before? It was mysterious, ancient perhaps, but beautiful in its contours and turns. He stood there for a moment longer, taking mental note of it, as he hoped to share its discovery with his sister. For surely, there would be something written of it in one of those books she had always been reading.

Though soon, he quickly remembered the task at hand, and brushed the thought aside. He then lowered the torch and pulled his knife from its sheath. He thrust it deep, wedging it between the stones to anchor his hold and climbed upward, to the top of the passage. After several forceful shoves with his shoulder and prying with his knife, he eventually forced his way past the rotting wood and out into an abandoned village.

It was for him, a relic of the past which he had never known. A once vibrant place, it now crumbled beneath the weight of its own decay. Trees had long since grown through parts where there were once roads and buildings. And a tangled knot of dead vines weaved in and around each of the structures, too weak to maintain their own walls.

It was a place that had long since been forgotten. And he wondered for a moment, how long it had been since people once inhabited this site as its streets once bustled with life.

What was left of it, had only but a little while longer before the forest would completely swallow it up and become lost forever. Now, the earth was reclaiming its land, nearly blotting out its existence entirely. Still, what was left of it, paved the way for his escape, and it remained a beacon which would serve to mark the preservation of his freedom.

*Many thanks, dear Sister*. He smiled as he thought of her in that moment.

But finally, he heaved himself over the edge, and rested on the ground to catch is breath. The covered shaft from whence he came, appeared to have once been a well, converted to serve as a tunnel from the city.

*Clever*, he thought to himself as he rose to his feet. And from where he stood, he briefly struggled to find his bearings. He searched his surroundings and could see the outer walls of Elsterheim stretched along the outskirts of the landscape, painting it as a monument of strength. From there, he would travel east, in search of his friend.

Several hours later, the sun was nearly set and there was nothing familiar that he could find in the woods where he stood. The night was nearly upon him, and the cold was wrapping its frigid fingers tighter around him as he searched in every direction. The foliage crunched and cracked beneath his feet as he carried onward, hoping to find a village or shelter to grant him solace.

Suddenly, he stopped. All had gone quiet around him, and it unnerved him deeply. Not a bird or animal in sight. There was nothing and he was alone. He carried on a few steps longer, gripping his hand tightly around the handle of his sword. He paused to listen and searched the woods for any movement that he could find but still, there was nothing. The hairs on his neck and arms stood tall as he felt the unshakable notion that there were eyes watching his every move.

Then he froze. The tip of a sharpened blade rested on the center of his back. He held onto the grip of his sword as he waited for the opportunity to turn and fight his assailant.

"Tis a fool's game, wandering the wood alone at night and without a horse." The deep voice behind him pierced through the silence deeper than the blade against his back.

"Turn around. Slowly..." the man calmly uttered.

Beowyn obliged and inched his body around toward the voice he heard. At the other end of the weapon stood Qereth, his friend, with a smile on his face. He chuckled aloud as Beowyn shoved the weapon aside and pushed him back out of frustration.

"Gods, friend, your face looks as though it had been ravaged by a beast. And you reek of shit!" he noted as he lifted his arm to his nose.

"Was it that whore at The Spotted Pig who did you in? I've always warned you against that one, but it seems that she's bested you after all. Tell me, Beowyn, is it those hearty thighs of hers or that enormous ass you can't seem get enough of?"

"It's the tits actually," he quipped as his friend nodded his head in approval and laughed.

"Indeed," he noted as he replaced his sword into its sheath.

"I've heard news of your escapades with Elwin and his army. I am glad to see you alive, my friend." He slapped his hand against the prince's shoulder as he led him deeper into the woods.

"And I you, Qereth," he replied with relief in his voice.

"Come," his friend ordered. "There is a stream up ahead where you can rid yourself of the stench, and my hut is further along the way."

As the darkness settled, Beowyn could hear the welcome sound of the stream his friend had mentioned. The water was frigid and quickly brought numbness to his hands and feet as he submerged them beneath the surface. He was hesitant to remove the rest of his clothes and expose himself to the biting elements but overruled his restraint with the need to wash the filth from his body.

He gasped sharply as he fought the impulse to withdraw himself from the water but scrubbed even harder before dipping his garments into the stream. Qereth bid his time as he waited by collecting tinder and wood for the fire he had yet to light.

"One thing is certain, Beowyn," he added, "your ability to maintain stealth is just as weak than ever before. Between your smell and iron clad feet, the hunt for game around here is scarce, to say the least."

Beowyn scoffed as he finished with the washing and pulled himself back onto the embankment, where his friend held out his own woolen cloak lined with animal skins.

"Thank you," the prince said as he eagerly wrapped it around his shoulders for warmth. The two men continued up along the stream's edge to where a small wooden hut rested against the towering roots of a large tree.

It had been quite some time since Beowyn had visited the place, but as they drew near, everything looked exactly as he remembered it. Qereth was an avid hunter and knew these woods like the back of own hand. Even in the dark, he could find his way, and it was always something that Beowyn envied of his friend. As they entered, both lowered their heads to make the shallow clearance of the door, and Qereth made his way directly to the small fireplace within the wall.

"You can hang your garments there so they can dry by the fire tonight." He smacked one hand of flint against the other which held his steel, and sparks then flew into the tinder by his feet. A few moments later, the sight of tiny embers glowed red in the night as a small stream of smoke emerged from the bundle he lifted to his face. As he blew, a flame began to consume the shredded moss and twigs between his fingers, prompting him to place it back within the fireplace and add more to fuel its hunger.

After he was satisfied enough with his work, he rose back onto his feet and lit several candles within the room. Beowyn observed his surroundings with the welcome ability again to see.

A single make-shift bed rested in the corner with a small trunk at its foot. Beside him, was a small table and one chair where a lonesome candle and a cup used to hold his cutlery rested. From the rafters hung a few small bundles of herbs to dry which he had gathered. Another trunk was fixed against the wall opposite him, where he assumed random miscellaneous objects were stored. It was small, but it had certainly served his friend well all these years.

"For such a skilled hunter, Qereth, I have yet to see any of the spoils you kill around here."

"Well, like I said, Beowyn, you scared them off." Qereth gently placed his bow and quiver full of arrows by the bed. "I've only just arrived out here this morning to start my hunt. That is when I found you wandering aimlessly like an idiot." He could sense that the statement had further meaning to it however and the man and reached into his satchel, from which he pulled a bundle wrapped in cloth and placed it on the table along with a biscuit.

"Here," he offered. "It's not much to fill your royal belly, but I'm sure it'll do for the time being."

Beowyn unwrapped the cloth to find several strips of dried meat tucked within it. He suddenly realized the pangs of hunger he felt at the sight of it and reached for a piece, pulling it apart with a stiff tug. The more he chewed, the more he realized he needed another and could no longer contain himself as he reached for one piece and then the next, finishing himself off with the biscuit at last.

Qereth glanced at him with amusement before tending to the fire once more as he knelt beside it.

"Tomorrow you can you make yourself useful and help me bring back a decent meal for us both to enjoy. But first, would you like to explain to me what it is that brought you to me in this state? Or shall I guess?"

Beowyn paused for a moment, forcing the last bit of food down his throat as he raised his head to meet Qereth's eyes.

"It's that wench from the tavern, isn't it. She bears your bastard..."

Beowyn shook his head at the notion before replying with a simple, "No."

"Ach, well carry on then."

Beowyn rolled his eyes but began with his introduction to Tanica and eventually led to their discovery by her father. Then came the deal between Elwin and his father and finally the news of the marriage which had been arranged, along with the disinheritance of his father's throne because of it.

Qereth remained silent through it all as he listened intently by the fire. One event led to the next, and finally came the personal grievances over his misfortune and the circumstances which he found himself in. Beowyn noted his desire to prove himself in some way or another and show his father that he was wrong. He needed to find a way to make himself worthy again, or at the very least, change his father's stubborn mind.

By the end of it all, Beowyn waited for Qereth's response as they both sat in silence together.

"Well?" Beowyn asked.

"I think I liked my story better," Qereth replied. Beowyn feigned a chuckle and remained silent as he waited for a response.

"Well, you certainly have a knack for finding trouble everywhere you go, my friend. But in truth, I do not know what I can say to help you in this matter. There is no direct answer, I think that will solve your problems as you so desperately desire. That is something you will have to discover on your own, I'm afraid."

Beowyn hung his head with disappointment but understood the truth in his words.

"I am but a humble servant of his majesty, the king. Merely a hunter whose only quandaries lie in whether I will find meat for the day or not."

He was a man of equal stature to Beowyn but whose blond hair formed a tight braid over the top of his head while the sides were shaved. The stubble on his face lined the sharp angles of his jaw where a small scar formed at the base of his ear.

The two had been friends since they were boys, and each thought equally of the other as a brother. His father was Aethel-wyn, an elder amongst Ludica's court and longtime adviser. And had it not been for his older brother, Qereth would've had to shoulder the burden of becoming the next elder and lord over their lands in Caelfall. Much to his own dismay. The man hated politics and anything to do with it. He was content with his place in life, and perhaps that is what led to his often care-free disposition.

After some time talking and sharing stories with one another, Qereth added a final stack of wood to the fire for the night. He then leaned his chair against the wall and rested his feet on the table in front of him as he crossed his arms over his chest and pulled his cloak tightly around himself.

"Get some rest, Beowyn, we'll have an early day ahead of us tomorrow."

The prince happily complied and laid himself down in the bed on which sat. The warmth from the fire spread throughout the room like a blanket as it popped and crackled beside them. A moment later, he shut his eyes and all that had happened that day disappeared as he drifted off to sleep.

The next morning however, before the sun had yet to rise above the ridge, Qereth shook the prince awake, jolting him from his slumber.

"Get up," he said. "There's something you need to see."

Beowyn looked to find that the fire had long since died down to coals, and he could feel the chill in the air as he rose from the bed. He quickly gathered his clothes and dressed himself, along with his equipment which had been laid down by his boots.

Qereth led him through the woods and quietly laid himself down along the side of a hill overlooking the road below. The two men waited, as they could hear the sound of horses approaching from the distance.

They peered over the top, where they could see his uncle, along with several of his men in tow.

"It's my uncle," Beowyn noted. "He must be rejoining his men in Taernsby where they are posted." A glimmer of hope emerged in his eyes as he entertained the idea of joining them.

He pulled himself forward as if to leave his cover only to feel the staunch grip of his friend's hand around his arm.

"Wait," he whispered. "That one there... I recognize him." He then pointed to a burly man amid his uncle's train as they led their horses along the road. His dreaded hair and dark, sunken eyes complimented the man's sour disposition, as he rode quietly atop his horse. From what he could recall, Beowyn had never seen the man before, as many times as his uncle had ridden into the city. But he had many men within his ranks. Far be it, that the prince should know all their faces upon first glance. Even one who rode so confidently at his uncle's side.

But Beowyn could see that Qereth was troubled. His friend lay quietly upon the fallen leaves as he carefully formulated his thoughts and made the connections in his mind.

"I've seen him before and I'm sure he's the one. I'm certain of it."

"What are you talking about?" Beowyn asked with a hint of frustration in his tone.

"A year past, I traded some veal along the border, and he was there at the post with several others from Graefeld."

"That. . . cannot be. Qereth, are you sure?"

"I am certain, Beowyn. I dare not forget a face that tries to cheat me out of my coin."

"It's a mistake. You must've recalled it differently, or perhaps—"

"That man is from Graefeld, Beowyn. I swear it on the gods."

He didn't want to believe it any more than Qereth, but the implications remained heavily in their midst. They both looked at one another and back to the caravan, moving slowly past their position.

"If this is true, then we need an explanation." He paused as he also began to work through the information presented before him.

"He means to regroup with his men at Taernsby, and I intend be there when he arrives."

Qereth nodded in agreement, and the two slowly dropped away from their position before heading back to the hut where Qereth's horse remained.

As Qereth pulled himself up onto the saddle, he lowered his arm and pulled his friend up behind him. The animal suddenly lurched forward as they quickly weaved in between the trees.

"It'll be nearly two days ride at their pace before they reach the town. We shall ride to Caelfall where I'll collect a horse for you and if we hurry, we can be there in time. I know of another route."

Beowyn acknowledged the plan, and they rode off through the trail. He couldn't seem to make sense of it all and soon found himself doubting Qereth's words about the man he saw. But he also never had any cause to distrust his friend and resolved to grant that trust yet again.

What he couldn't bring himself to understand, however, was the reason for his uncle's betrayal. If it were even the case... But for what cause could his uncle possibly have to bring this man among his ranks? This same man of Graefeld who only just walked freely among the walls of Elsterheim not a day before...

# CHAPTER 7

FOR NEARLY TWO DAYS, BEOWYN and Qereth rode unrelentingly toward the southern border of Faermire, stopping only to allow time for their horses to rest. As they approached the small town of Taernsby, it appeared only as small dots along the horizon from where they stood.

"We'll need to find a way into the town unseen," Beowyn noted. "They could arrive at any moment." Qereth searched their surroundings and directed the prince to a small forest further to the east.

"We can stow our horses there," he suggested. Beowyn nodded with approval, and they ushered the animals into the woods, where they secured them to a tree. As they departed, the two were careful to avoid detection, hiding behind anything that they could find. Time, however, was quickly passing them by, and they could soon see Sidonis approaching with his men along the main road.

A large contingent of Sidonis' men remained scattered throughout the town as they collected the bodies of dead civilians and soldiers alike following the raids which had been reported. A large pile of bodies sat just within reach of Taernsby's edge, where a wagon was fixed beside it. Several more bodies were piled inside, ready for transport to a mass grave which had been dug in the fields.

"Gods, look at this place..." Whatever mention of minor skirmishes that took place here, far underestimated the true caliber of what he saw before him. The place had been ransacked, left on the brink of utter destruction. "This was a slaughter."

As two men added another corpse to the heap, Qereth rushed toward the bodies once their backs had turned.

"Qereth!" Beowyn watched in shock, as he leapt into the wagon for a closer vantage. He shook his head in disbelief as he then searched the area, opting to hide himself among the bodies in the pile.

Moments later, they could see Sidonis arrive at the town's center and was greeted by his men. He gave orders to some as he remained on his horse and called for the man whom Qereth had recognized earlier on the trail. They spoke privately with each other briefly, and the two then directed their horses up the hill to the city fixed upon the Golis Bluff.

They're headed to Graefeld... he thought to himself as he looked to the wagon where Qereth lay. His friend remained lifeless among the dead and he was left alone to sort through it all himself.

The small town was fixed just beyond the border of the two kingdoms of Mistelfeld and Faermire. It would've hardly been a blip on the map for anyone to find, if it wasn't for the trading post it offered to those who crossed along the king's highway.

Beowyn had only ever been there once, and it had been rather forgettable to him at the time. With only minor businesses present to offer essential trades like the local blacksmith or the market, he never sought out the opportunity to return. Though it served its purpose at the time, now, plumes of smoke emerged from the charred remains of structures that were once functioning buildings.

The streets were empty aside from the pools of blood which had saturated the ground. The soldiers who remained sifted through the piles of rubble and wood, looking for what may be left to salvage for their own pockets.

Until now, there had been peace in the land with Graefeld, since the war had ended so many years before. Though it was more of a truce, agreed upon only due to the substantial loss of life over the last remaining city that was left of their kingdom. The Golis Bluff was Graefeld's only vantage, inaccessible by the sea from the towering cliffs of basalt columns upon which it stood. And the singular access point left the kings who fought for the land at a stalemate. Over time, infighting amongst the leadership further degraded the city into a rabble of factions fighting merely for their survival. The highway stood as a means to some civilization as they traded and sold for what they could glean, but remained cut off from the rest of the world. Eventually, many had left to find a better life elsewhere.

Graefeld was often found to be the one blamed for the upsurge in attacks on people who traveled the king'sroad in recent years and thus, further efforts to secure Faermire's border was made. Taernsby became the new military out-post for those who had been all but exiled by the king, Beowyn's uncle included.

As he searched for another spot to move to, he shifted his sight to find another body being thrown onto the wagon where Qereth lay. The two men rambled on over frivolous matters and turned away again to fetch another corpse. He cursed beneath his breath when the sound of his uncle's voice suddenly called over the men he governed.

"Send a party out and collect the lord of land for me. I wish to have a word with him. . ."

Several soldiers rose from where they sat and volunteered themselves as they gathered around their horses and rode off to the north, past the area where they hid.

The pounding of hooves upon the softened ground, flung mud all around with some splattering on the bodies which faced the road. The stench wafted further into his nostrils as he pulled his head into the leather sleeve of his jacket. He suddenly found himself looking into the eyes of another who stared passively into his own.

The realization left his heart to skip a beat as he gazed into the face of a woman, long since buried amongst the others. Her pale face and ashen lips lay hidden behind her dark brown hair which fell like a curtain onto another beneath her. Her eyes had glossed over and the once hazel shade which brought life to her flesh, was fading into obscurity.

He lowered his head and shut his eyes, pulling himself closer, forcing his body to go limp as he could hear their footsteps quickly approaching. From the depths of his core, he wanted nothing more than to leave this place, but found that this was the one spot where he could be safe.

Sidonis surveyed the landscape before him as they rode up before the city. What was once a beacon of power and strength, showed nothing more that the battered remains of a feeble and dying man. Graefeld's defenses were lacking as were the walls, which needed only a strong gust of wind to knock them down. He despised it and all who dwelt within the wreckage, considering them to be little more than the rats they ate.

As they entered the gates, he looked only to the palace where Helgisson stood awaiting their arrival. Many watched the pair from the street with apprehension as a thick cloud hung overhead.

Many of the buildings had become dilapidated, some threatening collapse, but the people seemed either unaware or simply lacked the desire to care. But with Sidonis, came a curious opportunity, and the numbers grew to see what he had brought to offer them.

As he dismounted from his horse, he casually removed a sack from within his saddle bag and threw it at Helgisson's feet. Several gold coins spilled out from the opening which had loosened from the impact.

"Your spoils of war," he said, as he opened his arms wide to offer his good graces. The man glanced down at the offering before him with discontent and curled his lip. He then turned his back and made his way into the palace. A smile emerged on Sidonis' face as he followed shortly after the man.

Several onlookers rushed to grab what they could as they fought to get past the soldiers for the sack, and Sidonis' bearded companion spat on the ground before finding a place to sit as he watched.

Inside, Helgisson took his place at the end of the hall where Sidonis approached. The former grandeur of its walls towered over them, revealing their insignificance within it. Faded murals of the ancients and the battles once fought lined the stones which surrounded them and the muted light from the sun emanated through the windows behind the man and his throne.

He was tall but lacked the fortitude of strength that his counterparts offered. His long yellow hair lay in dreads upon his shoulders and his beard grew untamed from his face as it sought to entangle itself with his locks. The ornate clothing he wore was collected from the stores of the kings long since passed and had begun to unravel at the seams.

The leather gauntlets he bore were still visible beneath his robes, just as it was certain he'd donned the rest of his equipment in case the need to use them in a fight ever arose. The man appeared ridiculous in the eyes of his guest, feigning power gained through the hands of another.

Sidonis brushed his foot over a large crack that had begun to form in the ground as he stood near one of the paintings before him.

"Truly fascinating, isn't it?" he quipped. "The ancients before us are immortalized forever in these images while those of us who remain, are forgotten to the winds. . . . What are we to be remembered for, Helgisson?" he asked as he turned his head to where the other sat. "What will you be remembered for?"

"The sins of my father," the man calmly replied.

"Indeed," Sidonis replied. "But I fear, there is nothing for me to even claim which I may be remembered for. Nothing even worthy of the utterance of my name when I am gone. So my existence is resolved merely to a petty dalliance with my enemy. Shameful really. . ."

Helgisson watched as Sidonis wandered through the hall and inhaled sharply as he raised his head toward the ceiling.

"I want more, Helgisson. I demand it,"

"Well, there is nothing for you here." the man replied. "You have seen it yourself, what people remain are like dogs who fight for the scraps. Or is it my throne you desire?" he scoffed.

"I already have it," Sidonis replied. "The only reason you sit there now is because I have done for you, what you failed a hundred times over. I killed the men who challenged you and slaughtered the ones who merely thought of it."

"You offered a solution to rid me of my enemies so that you could create one for yourself. The scoundrels are dead, but now I face Ludica, and have barely an army left to defend these walls."

"My brother shall be dealt with."

The leader of Graefeld paused as he considered the Sidonis' answer before he suddenly erupted with laughter.

"You are a mad man, Sidonis, and I am equally so for partaking in your schemes."

Sidonis feigned a smile before his expression turned bitter and callous. He waited for the other to calm himself before continuing with his plot against the king of Faermire.

"Ascferth is dead," he uttered stoically.

"So?"

"So, with his death, Gwenora seeks to align herself with my brother as she knows Ceolfrid will drive her into the ground. He will in time attack Mistelfeld and lay siege to the land along with that pet giant of his from Helmere."

Helgisson's brow furrowed, as he soon made the connection.

Graefeld had long been entangled with hostilities against Mistelfeld before Faermire took what remained of their lands. And the death of their king meant that others sought to seize an opportunity to strike.

"And what does this have to do with me?" The incumbent king interjected.

"Everything Helgisson, so long as I have your loyalty." Sidonis replied.

"You lured Astor and the others into Taernsby, only to slaughter them all. Who is to say that you will not also betray me so easily?"

"Now, what good would that do for either of us, Helgisson?"

"You plundered your own village to cast the blame on my people. That was not part of our agreement, Sidonis."

"A necessary evil, I can assure you. And one which the gods have smiled upon apparently. It only means now that my plans must be altered, as we have little time to spare.

"Ceolfrid will reconsider his plans if Ludica agrees to pledge his armies for the protection of Mistelfeld. But I will offer instead to grant the arm of Faermire for his hand in taking the land so long as I am to be made king over my brother. You will help me take the throne and be granted spoils far richer than what you've earned this day.

"Grant me your fealty, and you and your people shall no longer go hungry. You will no longer scrounge for the scraps of your enemies, and you shall trample over those who once crushed you."

It was an offer he knew that the sullen king would not refuse, but it only meant that he could not fail in his plot. The gods had heard him, that much was certain, and the sacrifices he made to them had been accepted. Their timing was impeccable, and he dared not waste the opportunity and the favor which they offered him in return. For once, the tides were changing, and he would see to it that this time, he would not fail.

He waited as the man considered the proposal. Moments passed in silence before he finally looked up from his seat and opened his mouth to speak.

"It is yours," he answered as a smile emerged on Sidonis' face.

Sidonis could see the spark of life returning to the man's eyes as he thought on the information presented. Helgisson rose from his chair with a renewed sense of confidence and approached the man who stood before him.

"Then tell me, my lord, what orders do you give your servant?"

# CHAPTER 8

BEOWYN HELD HIS BREATH AS he waited for the soldier to pass him by. The faint sound of urine splashing onto the ground behind him had finally subsided and the man walked on. The others called to him as a rider came with a prisoner in tow. As his footsteps drifted away, the prince pulled himself back away from the bodies on which he laid. He contemplated his next move, calculating also how he would get his friend out of the wagon.

Moments later, Sidonis returned to their camp at a distance from where they lay. His men then presented the prisoner they had previously obtained to him. The man's head had been covered in a sackcloth bag and his hands were secured tightly behind his back. He panted heavily and whimpered as the cover was ripped from his face.

Below the mask, Beowyn could see clear as day, the face of the local nobility, Rodmar, whose lordship governed the southernmost lands of Faermire. His rotund belly shifted rapidly as he panted beneath the tightened rag around his mouth. His face also was strained with sweat and tears as the men forced him to his knees before their leader.

Sidonis greeted the man with a smile and a faint remark about the travel he endured.

"I hope it wasn't too much trouble for you to come and see me on such short notice. But I am grateful nonetheless," he remarked.

Rodmar's muffled voice was reduced to muted cries for help and pleas for his life that were left unheard.

"Now it should come as no surprise to you my old friend that we are in trying times. Threats of war and treachery fill these lands and perhaps it is by the hands of the gods, or simply happenstance that you play a part in all of this," he continued.

The elder shook his head as he fought for his voice to be heard. The weight of his body pushed heavily onto his aging knees as he quivered from the pain. His once clean tunic was caked in splatters of mud and stained with sweat and drool which ran down his chest. By the looks of him, he had been pulled from his bed as he slept. His thinning white hair had been frayed in every direction as his beard followed suit.

"Oh yes," Sidonis uttered as he smiled at the man, seeming to answer the elder's muted objection.

"My brother is too weak to see that the very men who 'counsel' him on matters of the land he rules and are meant to be beacons of his piety, suck the very life from this kingdom like the leeches that you truly are... And I intend to open his eyes to this truth you see. Whether he likes it or not, he will see the filth that runs amok. Starting with you..." He slowly lifted his knife to Rodmar's face and traced it down to his belly.

"Do not think that your foul deeds have gone unnoticed dear friend. I know all that you have done to your subjects and what you have taken from them and especially the king. Your own people stood and watched as my man here walked into your very home to collect you and spat at the ground where you stood." He paused for a moment to watch as the shamed elder shook his head crying still for his life.

"Now what I can't seem to figure is where you could possibly be hiding all your spoils, Rodmar. Perhaps in here..." He added as the tip of his blade stopped at the man's navel.

"Let us see if I am right." The man's eyes suddenly widened as the knife was then thrust into his belly and drawn across the width of it. His voice went silent as the shock rushed quickly into his face, turning it nearly as white as his hair. Blood poured like water from the gaping wound as a portion of his entrails shortly followed. The yellow fat beneath his skin clung to the sides like curdled butter and the old man watched briefly with horror in his eyes only to fall over dead into the mud seconds later.

Sidonis also remained quiet as he waited for the man's life to drain out before him. He then looked to one of his men as he wiped his knife over the elder's tunic to clean it.

"Sever the head and give it to my brother as a message. I want it placed in his chambers is that understood?" The man nodded and the others watched as he carried out the order.

He then called over two others to himself and approached his horse with them in tow.

"The rest of you will remain here until you receive further orders from me shortly! I have a war to wage." As he rode off with his party, the men carried on as they had before, gathering what few bodies remained in the town to bury.

Beowyn turned himself back as he worked to slow his rapid breaths. He watched in disbelief at all which had unfolded before him and struggled to reign himself in once more. Though as he carried on, the wagon where Qereth had been hiding creaked and moaned as it inched its way on toward the gravesite. The two soldiers who sat atop the bench casually carried on in their conversation as the horse was nudged along.

Meanwhile, the man ordered to deliver Sidonis' message had already begun to make his journey back to Elsterheim and Beowyn cursed beneath his breath. He then retreated from his spot and kept his eyes on where the wagon was headed desperate to help his friend.

Night had begun to fall over the land as the wagon made its approach toward the grave and all was quiet around them. The turning wheels and crackling wood were all that could be heard as the wind blew softly over the empty fields around them. They each lit a torch and pulled the horse to a stop.

As they dismounted, one of the men began to complain about his discontent with their lot of the work as the other listened. They went back and forth over frivolous matters and began to joke with one another as they pulled at a body from within the wagon.

Together they heaved it into the pit and watched as it hit the bottom with a thud. Then as one turned back toward the load, still laughing from the other's comment, Qereth leapt up from his place and drove his knife deep into the man's face, killing him in an instant. The remaining soldier then quickly fumbled for his weapon only to have his throat slit from behind.

His lifeless body was guided into the pit as it fell, revealing the prince who stood along the edge as he looked to his friend.

"Took you long enough," Qereth quipped, and he lowered himself from the wagon.

"We haven't much time," Beowyn uttered. "I must return to Elsterheim at once."

# ELSTERHEIM

She heard a loud crash from a distance and the queen's piercing voice followed shortly after. The woman's enraged shouting came after a young servant girl had apparently dropped a tray in her presence. As Estrith approached the scene, she could see the servant struggling to conceal her tears as she fervently offered up her apology to the royal.

"Well don't just stand there! Clean it up, you filthy wretch." Richessa hurled further insults at her before she finally left the girl to tend to the mess, and Estrith rounded the corner to help her. The servant was shocked to see the princess kneeling at her side before she quickly lowered her eyes back toward the ground.

"No milady, please. You mustn't concern yourself with such things."

"Don't be ridiculous," Estrith replied. "This is my home; I am free to do as I please. Here." She lifted two chalices up from the ground and watched as the girl cautiously accepted them. Still shaken from the ordeal, Estrith attempted to ease her angst with a reassuring smile, but to no avail. The servant struggled to avoid her gaze and began to mop up the spilled drink with her apron, while her hands trembled.

As she finished with the last of what had remained, the girl quickly bowed herself before the princess and recused herself,

"Thank you, milady."

Estrith only had time enough to offer another reassuring smile before the servant was gone, leaving her alone in the hallway once more. She sighed, and slowly rose to her feet, only to notice the sudden anger she felt from within as she stood.

Richessa had been known to be foul in her treatment of the servants, but it didn't diminish the outrage that Estrith felt at that moment. Such a bitter disregard for humanity left a sour taste in her mouth, and she wanted nothing more than to offer the woman a hardy slap to the face.

But she soon remembered what she had seen of the queen and her uncle. Knowledge of such an affair could mean severe consequences for the woman as it was justly due, but then it would also mean the same for her uncle. As much as she hated Richessa, she held no ill will toward the man aside from his poor judgement. And having such knowledge should not be handled so lightly.

Yet still, the sight of the pair together had been etched into her memory, and it cycled over and over again in her mind, only fueling the outrage within her. Something needed to be done, and who better to do it, than the one person with the greatest leverage? If ever there was a time to confront the witch for her offenses, then now would be it.

The more she thought about the matter, the harder she found it was to restrain herself from doing so. She knew that she had wanted to wait for the right time, whenever that was, to reveal Richessa's dirty little secret, but alas, she could no longer wait. She wanted nothing more than to see the terror in that woman's eyes and laud it over her as she so richly deserved.

With one last ounce of justification, Estrith made her way to follow the queen and approached her chambers. She hesitated briefly, then knocked on the door. A moment later, she was greeted by the queen's maid, who lowered herself in respect.

"I need to speak with the queen," the older woman humbly acknowledged the request and shut the door once more. For such a well-respected position amongst the help, it proved to be more of a curse for the poor woman who had apparently aged well beyond her years.

As the queen granted her access, she couldn't help but feel a pit of nervousness rising within her gut. The maid escorted her to where Richessa was seated next to the hearth while she focused on her needlework by the light. The queen offered only a single glance at her direction to acknowledge her presence and remained quiet for a time, before she finally relented.

"I doubt you've come to watch me stitch. Shall I make presumptions as to why you are here?"

Before she had arrived, Estrith felt as though she had formulated the exact words for Richessa in her mind, but now in the moment, she was completely at a loss. Faced with the reality of her decision, she was forced to deliver. And rather than projecting the confidence that she had once imagined, she stood before the woman like a bumbling fool.

"Well?" she continued. The queen's casual demeanor served to reignite the animosity she briefly lost.

"I— I know of your misdeeds Richessa."

"Speak louder child, your grumbling vexes me," the queen kept her focus on the work within her lap.

"I know of your affair with my uncle. . ." She needn't raise the tone of her voice, for at once she knew that the woman had heard her. Richessa suddenly stopped and lowered the fabric in her hands. Yet as her head remained lowered, her eyes shifted up to where Estrith stood.

"Leave us," the queen hardly needed to finish the sentence, before her maid had already left the two women alone in the room. "Then, tell me, Estrith, what is it you know of my affair?" She gently placed her work at the table beside her and slowly rose to her feet.

Estrith could feel that same nervous pit begin to overtake her.

"I saw you with him, the day of the consecration. I saw you embracing one another, and I saw you kiss my uncle before you hid yourselves away." Richessa chuckled softly beneath her breath as she approached the princess. And as much as Estrith tried to avert her gaze from the queen, she needed to see her response directly. But instead, all she could feel was the queen's intense glare, over her body, studying her through and through.

There was silence between them for the length of an eternity, and she found herself taken aback by the gentle grin which subsequently emerged on Richessa's face.

"You know, there was a time when I wasn't much different than you."

"We are nothing alike."

"Oh, I beg to differ. You see, I know what it is you want in life... freedom. It is what every woman cursed with our place in life desires. But the more we long for it, the more it seems to elude us, doesn't it?"

The longer that Estrith stood in that room, the more she had come to regret it. The gall this woman had to compare herself to the princess was reprehensible at best, but she remained silent, and listened as the queen carried on. "I had hope once, just as you do now. Hope that one day, the gods would hear my prayers and grant me the freedom that I so desperately longed for.

"Women in our position are destined for a single purpose, and I'm sure you know it. But as often as I prayed, and as often as

I made sacrifices to the gods, they did not hear me. I was not much older than you when I was to be given away in marriage to your father. I knew not whether he was a kind man, handsome, or even honorable, but those matters were inconsequential. For I knew that regardless of who he was, I would forever lose myself, and become lost in obscurity. Every aspect of who I was before was to be stripped away entirely, and I would be tasked with the sole purpose of producing another heir. Anything else that I had to offer was cast aside, like the chaff in the wind. I knew all these things, and yet even when they came still came to pass, it did not lessen the pain that I felt.

"And as the years pressed on, I found it harder to breathe. The very walls of my existence had begun to snuff out what life remained in me, and the water I drank became bitter.

"We do not have the luxury of thought, or expression. And any decisions you wish to make are made on your behalf. That is the truth of it. So, I did the one thing that offered me even a glimmer of hope, the one thing that allowed me to feel alive, even if just for a moment.

"Sidonis offered me that moment..."

For as much as Estrith wanted to hate Richessa, she knew that there was truth in the words she spoke. The woman had confirmed her greatest fears, bringing them to life the more that she carried on, and it terrified her.

The confidence in Richessa's demeanor however, had slowly faded, and for the first time, Estrith caught a glimpse of her fleeting vulnerability. Though, she could not help but feel the pangs of manipulation beneath her grievances still. Whatever truth remained, there was still the matter of their transgressions against her father.

"Do you love him?" she asked.

"Does it matter? The idea of companionship or love even, means nothing, Estrith, when your own existence is reduced to little more than a shadow. You see, the truth of the matter is that we will never be free. Even love cannot help you escape the shackles that we are destined to bear. Surely, you know this child. Even as your marriage is soon at hand."

"Marriage? Wha- what do you mean?"

"Why, to Ealric of course. . ."

To hear either the words marriage, or Ealric spill from her mouth, let alone in a single phrase suddenly made her weak in the knees. It was a lie, it had to be.

"Ealric? That's not possible. My father would never allow it! He- he never even spoke of this to me. You are mistaken Richessa, surely."

"On the contrary! The young man made it very clear of his intent for you at the hall. And besides, such a union would prove most favorable to Ludica. Not only would your marriage to Elwin's son further secure peace between our lands, but he could rely on you to provide the information he needs from Elwin. An alliance he could better trust, rather than your brother, no doubt. A necessary sacrifice for the greater good, as he would put it."

She couldn't bring herself to believe the words which Richessa had spoken. For once her malevolence revealed itself wholly to Estrith, and it took everything for her to restrain herself. She could no longer discern whether it was terror or anger that she felt and wanted nothing more than to hide herself away forever. And if by some ill fate from the gods, her words were true, then she should've escaped with Beowyn when she had the chance.

"You're lying Richessa."

"I wish for your sake, dear girl, that I was." Estrith remained frozen where she stood, even as the queen gently placed her icy fingers upon her shoulder. "I did not make mention of it, because frankly it wasn't my place to do so. And hearing the news would have only made the anticipation that much worse for you. But there is still hope for you, yet," she continued as turned back toward the hearth.

Whatever leverage Estrith thought she once had, suddenly felt as though it was slipping through her hands, and she didn't know how to stop it.

"There was mention of Ealric's intent for you, but neither your father, nor Elwin had come to a definitive agreement. It seems that as favorable as it would be for Ludica, he still cares for you in his own way, and could not yet bring himself to fully offer his consent. I could change his mind. He only needs someone to show him that such a sacrifice is far too great to justify such little gain."

Richessa was careful to keep her eyes fixed on Estrith as she lowered herself back into her chair and waited for her to process all that she said.

"I only need the assurance that my little secret remains just that. Grant me my morsel of freedom, Estrith, and I shall offer you, yours..."

She could only seem to feel that deep down, Richessa's words were all just a sick ploy to manipulate her. But what if they weren't? She could at once, tell her father of her transgressions upon his return, but still risk the possibility of having to face a marriage with that monster of a man. Or she could trust that for once, the queen was capable of offering her aid, if even to save herself, which was more along the lines of her character.

After a further moment of agonizing consideration, Estrith finally looked to Richessa and relented,

"Agreed…"

But as soon as the word had left her mouth, she regretted it. It felt like a betrayal, not only to her father, but more so, to herself. Was the price for her freedom so cheap? She began to fill sick to her stomach and could only watch as the queen smiled back with acknowledgment.

"Very well," Richessa replied.

And as the two remained within the stifling silence which had quickly filled the room, Estrith couldn't help but feel relieved as a knock came at the door. They each turned to find that Richessa's maid stood before them once more, announcing the arrival of a visitor for the queen.

"Who is it?" she asked.

"It is a man," the maid replied. "He says that he brings for you a message from Taernsby."

The man arrived in the city upon his horse and approached the palace gates directly. The bustling town carried on around him as though the two were unaware of the other's existence. He towered over them, wedging his way through the crowds and finally dismounted as he arrived where the guards stood at the palace entrance.

"I require an audience with the queen," he ordered bluntly. Being the right hand of Sidonis himself, the man was well known in the palace as he had often accompanied the king's brother whenever he arrived. Though many were unaware of his name, his face was easy to remember.

He held an air of arrogance about him, seizing claim to a privilege that he was not due. His dark cloak wrapped around his shoulders and draped heavily to the heel of his boots. The leather armor which covered his arms and chest made him appear larger than his lean stature hidden beneath it.

Unlike many men who often braided their hair into thick locks or let them flow loosely upon their shoulders, this one opted instead to shave his head completely. The dark stubble which began to grow from their roots followed the contour of his skull and face which had been equally shaved. He held a large scar down his forehead and brow to the gaunt of his cheek, scowling at nearly everyone in his presence regardless of who they were.

As he waited for the approval, the gates finally pulled open revealing a representative of the king's staff. He casually followed the servant's lead, with his horse in tow toward the stables and scanned the grounds as they walked. It appeared to be empty aside from the occasional keeper or attendant as they passed them by.

And as he led his horse into the stall, the local stable-hand greeted the man while reaching for the reigns. The man however, curtly shoved his hand aside and personally guided the animal to where the hay had been drawn.

"Fetch my horse some water, then be on your way."

"As you wish sir," the lad acknowledged. "Shall I just remove your saddle for you also?" The stable-hand then found his hand in the man's grasp once more, feeling the tightening grip of his fingers around his flesh. The packaged which had accompanied him, sat only inches from the lad's grasp, but still remained safely tucked away.

"Forget the water," the man ordered. "Just be on your way."

"But I still need to—" Before he could finish, the lad took a forceful shove against his chest as the man's face suddenly turned sour.

"Reach for my horse again, and I shall cut you down."

It was obvious to note the utter confusion in the stable-hand's eyes, but he was happy to comply.

"Seeing as how there are no other steeds to tend to, I-I suppose that my morning ale is calling."

"Suppose it is." He remained a moment longer to watch the young man leave and turned to find an elderly woman waiting at the opposite end. She remained silent, only beckoning him as she made a gesture toward the courtyard. He nodded and followed her lead, eventually making their way up the stairs toward the queen's chambers.

For once, it was quieter within the castle. The king had apparently taken the whole of his staff on his little excursion to Mistelfeld. But it was all for the better, in this case. Their absence would only serve as his benefit in the end. Less of a risk for his own life...

Once they approached the door, the queen's servant stopped and entered the room alone to announce his arrival. Shortly after, the door slowly opened before him, where beyond the way, he could see the queen seated upon her chair, and the princess standing before her.

Estrith was surprised to find her uncle's cohort enter the room. His ever-smug expression caught her attention at first sight. She never much cared for the man, even though the two had never spoken.

But he had always given the impression that he would just as rather kill everyone in the room, than be bothered with their company.

She hardly had the chance to process his arrival, before Richesssa promptly ordered her out of her presence. But as she turned to leave the room, she inadvertently locked eyes with the man while crossing his path and the same stoic expression remained upon his face. He seemed to make it a point to stare her down, even as he lowered his posture in respect. But he quickly shifted his focus once she was out of his line of sight. And thankfully so. His dark eyes crawled over her as if they were searching for her every weakness.

Once the door had shut behind her, it should have been the end to any thought which was owed the man, but there was something about his arrival which had perplexed her to no end.

It was just days before, that he left with Sidonis back to Taernsby, but now he appeared again, only having returned alone to the castle. With her father gone to Mistelfeld and the remaining elders returned home, there was no business he could possibly have here that she could not reason within her mind. Let alone with Richessa.

There was something unsettling about the whole of it to her, and the only solution was to find the answers she needed. But how she would get them, she didn't know. The door was far too thick to hear their conversation, and there was no one else with whom she could inquire as to his business there. Though perhaps, the queen's servant would be able to help.

Thankfully, the woman was never far from Richessa's presence, and she found her sitting patiently at the end of the hall. There was a single chair tucked away beneath a torch which also served to provide her with the comfort of warmth during her momentary breaks. And it appeared as though that single moment of quiet, granted her the peace that she so desperately needed, even if it was so brief. Estrith almost regretted having to strip her of that peace, but the circumstance demanded it.

The elderly woman rose to her feet, though was careful to avoid aggravating the pain she felt throughout her joints. She kept her hands clasped within the sleeves of her gray dress. And all that stood in contrast to the solid tone of her clothes, was the white apron which had been fixed across her front. The woman took careful attention to the state of her appearance, and even the veil which covered her hair rested perfectly in its place.

"My Lady," she uttered as she bowed herself to the princess.

"What business brings that man here?" she asked as she glanced back toward the room.

"He did not say, my Lady. I met him at the stables and escorted him here directly."

Although she was hopeful that the woman would grant her a rewarding response, she still found herself at a loss.

"Very well. Was he alone?"

"Yes, my Lady." The servant appeared hesitant, but offered just a little bit more, much to her relief. "He was rather protective of his horse. Though he does not strike me as the loving type..."

"Indeed." Estrith smiled with approval and thanked the woman before racing off toward the stables where she eagerly hoped to find the reason for the man's arrival, whatever it may have been.

Richessa waited patiently as the man approached her and she scanned him from head to toe.

"My Lady." He bowed passively, somewhat annoyed by the incessant formalities.

"What news do you bring?" she calmly asked. But the posture she held was as rigid as the aura she so often portrayed. Her tight red curls were pulled loosely behind her back as she wore her crown with pride. And she continued to study him, just as she was keenly aware that he did just the same.

"My lord sends word to my Lady by way of a message for the king."

"What kind of message?"

"The head of lord Rodmar." It was hard to conceal the twinkle in her eye at the words he offered, and a smile quickly emerged upon her face.

"My lord says that you know of what is required once the message is received."

"I do," she quickly responded as she rose to her feet with a sense of anxious delight. She nervously rubbed her hands together as she paced the room before him.

"Is it secure? Where is it?"

"Shall I fetch it for you?" She could sense the unwavering sarcasm in his tone and glared sharply at him.

"Of course not! No, no, I'll have my servant fetch it to my husband's chamber."

She opened a small chest amongst her belongings and retrieved a small bag filled with coin which she then tossed to him. The two spoke further with each other regarding Sidonis' plan before she finally gave him leave to go. He bowed once more before her and finally left the room.

After he departed, Richessa returned to her chair as she ran through the information which had been presented to her, slowly lowering herself into its embrace. The words which Sidonis had spoken of when last she saw him gave a certain hope, though distant in her eyes.

Far be it that she should have doubted his words at the time, but it was his tenacity that she admired. Like sweet hyssop, his machinations of grandeur were to her, and she reveled in the idea of all that he offered. Perhaps it was her own words which pushed him to finally take action, but the more she thought on those things, the more she desired him.

Whatever it was that happened to charge him toward action now, made no difference to her as it only served to make it all that much more real. And she found it to be both arousing and nerve wrecking all at once...

As Estrith made her way to the stables, she found herself constantly looking back, expecting to find the man standing right behind her. Though she constantly tried to reassure herself, to no avail, her fears were only worsened by the sudden appearance of her younger brother as he leapt out before her from behind a pillar. He flung his wooden sword at her, swiping and jabbing with a playful fury.

But she nearly screamed, grasping her chest to steady her racing heart, and sharply cursed at him beneath her breath. The boy laughed, satisfied with a job well-done, but quickly took interest in her mission.

"Where are you going?" he asked, curiously taking his place at her side.

"Nowhere. Now leave me be."

"Then why are you walking so quickly?"

"I'm not. And lower your voice, Siged, please!" Irritated with her bothersome companion, she glanced over her shoulder once more.

"What are you looking for? And why do act as though someone is following you?"

Young Siged followed closely behind his sister as she desperately tried to ignore him. However, her efforts were futile, as he soon danced around her while she walked, asking more and more questions.

"Siged, please! If you are going to come with me, then you must be silent." She hissed the words from behind her teeth making him plainly aware of her frustration.

"Fine." The boy quickly agreed with a smile on his face, and for once, there finally came the silence she so desperately craved. Then eventually, they came upon the stables. Though with as many questions as her brother asked, she needed a way to be rid of him for fear that he'd only hinder her efforts. So, she contemplated her options and finally came to a solution, however weak it may have been.

She prompted him to keep watch across the yard and quickly sent him on his way. And surprised with her success, she quietly proceeded into the stables. Inside, she could see the man's horse feeding alone within its stall. It ignored her cautious approach and continued to eat as she laid her hand on its back and gently stroked its body for reassurance.

She glanced over at the door and drew her hand back, stopping as she took notice of a large woven basket strapped to its saddle, weighing heavily against its side. A faint stench emanated from within it that she could sense and hesitated for a moment before she continued.

She unhooked the buckle which secured its contents and slowly lifted the lid from the top to look inside. She then rose higher up onto her toes to gain a better look when she could see a large cloth over the source of the smell which grew ever more rancid.

One moment led to the next as she lifted the cloth out of the way and saw what appeared to be white hair within it. It couldn't have been what she thought it was but pulled herself in for a closer look as she used the tips of her fingers to shift the object into plainer view.

Suddenly, staring back at her was the grayed face of the elder, Rodmar's head. The eyelids drooped heavily so that his pupils were barely visible, and his mouth lazily gaped open as the dried blood pooled at the bottom of the basket.

She gasped and nearly lost her footing as she gripped her hand over her own mouth to keep herself quiet. She began tremble and her breaths grew quick, as tears began to well within her eyes.

Everything in her mind went blank in an instant and she wanted nothing more than to be gone from that place and scream. It was all she think to do, so she turned herself to run back through the door when a sudden wall appeared behind her and forcefully grabbed her arms.

"You of all people should know, lady Estrith to keep your eyes from where they don't belong..." Sidonis' man glared down at her from above with anger drenched across his face.

But before she could scream, he shoved her into the wall as she tried desperately to fight him off. The two wrestled for what felt like an eternity to her, and she could feel the tightening grip of his hand around her neck. He forced her to the ground where her feet slipped and thrashed among the hay beneath her.

Darkness began to form around the edge of her sight and all she could see was his scowling face above as he locked his arms and squeezed his fingers tighter around her throat. Her hands slowly began to loosen from his grasp and her feet had begun to go numb as the sound of the world around her began to fade.

Suddenly the man cried out in pain as he pulled his hands away, leaving her gasping for air on the ground below. She struggled to regain her senses and cradled her neck with her hand as she coughed and gasped as he writhed before her.

He forcefully yanked at a pitchfork which had been thrust into his side and threw it down as he searched for the culprit.

Young Siged stood in shock as he witnessed the man before him cursing at him while he struggled to regain his footing. He pulled his hand into the wound and lifted it back to reveal fresh blood running through his fingers.

The boy continued to stare as if locked in a trance as Estrith gathered what strength she had in her body to cry out to him.

"Siged run!" He suddenly snapped back to reality at the sound of her course voice and began to step back when the man snatched him at the nape of his tunic. He struggled helplessly against the raging man and was thrown effortlessly into the wall behind him. The sound of his fragile head smacked against the stone as he fell lifelessly to the ground before them.

Estrith gasped with horror and reached for the blood-stained pitchfork which had fallen within arm's reach. And fed up with the scuffle at hand, the man reached for his knife and lifted it into the air. As he turned to finish the job, she thrust the four-pronged spear into his chest with all her might.

She stared him in the eyes as he looked back at her in disbelief. Blood began to trickle from his lips as he slumped down onto his knees and died. His body remained fixed in its position by the tool still left impaled in his body and he rested in silence as she ran toward her brother behind him.

She gently lifted him into her arms and could feel a softened area at the back of his skull. Blood began to drip from his ears, and she gently rubbed his chest and cheeks desperately hoping to see his eyes open, repeatedly calling his name.

"Siged? Siged, wake up. Please!" He lay quietly in her arms, and she was helpless to do anything for him in that moment. She then began to sob and threw her head into the air as she screamed at the top of her lungs.

"Help! Somebody help me, please! Help!" She screamed repeatedly as she pulled him closer into her chest while the world around her disappeared.

# CHAPTER 9

## HELMFIRTH, KINGDOM OF MISTELFELD

LUDICA LIFTED HIS EYES, STARING up at the steep cliffs which towered over them while the ship drifted along the river. Unable to even see the city of Graefeld which rested upon the bluff, he shook his head as he pondered all which was unfolding before him.

Left alone in silence for once, he found himself wondering if the decision he made those years ago was coming back to haunt him once more. Had he angered the gods perhaps? Or was it simply a test? One question arose after another, and he soon felt that perhaps it was better he not be left alone to his own thoughts after all.

The sky was clear for once, but the cold winds still held their bite. The warmth he could feel upon his face from the ever-elusive sun brought comfort even if just for a moment as the ship carried on.

They were nearly upon the shores of Mistelfeld, and he couldn't help but feel a small sense of nervousness once they approached. The city rested not far from the coast, and from what he could tell, it was just as grand as he remembered it so many years ago.

Considered once an enemy of the king, Ludica was asked to return, with the promise of peace from the widowed queen.

The birds flew overhead, crying out in the wind to each other as if announcing their arrival to their shores. Then, one by one, he could make out the figures who stood along the dock as they waited for the ship. The queen stood among the center of the party, with her calm expression unwavering.

He smiled slightly at how the years had served her well in her old age. She was certainly smaller than he remembered, but she stood taller and more confident than ever with her gray hair pulled behind her back. Her hands were clasped loosely together in front of her, and her golden crown stood out against the green cloak draped majestically around her body.

The rest of the men who stood around her were of no consequence to his attention as the sailors drew the ship in against the dock. Sgell accompanied the king as he directed him to the ramp which led them to her, and Ludica gladly accepted.

Everyone, including the queen, remained silent as he approached her.

"May the gods favor you, Gwenora." He offered a bow of good will, then kissed her hand as she presented it. All eyes were upon the king and his envoy, some with curiosity, while others carried either skepticism or contempt. It didn't come as any surprise to him, seeing as how the two kingdoms had been at odds for some time.

"I hope your journey fared well."

"It did, my Lady. The waters carried us with ease."

"Good..." she replied, obviously growing weary of the petty formalities. "Come Ludica. Let us welcome you and your people as honored guests upon our land."

While doing so, Ludica took note of her sharp glance toward an elder who stood at her side, emphasizing the word 'honored', while doing so.

"And what a pleasure it is indeed..." The elder was happy to return the gesture to the queen. "I am Ordric, a member of her majesty's high council. I must say, the other counselors and I were rather surprised to hear news of your visit so suddenly. An impulsive decision by the Lady, but a sincere one no doubt."

Ludica remained silent, resolving only to observe the members' exchange. It was clear that neither she nor the counselor agreed on much of anything regarding matters of the state. The queen cracked her lips to fire back at the man but seemed to have found her restraint just as she began to speak.

"Sincere indeed, lord Ordric..." she resolved instead, to directing her fullest attention toward Ludica, and offered a courteous smile before turning back toward the city. "Shall we?"

Their travel through the streets were marked with bustling activity and the many aromas which filled the air the further they moved along. The people were quick to pause their business and lower their heads in reverence as the queen passed. Many, however, took sudden notice of the king and his envoy, sparking gossip amongst the crowd. All eyes were fixed upon the queen's guests and the news of their arrival would soon spread like wildfire.

Her gaze did not falter as she continued and finally led the king through the palace and into the room. Her servant was quick to remove her cloak and the counselors gathered before the throne as they waited for the queen to be the first to take her seat. As she casually lowered herself down, she directed her hand toward an empty seat which had been provisioned for Ludica as her guest. The group of men, then parted to give way for him to pass.

He scanned the large room around him, noting a somewhat similar layout to his own, but with a woman's touch no doubt. The torches flickered around them, and the hall stretched high into a dome where the sun's light peeked through. The hall was dressed in a simpler tone, but Mistelfeld stood out in many areas where Faermire lacked.

Gwenora had wasted no time in changing the order of everything around her once her husband had passed, that much was obvious to him. But the man hardly even noticed the clothes on his back at times enough to pay any morsel of attention to anything else from Ludica what remembered. What was clear to have never changed however, was that Ascferth was a scoundrel and a fool.

But before long, the order of business took the stage, as Ludica found his seat, prompting him to break the rigid silence which had filled the air.

"I've heard talk of the king's funeral at Stathmor. A bit archaic, wouldn't you say?" Ludica asked.

"One must not stray from tradition, Ludica. I'm sure it brought him closer to the gods nonetheless."

"Indeed," he chuckled. It was not a typical funeral in those present times, but Gwenora had ordered it out in a way to properly dispose of the king without blatantly spitting on his grave for all to see. She loathed the man, as did many around her. There were far fewer who found any sort of benefit from his reign unless they too could profit from it as well. And when he wasn't drunk, he squandered what remained.

The queen had long since established provisions for the kingdom and ruled the land as his proxy, even as he lived out the remainder of his years. Many were grateful, as she'd prevented Ascferth from bringing the kingdom to its knees. Some, however, sought to usurp his throne, but the queen had proven her right time and again. Even as others challenged her outright. Ordric was certain to have been among them.

That same man then came forward to interject,

"My queen, with the arrival of our new guest, perhaps you should like to advise the council of your intentions, so that it may be made clear to those who are unaware."

"You, being the chief amongst them lord, Ordric. But as I am sure you all know, Ceolfrid's scouts have been spotted at our north-ernmost border. The news of his cousin's death can only mean that he now intends to invade us."

"We do not know that," Ordric replied. "Such presumptions will only lead to the unnecessary deaths of our people. It could be, that he merely desires an audience with the queen, a renewed truce, if you will." The man no longer directed his words toward the queen, but instead turned his attention on the others who stood around him.

Some nodded in agreement, as others began to whisper amongst themselves.

"If you truly believe the nonsense you speak, Ordric, then your hubris knows no bounds. The only reason why Ceolfrid withheld his army from our land, is because it was his blood which held the throne. And without Ascerfth, then there is no truce. He believes himself to hold the rightful claim over this kingdom and will do whatever it takes to make it so.

As long as I shall live, that man will never take my kingdom from me. Which is why Ludica has come. With Faermire at our side, then Ceolfrid will be forced to stay his advance. He cannot overtake us with our armies combined."

"And what of Helmere?" another counselor interjected. "Ceolfrid's confidence is led by the hand of his giant. Nurrock, who leads his savage followers with a dragon no less!"

"The beast lost the use of its wings at the siege of Prohn years ago. It's no better than a pet trophy now," another replied.

"That 'trophy' still spouts fire from his mouth and can still maul twenty men in an instant. Wings or not, I have seen it with my own eyes!" The court suddenly erupted into a frenzy of voices, as those present began to argue with one another.

Ludica watched silently from his chair as the council debated for some time. All at the behest of the one man who vehemently opposed the queen every chance he got. His plan had worked however, and the queen's intent to unite the two kingdoms would not come so easily for her.

Though finally, Gwenora rose from her throne and lifted her hand in the air, silencing the chaos before her.

"Be that as it may, gentlemen, our chances stand to be greater if we align ourselves with a formidable ally. Ascferth made Ludica an enemy those years ago, but I now advocate for peace." She turned to the king who sat before her and the members of her party. "I ask that Faermire make an allegiance with Mistelfeld, one which shall stand the test of time. So that both our lands may be prosperous in the years to come."

"There will be no prosperity my queen, if we make allies of the man who stole Ceolfrid's bride. He will most certainly see it as an act of aggression and take action against us. We must instead go to him first, grant him an offering of peace so that he may look favorably upon us," Ordric interjected once more.

"I will not be made a coward and a fool. Especially not on the advice of such half-witted counsel. And counselor's you are... As I am sure you are aware, I am queen, and the decision is still mine to make. My plans for an alliance are not a request."

"My Queen, you must—"

"What say you, Ludica?" Gwenora was quick to end Ordric's words, turning instead, to face her guest.

Now tasked with the obligation to provide an answer, Ludica uncomfortably adjusted himself within his chair. Ordric had done a fine job of disrupting the balance within the court and he couldn't help but find himself also weighing the risks which had been voiced.

Although Ordric's intent was clear, the words he spoke regarding a new alliance proved to be problematic indeed. Ceolfrid would no doubt see the alliance between Faermire and Mistelfeld as a direct threat to his power. But so it would also stave off an attack, if not for a time. If Ceolfrid could take Mistelfeld, then it would only be a matter of time before the fight would be brought to his own borders.

And so, it proved that the war which had been fought so many years ago, had never truly ended. Only time had brought about newer circumstances, ushered in by the very same faces. Truces and treaties no longer mattered if it no longer benefited the parties at hand. And the only people a person could trust, were the ones whose motivation just so happened to align with their own for a time. Old friends became enemies, and old enemies, were now asking to become friends.

These were trying times indeed, and once again, Ludica stood at the crux of it all. Even with all the years that had passed, the dread he felt in that moment, had begun to haunt him once more. However, in his youth, when he was quick to race toward the fight, he now hesitated to even lift his feet. If time had proven anything to the king, it was that the nature of man would always lead them to war.

He paused for a moment longer and looked to the queen, whose eager eyes were fixed with anticipation. The option to forge an alliance was a risk, yes, but the queen had taken an even greater risk in placing so much of her trust in a man she knew the least. Though such a decision could not come with such haste, as he saw it. Ludica cleared his throat and addressed the queen as well as those who stood within the room.

"If it pleases the queen, then I should like the time to consider your offer. As well as it might benefit us both, I must also take in account, the stakes which we face as well."

He could see that it displeased the queen to hear his response, but she made the effort to conceal her expression. Ordric, however, found hope in the prospect of his declination and bowed with respect to the king of Faermire.

"A most wise decision, my lord. Such rulings should not be taken so lightly as others might. And I am humbled by the wisdom which you so greatly display here in our presence."

The man made sure to waste no time for the queen to protest and quickly took his leave, prompting the others to follow shortly after. Then, when once the room was filled with such clamor, the king now found himself oppressed by the onerous silence which was left behind.

Gwenora stood atop the stairs and slowly released the rigid tension within her shoulders. She sighed, and gently shook her head from side to side as she looked at the king.

"A wise decision indeed," she noted. "Though what a pity it is. I was hoping that his bitterness would kill him in due time. But judging by the smile on his smug little face, it only seems that you have only added years to his wretched life."

Ludica chuckled and offered his hand up to ease her down the steps. In her old age, the woman gladly accepted the help, taking one careful step after the next. As she reached the bottom, she stood nearly only half his height, yet still commanded his attention just the same.

"Time has proven to be our greatest enemy has it not?" she asked. "Soon enough, I will no longer be able to hide my ailments from those who wish to see me weak."

"Well, do not forget Lady, that those who wish to see you weaken, have only to look at themselves also. Time is equally a cruel bastard to us all."

"Hm, well the years have certainly worn heavily on you, Ludica, but not your good looks, that much is certain." He stroked his peppered beard and nodded his head with a smile.

"How are the children?" she continued.

"They test me daily." He paused for a moment as he thought about each of them. "But they are well," he added.

"Beowyn is too much like myself in my younger years, and the price for it against me is heavy. And Estrith... she grows to look more and more like her mother as the days pass. Emelyn is all I can ever see when I look into her eyes now."

Gwenora lowered her head as she smiled, masking the sadness behind it.

"I should like to see them one day," she noted. The room became silent once more as she reminisced on the memories of her past.

"In all my years, the gods have only ever heard me once. The bastard demanded a son but could get nothing. I reveled in it as

I watched him suffer the knowledge of his plight. No matter the woman he forced into his bed, all that remained was his shame."

"But there was Emelyn..." Ludica added.

She scoffed at the notion that her child had belonged to Ascferth.

"Emelyn was not his blood," she replied with a smirk. "I made him believe it was so once I found out that I was with child, but the moment my child was born a girl, he wanted nothing to do with her. Yet, she was everything to me..."

"As she was to me," he dolefully replied, recounting the loss of his first wife.

"You were good to her, Ludica, and I am forever grateful to you for that. Her death was not in vain, you know this."

"Yes," he answered. Though he could feel the pain of her loss creeping into his heart once again. The day she passed renewed itself to him as he watched her life slipping from his hands. The newborn children she bore to him cried aloud together as she reached out to them one last time. Her face grew pale, and her strength weakened with each passing moment as he stroked her face and soft auburn hair. It was the last time he had ever cried, and she spoke the words to comfort him while he sat by her side.

He couldn't bear to look down at the blood-stained sheets beneath her and kissed her hand as it fell limp against his own. Her small hand rested peacefully between his fingers as he called her name over and over again, pleading with her not to leave him. But his beloved wife was gone, and there was nothing that he could do to stop it. The newly crowned king was helpless to prevent her death, and it grieved him all the rest of his days.

"My daughter could never gain Ascferth's favor except in her death, and it brought about merely the opportunity for war at her own expense. I hated him for many things throughout my life, but for none more greater than that."

"Your people believe that I had stolen her from Ceolfrid."

"Please," Gwenora replied. "Ascferth knew that she was promised to you alone. It wasn't until Ceolfrid's father sought to use her as his way to control Mistelfeld, then he connived his way into the mix. They made you an enemy, and cost me the ability to see my daughter ever again."

"Either way, it seems that war may be upon us yet again," he replied.

She hesitated briefly then gently placed her hand upon his arm.

"Get some rest tonight, Ludica. Then tomorrow, there is something that I should like to show you."

Gwenora presented a reassuring smile before finally taking her leave. As Ludica made his way out into the yard, he was then greeted by his servant, who offered him his cloak. The king inhaled sharply, feeling the ice-cold air that permeated his chest. The chill of winter gripped his body, and life was suddenly renewed within his weary form.

"Your stare is as cold as the air about us, Sgell."

"Forgive me, Lord."

Ludica turned to the man who had served at side since the day that he had become king. His dark skin stood in contrast to the bright colors of his tunic, and he drew many an eye upon his appearance, for he was foreign to these lands. And if the color of his skin did not draw their attention, then his accent was certain to do the trick.

"Tell me, my friend, shall we join Mistelfeld? Or leave them to fend for themselves?"

Though the man stood as Ludica's aid, he presented himself always with a certain confidence that lacked in many of those who served a similar place. And though he humbly lowered himself before the king, it was clear that his place had been well-earned throughout the years.

"It is not my place to say, my Lord, but since you ask. . . I believe that the threat Lady Gwenora faces does not only lie beyond her borders. To make an enemy of Abensloh could mean that you also make an enemy within the walls of Mistelfeld. If I were to advise my Lord, then I would say that it would be best to avoid two enemies, when you can have none. For the sake of our people, this war is not ours to fight."

"Perhaps not now my friend, but it soon will be. . ."

In the dead of night, Ludica was greeted by a member of the queen's personal guard. The sun had still yet to rise over the horizon and all was quiet within the realm. Sgell approached from beyond the way and offered the king a reassuring nod as he joined the pair.

"The horses are ready my lord, and the queen shall meet you at the gate."

Ludica looked to his servant who then passed a hesitant glance at the guard.

"The horses. . ."

"Yes lord. The queen prays that you mind her discretion but asks that you make haste to join her. There are some who have eyes and ears throughout the city." Her guard made certain to avoid the king's gaze.

"Indeed," Ludica replied and reached for his cloak as he followed the men down the corridor.

Led only by the flicker of the torches' light, the men swiftly made their way further along the cobblestone path and out into the cold morning air. He looked on to find that Gwenora had already found her place atop her horse and greeted him with a smile.

"Care for a morning ride?"

"I'd hardly call it morning, Gwenora," Ludica replied as he mounted his horse. "Do you often make it a habit of sneaking through the night?"

"Only if the situation calls. Which it certainly has, as of late..." She added.

She then urged her horse forward, leading the way with her men close behind. Ludica and his guard then followed, driving them forward into the night. The sound of the beating hooves carried the group onward to the north, and the sun soon began to peak its head over the jagged hills which surrounded them. The horses led them amidst the web of expansive streams that overflowed from the cascades beyond the way. And the once green expanse had turned pale beneath the winter sky.

As they finally reached their destination, Gwenora brought her horse to a halt, overlooking the valley from atop the ridge. The others quickly followed suit, and the king paused to survey the landscape before them.

Down below, the charred remains of village huts had been burned to ash, and dozens of frozen bodies littered the field in front of them. He noted the bands of earth which had been scorched throughout the land, like the breath of fire had thrown itself to no end.

The queen then looked to Ludica, revealing the dread in her eyes. It was a feeling he carried all the same, as the scene presented itself before him. He remained quiet, shuddered by the disbelief which now carried him, and the bitter winds cut even deeper than before.

"There are others further north," she uttered. Her solemn disposition revealed the truth behind the woman's intent. That much was now clear to him.

"It is not merely conjecture, upon which I make my plea, Ludica. This is Nurrock's doing. And the savage only moves at the behest of his master. . . Ceolfrid intends to send me a message."

Even from where the party stood, it was clear that the giant king of Helmere had destroyed the village with the aid of his beast, the dragon. But the truth of what had been revealed was something that the king could not bring himself to readily accept. For the king of Abensloh no longer desired to remain dormant within his stronghold to the north. It was clear now, that the man wanted to finish what was started those many years ago.

"There are no survivors?"

"Word has not yet spread, if that is what you mean. But it is only a matter of time before some like Ordric discover what has happened and use it to advance his own causes. People will begin to flee, and they will use that fear, to demand we bargain with Ceolfrid. If we do not act now, then my people shall lose everything, including the safety that they so eagerly demand. Under Ceolfrid's rule, there will never be peace."

It was apparent to him, that the face of war had already begun to rear its ugly head. And that whether he liked it or not, Faermire would need an ally just the same. For there were no others upon which he could call when the tides of battle would eventually rise to greet him.

Suddenly, he could feel the cold winter winds upon his face begin to shift. He looked at the ornate flag which had been fixed to her guard's spear and watched as it flipped within the gust. First toward the east, and then to the south. It shifted and writhed as it was yanked in every direction.

The gods were finally stirring, and they were hungry for blood.

Ludica turned to Gwenora once more and tightened his grip on the reins as he finally offered her his treaty.

"You shall have it," he uttered and looked again toward the hollow and charred remains down below.

# CHAPTER 10

BEOWYN AND QERETH RODE TO the gates where they were greeted by several soldiers ready to seize the prince. Having escaped their charge only days earlier, the guards were more than eager to ensure that they wouldn't lose him again. Beowyn was quickly surrounded, leaving his friend to wrestle with the guards' hold on him and the struggle ensued.

"Let go of me!" Beowyn shouted. "I need to speak to the king!" His commands were ignored, and Qereth continued to throw himself into the mass, throwing his fists at any man within arm's reach. But finally, Eohric, the captain of the guard interjected on their behalf.

"Release them," the man calmly uttered.

"But sir! the king's order—" a soldier replied.

"Release them, now," Eohric interjected, reinforcing his commanding tone.

The guards looked at one another, hesitant to obey, but finally relented to the order. And as their grip on the men were loosened, Beowyn and Qereth were quick to shove the guards away. The prince tugged forcefully on his cloak as he took the moment to collect himself and turned to face Eohric once more.

"Where is my father? I must speak to him at once."

"The king has gone to Mistelfeld upon their queen's request, lord Beowyn," the captain replied.

"Mistelfeld? When will he return? It's urgent, Eorhic." The man could sense the frustration in the prince's tone as he followed him.

"We have sent word for his swift return. It is your brother, my lord... he is dying".

"What?!" The prince stopped in his tracks as he looked back at the man in shock. "What do you mean he is dying? What happened?!"

"There was... an attack."

Beowyn and Qereth looked at one another in disbelief, and the prince quickly reclaimed his horse as he rode on toward the castle with Qereth in tow. The two charged through the streets, shouting at passersby to move aside, before jumping down as they entered the palace gates.

He ran directly to the boy's room to discover his brother's condition. As they entered, Beowyn stopped himself just beyond the threshold to gaze upon young Siged lying unconscious in his bed. Estrith remained by one side and the boy's mother sat on the other, both gripping his lifeless hands. His head had been wrapped in bandages and his skin grew pale beneath the tender candlelight.

His heart sank at the pitiful sight of the young boy whose life barely hung in the balance. Beowyn struggled to catch his breath as he approached the bed, and Estrith leapt into his arms, weeping at the sight of her brother. As she pulled away, he took note of the fresh bruises and markings along her neck and face as she struggled to avoid his eyes. He reached for her face, but she quickly turned herself away, suddenly finding Qereth behind him, and the two embraced one another as her friend strove to comfort her.

Richessa glanced up but for a moment and returned to her son as she wiped the tears from her eyes.

"Who did this?" Beowyn asked as he reached down to touch his brother's chest. Siged's breaths were shallow, and his skin was cold to the touch.

"It was Sidonis' man. His name I cannot recall but—"

"The heathen tried to attack me before turning his wrath on my son!" Richessa interjected, as she turned back to face them them. "When I wouldn't give him what he wanted, he sought to quell his wrath elsewhere, and I curse him with every fiber of my being!"

"Where is he now?" Beowyn asked.

"I killed him," Estrith said coldly.

Surprised by her words, he reached out to her, offering up his hand in consolation.

"The healers have done all that they can for him, but they say his life remains at the mercy of the gods. Beowyn, they do not hear me," she whimpered as the tears began to flow heavily from her eyes once more. All thoughts of anything else in his mind had vanished as he looked upon his young brother.

"I've entreated them more times than I can count, but Siged remains quiet, and his eyes will not open. I don't know what else to do!"

She covered her face with both of her hands and hopelessly sank back into her chair as Qereth stepped forward while she cried.

"I may know of way that we can help him," he uttered before them. All eyes suddenly shifted to the man where he stood, as they waited for the answer they all so desperately sought.

He shifted nervously before continuing,

"There is a sorcerer who dwells within the Donnorath Wood, just beyond our land at Caelfall. People have spoken of his powers, but none dare enter the wood for fear they may never return."

"Then I shall go to him," Beowyn replied.

"But what if—"

"I cannot just sit here and wait for my brother to die." He knew the question that Estrith posed before it even left her mouth, as it equally haunted him. "I must do something..."

"If we leave now, then we may just get there before nightfall," Qereth added.

"Then we haven't the time to waste."

Neither Estrith nor the queen objected to their quest, though it posed such great risk for all involved, including the boy.

"Gather the horses, Qereth, I shall join you shortly." His friend nodded and hugged Estrith once more, offering her words of consolation, before finally departing. Beowyn then approached his brother and whispered a promise into the boy's ear as he looked to both his sister and the queen once more.

Time was of the essence, but the sight of Siged lying at death's doorstep, gutted the prince who stood beside him. Beowyn wanted nothing more than to remain at his side and bring comfort to his brother when he needed him most. But with each passing hour, the boy's life continued to slip away. And soon, all hope would be lost.

As he stood, Beowyn couldn't help but thank the gods for ushering their swift arrival. Had it not been for their hand, then the opportunity to save his brother's life would most certainly have passed them by. But now, whatever plot his uncle schemed beneath the shadows, would have to wait until his brother could be saved.

"Remain strong," he told them both. As he left the room, he made his way directly to his own, where he found the small wooden snake that Siged had carved for him. In that moment, all he could do to hold himself together was to grip it tightly within his hands before placing it within the opening of his coat, resting firmly against his chest. With it tucked safely away, the man turned and met his friend down below.

As the two made their way toward Donnorath Wood, Qereth couldn't help but notice that sinking feeling within his gut. Many throughout the kingdom had heard of that sinister place, but none more so than he and his people who dwelt within of sight of it.

Those who lived at Caelfall dared not look toward the forest at night, as many claimed to have lost their children or their loved ones to it. It called to those who gazed upon its darkness and the sounds which came from within at times could bring a grown man to his knees.

Only those who sought to end their lives or face the wrath of the gods directly would step foot among the woods, and he wasn't sure which would be their fate.

Beowyn, however, faced the terror head on as he drove his horse further through the land. The prince was too naive to comprehend what dangers they truly faced in that place, but perhaps that was not to his detriment. It was clear that he was driven only by the love he held for his brother and he would stop at nothing to save him. Though Qereth still could not help but feel a morsel of regret for having even mentioned the woods at all...

Yet still, they rode; faster and harder as the day's end drew near. The vast darkness of the forest shrouded the horizon before them, and Qereth looked off into the distance at Caelfall. There at least, he could find some glimmer of hope and escape the dread of what lay before them.

"Gods protect us," he whispered to himself as they came closer to their destination. Qereth had always prided himself in his ability to ward off the dangers that drew near, whatever they may have been. But when it came to the forest beyond his home at Caelfall, well, that was another matter entirely.

But suddenly, as though a certain line had been crossed, their horses pulled themselves back and reared up into the air, nearly knocking the men from their saddles.

"Woah, woah!" Beowyn struggled to keep his horse from bucking him as it continued to ignore his commands.

"We must turn back, Beowyn! There is only death which lies in wait for us there!" Qereth could no longer contain his terror in that moment as he nearly allowed his horse to carry him back to safety.

"Go if you must, Qereth, but I am not leaving until I find the sorcerer!" He drew his horse back until it no longer fought against him and dismounted, tying the reigns to a small tree nearby.

Returning himself to the plight at hand, Qereth relented and followed suit. He grabbed what equipment he could before the two departed, drifting further into the forest. Each step which drew them in made their entrance close behind them, as though a tunnel had been shut. And soon they were lost amongst the fog of the deep, and the groaning trees which surrounded them. The world outside this place could not pierce the veil which separated them. And soon the men found themselves no longer alone. They could feel the sense of watchful eyes upon them and all around them at once. Though there was nothing that they could find.

"Which way is it?" Beowyn asked.

"I-I do not know." Everywhere his head turned, Qereth could no longer make any sense of where they were, or even from where they had come.

"It's said that he dwells within the heart of the forest, but I cannot say for certain..."

Beowyn cursed quietly beneath his breath as he weighed the dangers that surrounded them now. It was his desire alone which kept him from his wit's end, but with each passing moment, Qereth could see that the prince too, began to feel the rising fear creep up within his anxious expression.

Was it a distant scream or the cry of an animal, they could not tell as they wandered deeper within. The silhouettes of the trees and foliage before them often appeared as hideous beasts or that of nefarious stalkers casting a wider net round about them.

Suddenly, Qereth could feel his foot plunge into the false ground beneath, which had turned into a small pit filled with rancid water. Taking nearly everything he could to keep himself from panicking, he pulled himself up with the help of his friend who had caught him by his arm.

The longer they walked, the more they could hear the noises grow louder around them. Even so much as to hear the faint whispers of those they could not see. Both men had long since drawn their swords and gripped them tightly in their hands.

"Do you hear that?"

"Of course I do!" Beowyn replied, as they both turned their heads to find the source of the voices they heard. Suddenly, a shadow shifted off in the distance that one caught a glimpse of, and then another.

"There!" Qereth pointed his sword at what appeared to be a large snake, or perhaps something else which scurried along their path. Another large creature seemed to drift past them only moments later.

Up above them, the trees swayed in a wind that they could not see nor feel, and behind him, Qereth could see what appeared as a creature both ox and man standing the distance. Just watching and waiting.

As he turned back around, two eyes glared down at him from within a shadow black as night. Then like a shimmer of light had shone over it, a wave of color emerged over the figure's skin, which showed that of a woman cloaked in scales from head to toe. Her eyes were orange and her hair dripped with blood.

Frozen in fear, he could only watch as she whispered words unknown to him and pressed her fingers onto his forehead, forcing his knees to go weak. He crumbled into pieces onto the ground and glanced toward Beowyn who was cast with a spell just the same. And towering above his friend was the oxen creature they had seen only moments before until a heavy weight had suddenly fallen upon his eyes. And within seconds, they were lost within a deep and heavy slumber.

As Beowyn awoke, everything around him was covered in a blurry haze so that he couldn't make sense of anything he saw. The sound of drums pounding in the distance forced him to lift his head, as heavy as it felt. His mouth was dry, robbed of anything to quench his thirst, and his limbs were like foreign objects that swayed back and forth over the creature who carried him.

The light of the flames carved a path along a dilapidated fortress. Its walls had long since collapsed through the ages and had been swallowed up within the woods. A relic of the old king-dom, it now stood as a haven for those who sought to touch the gods.

Over time he regained his sight and could see that Qereth had been given more control of his senses, fighting to free himself from the clutches of their captors.

"Beowyn! Beowyn wake up!" A loud horn bellowed around them as they were carried further within the old castle's walls. Both people and half-bred creatures alike approached the men as they droned on with chants of the old language. He was helpless against their touch, some whose faces were marred with self-mutilation and others with diseases he had never seen. Each one covered their bodies in clay and paint like that of the dead.

They were carried to a large circle where stones had been laid and a cauldron placed over a fire at its center. Behind it, a frail man covered in markings, ordained himself with a crown of antlers over his head. He lifted his arms to the night sky and uttered words which seemed to spill from his lips like the tar that ran down his chin and neck. Black ash was smeared across his eyes, and he began to tremble before them.

As he spoke, a cloud began to emerge from within the cauldron and lifted itself into the sky. Swirling and twisting within itself, he could see the faint blue hue of images emerging inside of it until it rose high into the air.

At its peak, the cloud erupted and emitted a light which had been cast over the circle, bright as day, until it finally settled over them all. The beating drums ceased, and all those around them fell silent as a young woman approached the man and kissed his hand. Both Beowyn and his friend followed her trail with apprehension marked within their widened eyes. The woman who, both delicate and fair, looked to her leader with a smile on her face, and walked to the ledge from where they stood. She appeared both content and elated to have been chosen and removed her robe before finally leaping to her death.

Beowyn gasped with terror and looked to his friend who had once again returned his focus on loosening his bonds. The prince also took his cue in that moment, and both men fought and thrashed over the creatures who held them upon their shoulders. Though finally the savages which held them released their grip and dropped the pair into the circle.

As he lifted himself to run, Beowyn suddenly caught himself at the sound of the man's steady and unwavering words.

"You are here for the boy. . ."

The prince paused, tempted still to run, but lured by the knowledge the old man presented.

"I-I am," he hesitated.

"Many who come to entreat the gods often receive the answer they do not seek."

"Are you the sorcerer? The one who has the power to heal?"

"I am called by many names, boy, but you may call me Gorhan." Qereth looked at his friend with a sense of apprehension about him. An expression like that of regret and fear for the lives he felt himself had endangered. It was far too great a risk to take, but the prince would not relent.

"I am here for my brother, sir." he said. "He was gravely injured, and his life now hangs in the balance. I wish for you to heal him."

The man approached the prince as he studied him from head to toe. He was smaller in stature but held confidence unlike any other around him.

"What will you give?" he asked with a grin.

"I have money." He removed a small bag filled with coin from within his coat and the man gladly held out the tendrils of his hand to accept it.

"I alone require your coin, but the gods I'm afraid, require something more." he mischievously added.

"But I have nothing left to give."

"Your blood. A life for a life…" In that moment, Beowyn couldn't help but recall the words his father spoke only days before. Had his life been meant for this moment? Had it always been his fate to give up his own life and claim to the throne for the sake of his young brother?

All he could seem to think of was Siged's face looking back at him with that smile he had always cherished. But his bright grin quickly faded as his eyes shut and his face grew pale. He then reached for the small wooden snake tucked away against his chest and clutched his hand over top of it before he finally answered,

"You shall have it," he replied, as he lowered his head.

"Beowyn, no!" Qereth reached out to his friend but was quickly pulled away. Gorhan then led the prince toward the cauldron where the flames grew hotter beneath it. The old man lifted his arm above the boiling liquid and cast a fine powder over the pot as a black plume erupted before them.

The drums began to beat yet again, and those around them continued their chant as Gorhan held his trembling hands over the fumes. Beowyn could smell a bitter scent and briefly turned his head away as he noticed his friend calling out to him amongst the countless voices.

"Do not do this!" he cried. "We will find another way!" He nearly considered it, as the thought of what lay in wait for him gripped his heart with terror. Death stood before him, and he began to tremble at the sound of their beating drums. In an instant, the man had signed his life away to the gods, and it seemed that they were more than ready to accept it.

Suddenly the sorcerer unsheathed his dagger and reached out to the prince as he tightly shut his eyes. He could then feel the shuddering pain flow through his arm and into the rest of his body. His hand quivered and he opened his eyes, shocked to find himself still alive. Gorhan continued to hold his hand above the cauldron as blood drained from the gaping wound in his palm.

Satisfied with his contribution, the man released him and watched as Beowyn cradled his arm against his body. He laughed aloud and reached a cup into the pot as he lifted the oozing liquid to the prince's face. It was thick like tar and smelled of a corpse. Though before he handed it to the prince, Gorhan looked sternly into his face and began to speak,

"A tower of many stones crumbles beneath the winds which have not been known. And I see you stand in the midst."

The prince couldn't seem to find any meaning to the sorcerer's words but took the cup from his hand and forcefully swallowed the drink before he could change his mind. He coughed and gagged at its foul taste but kept himself from retching back what he had consumed, for fear that the spell would not work.

He then looked back to his friend, who stood and watched him with dread. All he could hear was the pounding of drums as they grew louder, and the fire grew hotter beneath his feet. He looked into the dark sky above and found himself helpless as he heaved his body back, releasing the spirit within him. Beowyn was paralyzed, incapable of resisting the sucking force he felt within his chest. When it was complete, he fell to the ground limp and cold, shivering from head to toe. Until finally everything went dark.

The sound of the proceedings round about him had gone silent in an instant and the call from Qereth disappeared as the world around him faded. There was nothing that he could see nor hear anymore. Even the life which flowed from his own heart had ceased in that moment and for Beowyn, son Ludica, the prince of Faermire, he was no more.

Yet in the distance, there appeared a light, if only as a flicker. Once more, and then another, it came to him and grew brighter, as he could hear the soft call for his name. Then, like a sudden wave had hit him, ripping him from his slumber, he flung his head up from the ground where he lay and began to vomit.

The black tar-like liquid from his cup spilled out of his mouth and over his lips as he retched repeatedly, so that nothing left remained inside of him. Qereth appeared by his side to lift him up as the two sat alone within the circle. Beowyn clung to his own body as the pain rolled through his veins like shards of broken glass.

"Here, drink some water." The prince accepted the offer and reached for it as he tried to steady his trembling hands.

"What happened?" he asked.

"After you drank from the sorcerer's cup, you looked to have given up the ghost before you fell to the ground unconscious. I thought you were dead but could see at last that you drew breath. So, I waited here beside you until woke."

"Where have they gone?"

"I cannot say," Qereth replied. "They departed into the night."

Beowyn could feel his friend's eyes resting heavily over him for some time and glanced back to confirm his suspicion. The look upon his face was something that he couldn't quite understand. Whether he was distraught or confused by what it was he saw, he wasn't sure, and it troubled him.

"What's the matter?" he asked, as he struggled to regain his balance.

"I-I cannot say for certain. But it looks as though you have aged overnight. Almost like some ten years have been drawn from your face, Beowyn."

"I can feel it so. But let us hope that his spell worked. Help me up."

Qereth was quick to oblige his friend and stretched the weakened prince's arm across the back of his neck. Step by step, the two men slowly made their way back into the depths of the forest, hoping to eventually reach horses.

As Estrith awoke, she lifted her head to find that she had fallen asleep beside her brother's bed. The flames from the fire crackled and hissed as she pulled the blankets of fur further onto his chest. She caressed his cheek and pulled his hand into her own, nearly bringing herself to tears once more.

Richessa had gone for the night, leaving the two siblings alone together and she prayed over him to the gods.

"Do not leave me, Siged, please. You must fight this." With no word still from her brother or Qereth, Estrith was left to carry the weight of her young brother's plight upon herself. Time was quickly passing them by, and all she could seem to feel was a dwindling hope for his survival.

She lifted his hand to her face and gently kissed it. As she lowered it back to the bed, a small tug against her fingers from his own sent her eyes up toward the boy's face. She was unsure of what it was that she had felt. Was it just her imagination or was there life in his grip, even if just for a moment?

Suddenly it happened once more, and she could see the fluttering of his lids before his eyes opened in front of her. Within an instant, Siged was awake, and she was content with the knowledge that Beowyn's journey was in fact a success.

# CHAPTER 11

## HELMFIRTH, KINGDOM OF MISTELFELD

THE MEMBERS OF GWENORA'S COUNCIL had gathered before the empty throne as they awaited her arrival. The great hall was filled with the blend of incoherent voices that spoke amongst each other. Up above them, the sun had cast an ambient light through the panes of glass which formed the dome.

The intricate details carved within the walls gave way to the awe-inspiring architecture throughout. And the true majesty of Mistelfeld revealed itself at the peak of each new day. Even the doors, which had scaled the height of its supporting walls, announced their elegance each time they were opened to reveal their guest.

The court reverberated as the thick doors were pulled apart, and all fell silent as Ludica appeared from behind them. Several members of the council bowed toward the king, as others spoke quietly amongst themselves. It was a sentiment he couldn't quite gauge, either for or against him, but he carried on, and greeted them all with a nod.

As he reclaimed his spot at the foot of the throne, he turned to find Ordric approaching him from within the mass. The old man took pride in his appearance, ensuring that neither a single hair nor thread was out of place. His gray beard had been neatly trimmed to match his thinning hair and the hem of clothes had been pressed well beyond necessary for the tunic he wore. Mistelfeld's colors were sure to be seen in whatever he donned, making sure that the color green was displayed for all to see.

"I have heard rumors of recent excursions with the queen as of late. I do hope that his majesty be careful to avoid any misguided persuasions, however genuine they may seem," he said.

"And what sort of persuasions might those be, Lord Ordric?"

"Some that should not be taken at face value. Whatever misconceptions Gwenora may have, we must not be so quick to rise against Abensloh. Ceolfrid is a brute no doubt, but cunning and wise all the same. We have only to make an audience with the man before we make any maneuvers which we will most certainly regret. Ceolfrid will listen to reason, I'm sure of it."

"Under the proper leadership, no doubt..." Ordic's sense of word play hardly made it difficult for Ludica to read between the lines. And it sickened him to see just how little the man cared to conceal his treasonous ways. But as certain as Ludica was that Ordric harbored such contempt for Gwenora, he was also certain to have his schemes afoot.

Then the announcement came, and the crowd turned to face the queen as she entered the court. All the men bowed and waited until she had properly seated herself upon the throne, then looked to her guest, the king.

And just as she portrayed the confidence in her trust of Ludica, he too, could feel the unwavering scowl from Ordic's face.

"Whether some choose to believe it or not, we are now faced with the grim reality that war stands at our door. Ceolfrid's scouts have been spotted along our borders, that much we know. But it is with that knowledge that we must come to terms that it will only be a matter of time before we find his armies gathered there to meet us.

"I will not stand by and wait for that time to come. For then, it shall be too late. But with Faermire's aid, we may be able to withstand Ceolfrid once and for all.

"Ludica has finally agreed to an alliance with our people, and it shall be settled by the day's end. From this moment forward, there will no longer be enmity between our lands and our people. Today will mark the day where we find everlasting peace."

It was customary in the times to forge an alliance between rulers formally. And so it would be, that a ceremony was set to cement their treaty, so that all who were present, could not dispute the claim, nor dishonor the vow. It was in essence, a ceremony in which all would take part, whether great or small.

Some within the crowd could then be heard saying,

"Here, here," while others began to murmur once more. Ordric could once again be found with a look of disdain upon his face and hardly uttered a word, until he turned to face the king.

"You have doomed us all," he said, before turning to leave the court. The members of his entourage followed closely behind, and the queen's eye glimmered with approval.

She remained for a time with the group within the court and conversed with those who eagerly supported her decision. It was a notable divide, as Ludica could see it. And soon, nearly half of Gwenora's leadership had left the room. Of course, one could not possibly satisfy the lot entirely, but such dissent could only mean that more trouble loomed upon the horizon.

Ludica respectfully bowed toward the queen, then finally re-cused himself to the balcony which overlooked the city. He had hardly any time to take in the air around him and cherished the moment at last.

The black sands of the shore lined the border of Mistelfeld as far as the eye could see. It reminded him much the same of his land at Elsterheim, as both kingdoms shared the river, Ethreal. Its vast waters carried the divide between the western kingdoms and the east. He knew little of the world beyond the river, aside from his dealings with Elwin and his rule over Valenmur, but that was more than enough for him.

Ludica had little desire to become entangled with the interests of those men, as he had plenty to contend with on his own. And that was becoming more evident to him as the days drew on. For there was no peace amongst the greedy and the proud. He could not, however, decide where he fell amongst them. For men do not ascend the throne and hold it for long, unless they too, can equally resist those who seek to take it.

But before long, the aging king found himself overcome by the cold, and soon he made his way back into the court. Inside, prepa-rations were already underway for the ceremony which would soon be at hand, and the fate of their two kingdoms would be sealed. He lamented the need for formalities in all aspects of his life, whether great or small. The king would just as rather sign the document and be on with it, but things in life never came so easy.

He watched as the servants moved hastily about and sighed aloud as he passed amongst them. Sgell awaited the king just be-yond the door and offered him a modest bow, before the two men made their way down the corridor. Not a word was spoken before he finally approached his room. He hesitated to enter through the door, as if doing so would only solidify his choice to carry on. And on the bed, lay the clothes that his servants had prepared for him. Ludica had never felt more alone at that moment, and the only solace he could find was in the presence of his friend, who stood silently behind him.

The ceremony drudged along just as he feared it would, but the disgruntled sight of Ordic's appearance brought some relief, if only for a moment. Despite the man's objection at the whole of it all, he still made it a point to be at the front for all to see. The court had been filled to the brim with people and for once, the king found himself stifled by the heat which enveloped the room.

Gwenora carried on with her speech and all eyes were fixed on her alone. She spoke with a renewed sense of veneration and carried herself with poise. The words drew her people in and the claim to power which she held, carried with it the right to call herself their queen. In all the years, no doubt squelched by the antics of her husband, the woman was at last free to lead her people in the way that she saw fit. No longer constrained by the shackles of her marital stature, she was indeed liberated. And Ludica could not help but smile on her behalf.

Though finally, she called the people's attention toward the king and all eyes were suddenly glued to him. The court was silent, and he looked to find Gwenora offering her hand toward him. He cleared his throat, then ascended the stairs as he rose to stand beside her. Before them, an ornate podium had been erected and it held a large parchment outlining the treaty between Faermire and Mistelfeld together.

He had read it before, but in that moment, the words appeared to him like a jumbled mess. He wanted nothing more than for it all to be done. Though finally, he watched as the queen took the quill and signed her name, then sealed her crest with wax beside it. It was a public declaration, and a sign for rulers of the land that would forge a new path ahead for them all.

He hesitated for a moment, but finally took the quill from her hand and signed his name beneath the queen's, then pressed his ring firmly into the melted wax beside it.

She smiled up at him to note her approval, then gestured toward the other leaders as they followed suit. Eventually the ceremony would come to an end, and the king could breathe once more. Though the people began to mingle within the court and Ludica found himself forced to entertain their enduring formalities. From one conversation to the next, he found no relief until his servant appeared from among them. And the man was careful to weave his way in and amongst the crowd as he made his way toward the hopeful king. Ludica couldn't help but smile at the sight of his friend but found the man's countenance far from endearing.

The king could see Sgell's solemn expression as he approached, and the man revealed a small note which had been rolled within his grasp. An urgent message no doubt, carried by way of a falcon. His servant was quick to escort the king aside, then leaned in to conceal his words from those around them.

"Forgive me, my Lord. But there is news of an attack within the palace."

Ludica could feel the grip of a rising pit within his stomach.

"An attack?" He struggled to comprehend the man's words as he looked him in the eye. The nervousness in Sgell's voice was noted, albeit contained beneath his stoic composure.

"It is the young prince, my Lord. Siged is dying..."

The world outside of Donnorath Wood appeared as though it carried a life which had never been known from the forest within. Entrapped by their wooded prison, the men had come to wonder what was real and what was not. For they could no longer discern reality from the tricks that had been played upon their minds.

The darkness both expanded and grew heavier all around them, just as it began to suffocate them all at once. The black trees groaned and ached all about them, entangling themselves even tighter together with the vines that choked them.

Even the light seemed to grow dim as they approached it. So, they quickened their steps. Until soon, they were running, stumbling over one another as though it were a race to the finish line. And just when it seemed that the light would disappear, the men leapt out into the field, where they rushed to the safety of their horses. Beowyn clung to its neck as he swallowed every fresh breath of air that he possibly could.

Finally, they were safe. Qereth made it a point to make it as far away from that place as he possibly could, as he mounted his horse and waited for his friend. Beowyn, however, took a moment to look back at the dark fortress which seemed to call out to him from within. It was a place where powers unknown resided and one where he knew he could never return.

He looked down at the wound that Gorhan had left in the palm of his hand and took notice of the black tar which seeped through his bandage. Whatever spell the seer had cast, it left a lasting scar both within and without his body. Something happened to him in that place, and he could feel that it still remained.

"We must hurry, Beowyn. Siged awaits us." Qereth appeared increasingly unnerved at the sight of his friend who remained standing, unmoved in the midst of the forest. Beowyn continued to stare on into the darkness, almost drawn to the call of its beckoning groan. When once, he could not stand to be in that place any longer, he soon found himself taking a step back toward it.

"Beowyn!" Qereth called to prince, as he tugged tightly against the reigns of his horse. Then the trance had been broken. He turned back to the horse and lifted himself up into the saddle.

"I'm coming," he said and looked to his friend. Qereth carried his angst over the whole of his countenance but pressed on as the prince led them away. They rode on toward the city, but both men remained silent, lost among their own thoughts. He was certain that Qereth worried much about the things that they had seen within the forest. Even time had seemed to slip them by, and all sense of reality felt as though it were only a dream.

The day had begun to stifle beneath the clouds which formed overhead and though they rushed to Elsterheim, Beowyn couldn't seem to rid himself of the rising cold within his bones. Whether it was from the spell which had been cast, or simply the winter setting in, he found himself cowering from the wind against his face.

Even still, he pressed on. For despite what they had been through, he couldn't be certain if his brother still lived.

Estrith couldn't keep herself from staring at the woman seated across from her. Richessa remained at her son's bedside for just as long as the princess did. Though not a single word was spoken between them since the day of the attack, and perhaps, it was all for the better.

She found herself constantly replaying that moment in her mind and though she couldn't bear the thought of it, she knew that somehow, the queen was involved. And as she tried to reason her way around it, she could only ever seem to conclude that it resulted in Richessa's treason. And if it was so, then it also meant that her uncle was somehow complicit with her in it all.

Such an accusation, however, would only serve to bring the queen's wrath upon her as she remained at Elsterheim alone. As her father had gone to Mistelfeld, and her brother now missing for days, there was no one left to support her word against the queen's. And until either of those men returned, then Estrith remained at Richessa's mercy. The very woman whom she believed to be responsible for Siged's plight, now sat only a breadth away from her, cradling his hand in her own.

She felt more like a prisoner in her home now than ever before. And the deal she had made with the queen drove Estrith to hate herself even more in that moment. She cursed the very notion that she could ever trust that woman, and it was Siged alone, which anchored her there.

The two women sat on either side of him, offering the boy comfort in the best possible way that they each knew how, but it still wasn't enough to wake him from his trance.

Hours had passed. And those hours soon led to days. By the grace of the gods, Siged's life remained, and Estrith could only attribute that to whatever it was that Beowyn and Qereth had done. But what should've only been a trip of two days at most, they were gone now for four. She had found hope for a time, as she saw the flicker of life in her young brother, but now, she worried in the absence of the other.

She grew anxious and found herself constantly looking toward the window as the sun began to dim. Another day had come to pass, and still there was no sign of them. Something must be done, she thought to herself.

"It has been far too long since they set off to Donnorath Wood. Perhaps we should have a party sent out in search of the prince."

The queen passed a glance toward the princess but remained silent for a time before she finally offered a response.

"Beowyn spends more of his time within the realm than he does here in the city. I'm certain that he can find his way back. We needn't waste the resources."

What little hope Estrith held for Richessa's compassion had been utterly crushed. The woman carried a defiant disregard for the very man who sought to save her own son's life. And so it was, hidden beneath that distraught and forlorn exterior, that the queen clung tightly to the seething bitterness which fueled her life.

Though suddenly, the door burst open, revealing her brother just beyond the threshold. Estrith leapt to her feet, both shocked and relieved at the sight of the man before her as she called to him.

Beowyn was winded, and the journey had obviously taken a heavy toll on him by the disheveled appearance he presented. But it made no difference to her. Her brother was home again, and in that moment, that was all that mattered.

Beowyn, however, had hardly taken notice of any other presence in the room as he made his way to Siged's bed. He gently clasped Estrith's shoulders to greet her, but quickly focused his attention on the young boy who lay before them. Qereth followed into the room shortly after, and greeted the queen with a bow, then offered Estrith a comforting embrace.

They watched as Beowyn knelt beside the bed and gently cradled Siged's hand. Their brother's eyes remained open, staring distantly into the ceiling. His color had since returned, and his breathing had steadied, though still, the spark of life had yet to return.

"Brother? I am here, Siged, it's alright. H-how are you feeling?"

"He has yet to speak, but he is doing well, I think," Estrith replied. "Whatever you did, it worked."

"He just needs time to regain himself that's all," Qereth added with a reassuring smile.

"Perhaps," Beowyn said.

As Estrith looked upon her brother for a moment longer, she reached out to him with growing concern.

"Are you alright? You look. . . ill. Or changed somehow, I cannot quite place it."

"I'm fine. As long as Siged is well, then that is all that matters."

"What happened out there?" She looked to Qereth, hoping that her friend would share what news her brother withheld. And just as the man nearly relented to her pressing gaze, the distant bells began to toll. Their father, the king, had finally arrived.

Richessa suddenly rose to her feet, as if by some means, the bell's toll was meant just for her. And in that moment, Estrith could see for once that there was fear in the woman's eyes. It was clear that her father's arrival meant something dire for the queen. And thus, her guilt was confirmed.

The woman was careful to mind her disposition however and straightened her dress before leaving the room. The others looked cautiously to one another and then to Estrith as she turned to face her twin.

"Beowyn, there is something I need to tell you. It's about Richessa, I-"

"Later Estrith, I need to speak with father. It is urgent."

And before she could stop him, the prince and their friend quickly left the room as she remained alone with Siged. Finally, without the queen's presence, Estrith was free to lean forward and kissed young Siged's face before reassuring him with a gentle smile.

Outside, both servants and guards alike, ran frantically about as they prepared for the king's return. Her family waited at the palace gates where she nervously joined them. Unsure of what she would even say or if she would get the chance to say it, she looked to the others whose gaze were fixed at the road ahead.

Beowyn's brow was furrowed with a certain determination in his eyes, and Qereth stood cautiously behind him. Richessa stood rigid and tall, as though to mask her angst within. Though her shoulders seemed to curl ever so slightly to the front, and her knuckles were held white against her dark dress.

She could feel the rising tension amongst the group, even within herself. Time seemed to slow before them, and the grip of her hands together grew tighter with each passing moment. Estrith had longed for her father's arrival before, but now, she didn't know how to face him. For once in her life, she felt the weight of the world upon her shoulders, and it felt as though it was too much for her to bear. As the king and his entourage approached the castle, Estrith could see the desperation in her father's eyes. The fate of his youngest child hung the in balance, and what little he knew of the boy's condition drove his feet faster upon the ground. Those present were quick to bow themselves in reverence to the king, but the man brushed the formalities aside.

"How is he?"

"He is awake now, my lord, and shows great progress." Richessa spoke first and kept her eyes fixed to the ground. He acknowledged her with a sigh of relief and greeted the others with a nod. Estrith opened her mouth to speak but heard her brother's voice instead. Though as he tried to interject, he too was cut short by their father's hand. The king's mind remained solely on the state of his young son. He passed through them unabated and proceeded to the boy's room.

As they entered, he promptly removed the gloves from his hands and lowered himself beside the bed, gently caressing Siged's head. And with words known only to the pair, Ludica whispered softly into his ear. With no response, he then grasped the boy's hand, prompting him to squeeze. But still, there was nothing. So, the king gently replaced his son's hand back onto the bed and rose to his feet, keeping his gaze fixed upon the ailing child.

"What of Sidonis' man?"

"He was killed amidst the scuffle, my lord," Sgell replied.

"I was speaking to my daughter." He then turned toward the young woman who couldn't bring herself to look him in the eyes.

"When I learned that he had returned alone, without our uncle, I sought to find an answer for his arrival. That is when I found the head of Lord Rodmar secured upon his horse. And when I turned to call for help, he attacked me. Only then, it was Siged who came to my aid. But suffered on my account..." She struggled to carry on as the memory of that day came rushing back, flooding her mind with all that had happened. As she nearly lost herself amongst her thoughts, her father had finally spoken, rescuing her from it all.

"Rodmar..." He repeated the name again, as if trying to piece it all together.

"She speaks the truth, father. But it was all by uncle's hand. I've seen it with my own eyes, Qereth and I."

"Uncle?" Estrith lifted her head at the realization.

Their father turned toward Beowyn and studied the man for a time. Then finally looked back to Estrith and then to Qereth.

"The three of you will join me in my chambers to discuss the matter further." And with nothing more to add, Ludica left the room with her brother and Qereth in tow. But as she turned to follow, Estrith could feel the sudden grip of Richessa's hand around her arm. She looked to the woman who could no longer conceal her terror and plead to the princess through the veil of her silence. The queen's eyes spoke louder than any words could in that moment, and so it was that now Richessa was at her mercy before the king.

Estrith paused for a moment, but pulled herself away, leaving the woman alone to her misery. As she then entered her father's chamber, she watched as the man lowered himself into his chair by the hearth. His eyes remained fixed upon her brother and carried the deafening silence with him.

"I will forgo the notion that your attempts to escape my command will go unpunished. But if what you say is true, then you will tell me everything of what you saw regarding Sidonis. Both of you..."

Beowyn and Qereth looked to one another before the prince took a step forward to give his account. He began first, when their uncle was spotted on the road to Taernsby, and then his venture into Graefeld. Qereth later joined in on the account of all they had seen as her father sat quietly and listened. Though the more they spoke, the more that she could see her father's grip tightening around the chair's arm. His focus shifted to his son, and then to his feet, remaining still, all the while.

The air was heavy amongst them, but her brother carried on. Estrith lowered her head at the tale of the elder's beheading and the message sent to Elsterheim, but nearly jumped as her father called her name. He ordered his daughter to speak of her account, and she struggled at first to find the words.

"I saw that he had arrived at the palace alone which drew me to question his intent. I-I knew that he had left with uncle only days before but had just arrived for reasons I could not understand at the time. That is when I had gone into the stables to discover what he had brought for you. When I discovered it, I turned to call for help, but he attacked me, and then Siged also. I did not know at the time that the man had attacked Richessa, as she said."

She paused again and considered for a moment whether to continue, or leave her previous revelation unspoken. But the words began to flow unconstrained from her mouth, as though the action was not her own.

"But I have seen them together before father. Sidonis and Richessa, embracing and kissing each other. It only made sense to me now after all that we have learned here today. But I do not think that she-"

Ludica suddenly threw his hand into the air, silencing her within an instant. Both Beowyn and Qereth stood with consternation at the news of their affair. And as though Estrith had been the one to betray her father, she cowered as he leapt from his chair, scattering the objects from the table beside him.

Fury was all that they could see in the king's eyes though he remained quiet. He grew cold as ice and stood like a tower before them all until he finally relented to the rage which seethed within his veins. He rushed past the trio and to the door as he flung it open. Though there she stood, the woman whom he once called Queen. Richessa's eyes were filled with tears which streamed down the sides of her face. Her hands were clasped prayerfully in front of her body as she threw herself at the king, pleading for her life.

All hope for what plots she could devise to convince her husband otherwise fell to the winds and all that remained of her stood before him. She grabbed for his chest, and begged him to hear her side, though he could stand to look at her no longer. The king plucked her hands from his body like thickened roots in the ground and threw her to the floor as he began to beat her.

She cried aloud as one smack followed another for all to see. All those around them stood in disbelief but remained helpless against his rage. Estrith and the others watched as she cradled herself at his feet while he relentlessly continued. The king ripped the crown from her head and pulled her by the hair until he threw her out into the yard. Both servants and guards alike, then approached the scene as he demanded their eyes to watch.

Richessa continued to beg and plead for her life as she threw herself around her husband's legs over and over again, even as he kicked her away.

Though finally, he could stand to see her no longer, and pulled his knife out, lifting it high into the air.

"If you will sleep in my brother's bed, then you shall die in it!"

She threw her hands up for one last plea and shut her eyes as he bore the knife down toward her body.

But against all sense or reason, Estrith could not bring herself to understand what was happening in that moment. Richessa's screams seemed to call for her and the young princess chose to heed it. The world around her seemed to fall dark as she raced into her father's path, nearly taking the killing blow for herself.

Everything fell silent and she raised her head up to the man before her.

"Please, father," she begged. "Let there be no death today. On this day which your son lives..."

She watched as he panted fiercely, restraining the rage once more beneath his chest, and dropped the weapon onto the ground.

"Take her to the dungeon!" He ordered, as his men promptly followed. They lifted the broken woman up by the arms and dragged her away as she continued to sob. All who watched could not remove their gaze from the queen until she finally disappeared beyond the gate.

Then left alone in the field, Estrith slowly pulled herself away from her father's wrath and lowered her head in reverence before him. Though finally, she could feel the gentle press of his finger under chin to lift it back into his sight. He stared at her for a time in silence, marking his gaze deeper into her fearful eyes.

"Have the elders gather their armies and send a message to Mistelfeld," he said. "War is upon us."

# CHAPTER 12

## ECRIN, KINGDOM OF ABENSLOH

THE CITY APPEARED SLOWLY, AS they crossed the ridge into Abensloh. Its walls stretched along the expanse of the lake which lay beside it. And the waters appeared almost black against the darkened skies above, as the rain carried on.

Sidonis had been to the capital only once, and it was years ago, before the Siege of Straefort. Much had changed from what he could remember. Ceolfrid, the king, learned from his father's mistakes, and added much to the city's fortifications. The sun's passive light was all that could be seen against the dreary skies above, casting a shadow over Ecrin. But within that shadow, there remained the strength and power of Abensloh's might. Sidonis reveled in it and grinned with pleasure as they approached the city's gates.

The capital was open to travelers and traders alike, funneling its patrons through the streets like cattle. The locals crowded the men, shoving their wares into their faces, and the music of the kingdom filled the air. Dancers paraded through the streets, raising their baskets to be filled with coin, and the local whores seductively waved to the men as they passed them by. One man nearly gave himself over to their enticing offer, but quickly returned himself to the task at hand. Sidonis continued through the streets, with only a single goal in mind, and followed the road up toward Ceolfrid's castle upon the hill.

The soldiers standing guard at the palace gates were donned in heavy black armor that presented them as shadows against the wall. Their helmets concealed their eyes as a long draw of black horsehair spilled over the top, and down to their shoulders. Blood red flags waved in winds as it pierced through the bland and muddied world around them, giving further credence to Ceolfrid's power. It was a sight to behold for the strangers who beheld it, and the men of Faermire stood among them.

"I am Sidonis, brother to the king of Faermire, and I have a message for Ceolfrid."

Only one soldier seemed to bother with their approach as he shifted his head toward the man, ever so slightly. He then contemplated the action before finally turning to leave their sight.

Sidonis and the others were left waiting there for some time as they pondered if he was ever going to return at all. Until finally, the small door that he had previously vanished through opened once again, and the guard curtly invited him in. The other two, however, were barred from entering the castle walls with hardly a word spoken to them.

"Just him," the guard ordered.

Sidonis proceeded in without hesitation as he left his men to fend for themselves within the city. The guard then led the man on alone into the palace until Ceolfrid's servant finally approached him.

The man was dressed ornately and presented himself with an arrogance much like Sidonis himself.

"The King has no interest in the frivolous matters of Faermire. So, state your business here to me now and I shall relay it to our lord."

"I shall relay it to him myself."

"You shall not!" The servant replied. "You will tell it to me here, now, or you shall leave. That is your only option."

Sidonis then scoffed with frustration before finally relenting to the man.

"I've come to present an offer of alliance with Ceolfrid as the future king of Faermire. I know he seeks to conquer Mistelfeld, and I will give my army to his aid."

The servant stared blankly for a moment at the man who stood before him. The words he offered came with nothing to support them, but he nodded his head and turned away.

"Wait here," he ordered.

After too much time had passed for his comfort, the servant finally emerged once again, appearing annoyed at the sight of the man before him. Sidonis' presence alone was enough to make the man scowl, but the servant pressed on, leading him to the king's throne room. Several guards stood nearby as the walls were draped in the same red banners that ran like blood along the stone. The music from within grew louder as they approached and two large doors slowly peeled open, revealing the festivities inside.

Ceolfrid sat in the distance upon his black and granite throne. Dancers swung their bodies before him as they threw streams of fabric into the air, moving like water amongst each other. The instruments carried music into the air like a spell which had been cast over all who were present, and many took part in conversations amongst each other as food and drink were scattered all about them.

The servant then urged him forward along the floor to present himself to the king. Each step which brought him closer to the throne brought more eyes upon the man, bringing with him, a new topic of conversation.

The king then raised his hand into the air, halting the music and the dancers alike, leaving Sidonis to approach him in further silence. Those who watched him whispered amongst themselves while others looked to the king for his response. The throne sat high above all the rest as Ceolfrid looked down upon the man who bowed himself before him.

"Sidonis, the king of Faermire... Now, Ludica I know. But you, I do not." The room was silent all around him, and he was suddenly at a loss for words.

"Now I must say, I was intrigued by the idea of meeting the great king of Faermire's own brother, but I suppose— well, I just thought you'd be taller..."

Sidonis could hear the faint snickering from those around him, and he feigned a smile while he waited for them to cease, before Sidonis continued,

"Perhaps the king would like to hear my offer in private," Sidonis replied.

"The king would not." Ceolfrid glared down at him before taking a sip from his cup.

"Whatever 'offer' it is that you have for me, it had better warrant my attention well. Or I shall make certain that you regret having stopped my party."

Sidonis then cleared his throat as he felt the heavy weight of all those who looked upon him, waiting for an answer.

"News has spread quickly of your cousin's death, and Gwenora seeks to form an alliance with Ludica as we speak."

"I know." Ceolfrid's demeanor was unrelenting, taking Sidonis by surprise. He scanned the room about him, as the king's patrons carried an expression much like his own. "What sort of king would I be, if I lacked my sources?"

"Then you know that he will no doubt accept her terms. The two kingdoms will soon become more than just a thorn in your side lord, King. But I can offer you Faermire's arm instead, once I am king."

"Then tell me Sidonis, how are you to become king? As I see it, you stand before me with neither the crown, nor the army. Just your word..."

"I will give you the whole of Faermire, itself."

His words struck a chord of intrigue with the mighty king, and he noted the change in Ceolfrid's expression, if ever so slightly. The king sat for a moment as he considered the notion and rose from his throne as all eyes were peeled on him alone. Then without a single word, Ceolfrid gestured for the music to resume as the dancers were quick to take their cue. The remaining patrons then followed suit, and resumed their conversations and festivities amongst each other, while Sidonis awaited the man's response.

He watched as the king took one final sip from his chalice, and nudged his head, signaling Sidonis to finally approach him. He followed the man to a private chamber behind the throne and stood in awe at the sight before him. Ceolfrid casually approached the ledge which overlooked the city, displaying the king's vast, and nearly endless expanse. Where his palace sat upon the hill, the view allowed him the pleasure of overlooking all that he ruled.

The city of Ecrin spread itself across the landscape, adding more to his power and rule throughout. And the distant fiery eruptions of the mountain fixed within the horizon, served as a constant re-minder that the gods found favor upon the man, the king. He was proud in every way, and he knew it well.

"The last time I saw your brother, he had stolen away my bride and nearly toppled my father's armies when we were at our weak-est. But by the grace of the gods, my father is dead, and our armies are stronger than ever. Yet still, the very name of Ludica and his legacy continue to vex me. So, tell me, why should I not cut you down where you stand?"

Even in this place, so far away, Sidonis was lost beneath the cast of his brother's shadow. No matter where, or to whom he ran, the man was constantly forced to dwell beneath the one he hated most. Ludica was the name which gutted him at his core, and Ludica was the one which had stolen everything from him. Even his own birthright.

Though born together from their mother's womb, Ludica was the one who entered the world first, and thus took upon him the inheritance of their father's throne and all that came with it. The brother who should have been his equal, treated him in everything as his lesser. But no more. Sidonis swore to himself that one day, that he would take back the claim which was his own.

"Because I too wish to rid this world of the blight which is my brother..."

"Indeed," Ceolfrid replied. If ever there was a morsel of weak-ness that Sidonis allowed himself, it was in that moment. And the king could see it, however so little. He then invited the man to di-rect his gaze upon the view which stood before them both.

"Look at my kingdom before you, Sidonis, and tell me what you see."

He paused for a moment, considering the words which he should say.

"I see a vast land. One which can only be ruled by a king who is worthy. And there is none more worthy than you, Ceolfrid."

The king of Abensloh chuckled at his response but turned to face him once more.

"I see a land full of prosperity," Ceolfrid said. "All who enter my kingdom, know that the gods dwell in this place. And it is by the gods which I have my power. But with such power, comes an even greater demand...

Our lands are divided, Sidonis. And a divided land cannot be a prosperous one. I have been given a divine right, you see. But it is by that right, that I must fulfill my purpose in this world."

The king stood nearly a head taller than Sidonis as he glared down at the man. Ceolfrid's broad shoulders carried him like a fortress dressed in fine clothes and jewelry. His metal crown bore sharp spikes all around its circumference, and the black in his eyes seemed to pierce into his very soul. His face had been shaved clean, revealing the staunch lines along the gaunt of his cheeks and the sharp point of his chin. Meanwhile, the golden hair which draped over his shoulders was pulled back to better accentuate his face and stood in contrast to the crown he bore.

Sidonis paused to collect himself before pulling his shoulders back and looked into the king's eyes.

"Then perhaps, my presence here, is meant to help you fulfill that purpose."

The room fell silent, as Ceolfrid studied him from head to toe. And for the first time, Sidonis let slip a morsel of fear into his eyes.

"Then tell me, why should I trust your word, when you are so quick to betray your own blood?

"To sully the land with the death of those whose blood you share are to be cursed among men, you know this. And to betray your own flesh, Sidonis, is to betray the gods themselves. If such a thing were permissible, I would've killed my cousin, Ascferth long ago and yet, it seems that I have been rewarded for my patience. I am blessed by the gods, though here you stand, asking me to align myself with the cursed."

"The gods are in constant need of change, Ceolfrid. One king rises, just so that another may fall. This is their way. So, to say that we know why it is that gods allow such things, is deny their very will. You are blessed indeed, lord King. That is why the gods have brought me here before you."

It was a great risk for Sidonis, using such a ploy against the king. But for one so mighty as the man before him, Sidonis sought to exploit the weakness of his superstitions against him.

"Go on," Ceolfrid replied.

"Faermire stands at the crux of the river Ethreal. From there, it divides the kingdoms of the east and those to the west. But the people of my land have a powerful resolve. If you were to try and take the land yourself, then you would most assuredly stretch your armies to the brink, even with Nurrock at your side.

"Let me rule my own people as your proxy, and your dreams of unity shall soon be at hand. My loyalty is yours, Ceolfrid, whatever the cost."

"Of that, I have no doubt Sidonis... But for one to sell his own brother's head for pleasure of his crown, it is a treacherous thing indeed." Ceolfrid considered the proposition a moment longer, then made his way back toward the court.

"You will join me tomorrow as we pay a visit to our dear friends in Helmere. Perhaps then, you may prove your loyalty to me."

As they reentered the court, the king waved him away like an unwanted offering and his guards appeared swiftly at his side. In a single moment, the knowledge of his presence was quickly forgotten, and the large doors were pulled shut in front of him. He stood alone to stare into the thick wooden wall that barred his entry as he was left alone once more.

He could still hear the muffled tones of the music beyond the door and scoffed aloud to himself. Though suddenly, the king's servant appeared from behind him and nudged him further along.

"I will show you to your lodging for the night."

"And my men?"

"I will tell them of your whereabouts, but they shall remain outside the palace. Where they sleep, is up to them."

And from one hall to the next, Sidonis followed the man throughout the maze of the palace atop the hill. Each new turn drove him further into his own thoughts, and as hard as he tried, he could not escape them. Soon, he found himself tormented with overwhelming realization of his insignificance. And in the grand scheme of it all, he still meant nothing.

The next day, Sidonis and his men gathered themselves amongst the king's caravan on the road to Helmere. Though they quickly found themselves lost within the crowd. And like a giant snake, Ceolfrid's train slithered along the road for hours toward the marshlands of the east.

What sun there remained for them to see beneath the winter sky, disappeared amongst the mist of Nurrok's kingdom. Helmere was a vast wasteland of marsh and soil too rancid for any crops to grow. Only a single road lead into the capitol city of Armagh from which all others joined, and much like the stories of old, Helmere was a place too foul for even the gods to dwell.

Torches were lit along the path so that its travelers could see as they traversed the fog and darkened skies about them. Animals screeched and hollered through the air, some were near and others far, though nothing could be seen. And large trees emerged from the waters like a withered hand draped in moss. Vines then curled and clung to all that remained as stones crackled beneath their horses' feet.

Sidonis and his men carried a watchful eye at all that appeared before them, as if the danger lurked in every direction. The people of Abensloh, however, carried on as though they were unbothered by it all. Clearly Ceolfrid and his people had taken this road many times before.

Though soon, Sidonis could spot a distant flicker of light growing brighter as it drew near. A large trail of torches then appeared through the mist as a new caravan had arrived to join them where the roads would meet. He studied the party, curious by their wayward appearance. The fellow travelers had adorned themselves as savages, caked in mud and paint, while they carried their instruments of ritual in their hands and on their backs. Not one had uttered a single word, not even the man who led them.

The king himself, then stopped his horse to lower his head in reverence to the man. The one known as Gorhan had arrived to preside over the ceremony which had been set in Armagh. Sidonis had heard of the man but had yet to make his acquaintance. He was known to be reclusive at times and appeared only when the gods were near. It seemed that the tales had proven true as to the man that presented himself before them. For the priest who spoke on behalf of the gods, made certain that none should forget his name. He was old and frail, but his name held the stature of the gods themselves. And all who would lay eyes on him, would be certain never to forget his face.

Those who followed the seer were like those who had been cast aside; the scourge of society. Many had the misfortune of being born with deformities, while others' scars were self-inflicted. Some were diseased, and some were simply the forgotten. But then, there were the creatures. The abomination of both men and Akorag joined together. Many appeared with both human qualities and of beast alike. They were the product of a union most unfitting for both the gods and of men. It appeared that there was truth in the rumors which Sidonis had heard, a most unsightly one. Though seeing them all together, Gorhan's followers created a most formidable mass; walking as spirits along the mist and keeping their eyes fixed on darkness ahead.

The sight before him brought a certain chill to his spine, and he was glad for once, to be near the back of the line, far from the intermingled presence of those who join the king's caravan. But all had gathered to celebrate the giant whose name was Nurrock. For yet another wedding was at hand, and the creature would take for himself an additional wife.

It was said that he stood at twice the height of a man and held a dragon for his pet. Though known as merely a runt amongst his own in the Skeleg lands, the half-bred creature escaped their efforts to consume him and ran south to dwell amongst men. There, he found his place within the swamps of Helmere and took on the name of king to the few who saw him as a god. Ceolfrid however, saw the creature as a weapon and a tool for his kingdom to be used.

The two lands dwelt in harmony together and those who knew of Ceolfrid's might, knew that it came at the hand of his giant.

Though as they approached the city, Sidonis found himself pitying the creature for boasting such a land as this. Nurrock's home was a wooden fortress which sat within a clearing of the marsh. Its walls were made of massive logs, driven to spikes at their tip and a large moat was forged all around its border. Small villages were sectioned off within the city's limit and consisted of those who deeply revered their king. The air reeked foul from the waters around them and only the glow of light from within the small capitol brought solace to travelers lost amongst the wasteland.

Ceolfrid knew very well that having a giant to fight on his behalf would require sacrifice to some degree. But to his delight, Nurrock was simple-minded enough to be satiated by the promise of what little Helmere had to offer him. The brute was not one to be reckoned with in a fight of arms but provided the means for a king of true wit to solidify his own power. Ceolfrid had gained everything from their bargain whilst also keeping his pet at bay. It was a clever tactic, and one which Sidonis envied deeply.

As the towering gate raised itself high into the air, The king of Abensloh and his new companion entered the Giant's keep with their trail of subjects following closely behind them.

Nurrock stood at the city's center for all to see. The rumors of his stature and might had proven true to those who had only ever heard of the giant. He towered over all who gathered around him and reveled in their praise. He was a warrior through and through and carried himself as the god he believed himself to be. Not an ounce of fat appeared on his sculpted flesh, and he boasted only his trousers and numerous scars as his apparel. His dark eyes sat deeply within his furrowed brow and the ink which painted the story of his might clung to the shaved skin upon his skull. He was fearsome in every way, nearly bringing Sidonis to stop in awe of the creature.

Nurrock opened his arms wide to welcome his ally and the priest, ordained by the gods. His deep voice rumbled in their presence for all to hear, and he smiled with delighted anticipation. As the giant's lips pulled back, his teeth appeared brown with rot, and he spoke with unwavering pride.

"My brother comes to join us!"

Ceolfrid lowered himself from his horse and approached the brute to happily accept the invitation. Crowds began to gather as they celebrated the guests who had just arrived, shouting praises to them both. The music carried on as the two kings greeted one another and finally turned to approach the great hall.

Sidonis and his men slowly followed the precession as it funneled in and around the large building which stood at the city's center. Hundreds of torches lit the night sky and large drums echoed as they pounded to the beat of the giant king's music.

His people were dressed in what looked no better than rags, but they carried themselves with a pride unmatched. Many dared not to even wear shoes upon their feet as they danced mindlessly around their god. His soldiers were all that brought credence to the state of his people, but even then, he found that they should be feared more for their stench, than that of their might. Sidonis could not bring himself to understand the savagery before him, but knew that when the time came, Nurrock's people would happily throw themselves upon a blade for him. So perhaps, in the end, that was all he needed to understand.

As Nurrock led his guests into the hall, Sidonis watched as Ceolfrid gave an order to his servant. The servant then came toward the men while they stood amongst the crowd.

"Follow me," the man ordered and led Sidonis into the hall where the festivities commenced. Ceolfrid presented his minstrels and dancers before the giant who accepted the offer and watched with delight as he ate and drank from his seat at the table. His chair sat larger than any throne or seat that Sidonis had ever seen. His hand grappled the meat of a boar's leg with ease and his cup appeared as a basin rather than any cup one might be offered.

As he approached, Ceolfrid casually waved Sidonis over and offered a seat next to himself. Nurrock sat beside a young woman who was stricken with fear. She was presented before the giant more than anything, as a sacrifice, than a wife. She whimpered and trembled before him as he caressed her body before the crowd. He examined the offering at hand to determine its worth to him and found himself nodding in approval. She would suffice, it seemed.

Ceolfrid leaned in toward Sidonis as he kept his eyes focused upon the scene before them.

"His queen killed the other, so now the creature demands another," he uttered with a grin. Sidonis could see the woman of whom he spoke, sitting at the other end of Nurrock's table with a scowl upon her face. She glared at the new bride with contempt in her eyes whilst seeming to plan her demise. Her dark hair matched the color of her eyes as they hid against the light and the sharp features of her face brought a terror to any who sought to threaten her place as the true queen. Whatever it was that the king had planned for the woman that night, held nothing against the wrath of his queen in the days to follow. The young woman's time was left short in this world, and she knew it.

With Nurrock's consent, the ceremony commenced and Gorhan approached the king and his new bride at the center of the floor. The hall soon fell silent, and the priest addressed the couple with words of blessing from the gods. As he carried on, the seer's followers created a line before them and began to play their own instruments as they chanted in words of the old language.

Nurrock then proceeded through the barricade of his people as they covered him with markings of paint along his body. His new bride was directed to follow her husband through the crowd, but she couldn't help but cower away from their touch. Even as she did, the giant, however, remained unmoved, waiting still for her with a smile upon his face.

Sidonis watched the ceremony proceed with curious delight and soon found himself enjoying the festivities which quickly followed. Ceolfrid enjoyed the celebration from within his seat as the others took the liberty of freedom upon themselves. And the night carried on, much like the drink which drove them all to madness. But it was the unwavering eye of the seer, Gorhan, which quickly caught Sidonis' attention. And as hard as he tried to avert his gaze, he couldn't help but glance back at the old man whose eyes were fixed upon him.

Even as the celebration continued, and the patrons became lost within the haze, the seer remained still, staring throughout his very soul. And soon, Sidonis found the drink to have lost its luster as the music became a drone against Gorhan's piercing eyes. One moment after the next, and the old man remained, staring. Though finally, he watched as the seer rose, and approached his seat from across the room.

In that moment, Sidonis couldn't be sure if he should be relieved or worried by the gesture and hesitated to even speak at the sight of him as Gorhan arrived by his seat. But before he could think of the words to say, the old man was suddenly upon him.

He remained silent for a moment longer, but finally leaned forward to whisper a word within his ear.

"Shall I bless the one who comes to betray?"

# CHAPTER 13

## ARMAGH, KINGDOM OF HELMERE

WHETHER CEOLFRID HAD TOLD THE seer of his plans or not, Sidonis couldn't help but feel as though the gods themselves were staring so intently into his eyes, waiting for his reply. In all his years, he cared little for the gods, seeing them merely as tool for man's convenience. Yet, here, in this very moment, he felt that he couldn't be more wrong.

The eyes of Gorhan were as black as night, so that even the torch's light could not reflect against them. Deep within the shadowy abyss, was where the gods had dwelt. And it was from that place that they demanded he speak. The frail man was merely a vessel; a tool for their use, and he alone stood with their undivided attention. For he was to be judged, and their scales moved in whichever way they deemed fit.

"Do I find their favor?" Sidonis asked.

"That depends," Gorhan replied. The seer finally removed his gaze from the man and looked toward the king of Abensloh. "Ceolfrid has asked me to bless his pursuit. But such an undertaking would require that I bond you to him as well as to the gods.

He wishes to ensure that you honor your word. So, to bless the king, means that I must also be willing to bless you."

"For a price, no doubt. . ."

"Everything comes at a price, Sidonis. Either at the hands of the gods, or. . . by other means."

Sidonis looked to Gorhan, unsure if it was to the man or to the gods that he now spoke to. Either way, the terms had long been set, and he was required now, to fulfill his obligation. Though, not a word was spoken before Gorhan found whatever answer he was looking for through Sidonis' eyes. The old man cracked a sinister smile and nodded at him with approval.

"I will bless Ceolfrid's pursuit as well as yours. But know this, Sidonis, there will be a time when I shall call upon you for recompense. And when I do, you will surely pay it. . ."

Every word clung to him like a chain wrapped tightly around his neck. Such a price it would be for Sidonis to claim his prize and for a moment, however brief it may have been, he almost regretted it. But such was the game. Every man in this world had his price, even amongst the gods that dwelt beyond the veil. And every price seemed to demand that much more of him, making sure that he would not forget his investors.

And just like that, without so much as single word, Gorhan snatched his answer from within the depths of his pawn, then turned back toward the center of the room. From there, the seer welcomed the king of Abensloh with a simple gesture, and Ceolfrid obliged him with a smile. The hall fell silent as the king rose his hands in air and all eyes went to the men before them. Ceolfrid waited, straining the intrigue just a little bit longer, as though he meant it for Sidonis alone. Until finally, he opened his mouth to speak,

"To my friend Nurrock, your might and strength know no bounds, brother. As a son of the gods, I am humbled by your truce and offer this gift of yet another alliance, if it pleases the king."

Ceolfrid gestured toward Sidonis and waited for him to rise before the crowd. Taken aback, Sidonis hesitated and cleared his throat, piercing the silence. He rose slowly from his chair and struggled to keep his eyes from wandering throughout the room.

"This is the brother of Ludica, king of Faermire. He has offered his loyalty in exchange for the life of the king, so that he alone may sit on the throne."

Those present began to whisper amongst each other as Sidonis could feel a pit sinking deeper within his gut. Nurrock's eyes shifted down at the man with noted distrust, before looking back to toward his friend, driven further by his curiosity.

"But just as you well know, a man's blood is sacred to those whose bond you hold. And that bond cannot be broken, lest he seeks the wrath of the gods."

Even as he spoke, Gorhan moved, and began to utter words of old as his followers chanted along in the shadows. Together, they each flowed as one, and Sidonis stood in awe as they continued in unison. The seer removed his dagger from its sheath, just as Ceolfrid pulled his robes apart and revealed the bareness of his chest. The drums began to beat once more and the king of Abensloh lifted his head again toward Sidonis.

Gorhan's words grew louder as he raised his hands high into the air, trembling and shaking with fervor. The old man then flung his head back, revealing the whites of his eyes, and a blackened ooze began to seep and spill from his lips. It rolled torpidly down his neck like tar and at once, the old man sliced his blade across Ceolfrid's chest. The king neither winced nor cried out in pain, choosing only to widen his eyes as they clung even deeper onto Sidonis.

He watched as Ceolfrid's blood trickled swiftly from the wound above his heart and the chanting continued. As the life streamed down, the seer was quick to catch what he could within his chalice, then lifted it toward the heavens. The old man uttered a few words more, then leaned himself over the cup, letting the dark substance drip from his lips and into the blood.

As Ceolfrid gently took it from the seer's hands, he then offered it to the man before him, drawing all eyes onto Sidonis alone.

"Drink of my blood... Vow before the gods here and now, that you belong to me. And to betray my blood, is to betray the gods themselves."

His words drew such a weight that Sidonis had never known before, and he nearly cowered at their utterance. The room fell silent, and even the giant's stature held no bar to the insignificance of the world around him. In all of his years, he had cared so little for the gods, yet in this moment, they demanded his very soul. And he was to present it to them in such a place as this, one where so many so eyes were held to bear witness to the occasion. Whatever plans he held before, meant nothing to the gods as they planned to grant him a new purpose. For his life was no longer his to claim, and to drink from that cup meant that he would accept their terms.

He paused, staring deeply into the chalice before him. Ceolfrid's blood within it had been consumed by the blood of the gods and turned it as black as the night sky above. It churned within itself as though it possessed a life of its own and it called to him with each passing moment. He stood alone, captivated by its movement, and pulled it closer to his face. And without removing his gaze, he spoke aloud.

"I shall drink it..." he said and pour the contents into his mouth.

All at once, he could suddenly feel a searing chill spread throughout his spine and the drink had begun to consume him from within. He grew weak and nearly gave himself over to the darkness which had overtaken his sight. Ceolfrid and all who were present became like a haze before him, forming merely shadows within a dream. He could hear the faint whispers of his name until all the remained was the darkness around him. Soon there was nothing but silence and all had gone numb. He was lost within the abyss, given over entirely to the mercy of the gods, and for once, he did not fight it.

Then hours had passed, or so it seemed. Though, as he opened his eyes to find Ceolfrid still standing before him, he wondered if what had just happened to him was real. The cup in his hand was empty and the great king of Abensloh stood before him with a smile of approval upon his face. What silence there once was, now began to let slip the distant sound of music and revelry all around them.

Soon the world appeared as it once did before he took the drink, but he cursed beneath his breath as he struggled to regain his composure. Ceolfrid could see it in his eyes, and he chuckled softly to himself.

"Enjoy the festivities... Brother." The king recused himself as he took his place amongst the others and Sidonis was left alone to fend for himself. Though as hard as he tried, the world continued to fade in and out before him. His head spun endlessly in circles, and he took his seat, hoping desperately to steady himself.

Meanwhile, the hall fell silent once more as Gorhan's creatures ushered a captive toward the center of the floor. Sidonis couldn't make sense of what we saw, uncertain if his mind were still playing tricks on him, or if the hooded figure before them actually bore skin which appeared as ashen gray. The woman, whose hands were bound in front of her, had long since given up the struggle to fight against her captors. And she hid beneath the sack which covered her face for what little solace it offered her. She had been stripped down to nearly nothing except the veiled garment which loosely hung over her shoulders. All could still see the shape of her figure as well as the parts which were certain to draw the eye.

Ceolfrid, along with the others leaned forward in their seats, intrigued by the prospect at hand. The old man however, remained silent as he scanned the room, driving his spectators further with curiosity. Then, all at once, he ripped the sack from her head, revealing the marvel beneath it for all to see. And it seemed for once that it wasn't his own mind playing tricks on him as he thought. Sidonis, along with everyone else, sat in awe at what creature stood before them all.

Her hair was dark like coal, though her eyes glowed like the faint embers of a kindling fire. Her pointed ears thrust through her jostled hair revealing the defining signet of her kind, bringing further credence to the rumors of old. So rare was it find such a creature as this, but one so pure was a true gift indeed. The elves of Aecorath did well to hide themselves throughout all the land and were sought by both peasant and king alike. For their beauty and their power were much sought of throughout the land.

She stood tall, though weak from the treacherous journey, no doubt. And though she looked both broken and defeated, it did nothing to mask the magnitude of her beauty. Gorhan looked little more than a feeble vagabond at her side, but he shouldered the creature like a prized trophy for all to see. And it was his prize indeed.

The elves had grown extinct throughout the ages, as man sought desperately to capture them. And what little of them remained in the world, were driven into the shadows, never to be seen or heard from again. Then soon, the word of their existence became a myth and that turned to little more than a story, full of tales meant only for the delight of children.

Yet there, in that very moment, one stood. And she was just as beautiful and alluring as the tales had always described. What Sidonis would give to be able to touch her, though, there he remained, forced to watch as both Ceolfrid and the giant rose from their seats to approach her. Even the queen of Helmere could not avert her gaze, enthralled by its beauty.

"What powers does it possess?" Ceolfrid asked. His eyes remained fixed upon the woman as hers lay heavily upon the ground beneath her feet.

"I have yet to discover that for myself," Gorhan replied. "But tonight, she is yours to discover. A gift to you from the gods. For tomorrow, you shall gather yourselves to war."

And with that final word, Ceolfrid at once took his liberty upon the creature, and the remaining festivities endured all throughout the endless night.

As Sidonis entered the great hall, Ceolfrid stood quietly before the fire which crackled and popped beneath him, merely offering a passive glance to acknowledge his arrival. His robes draped open at his side, and he casually bit his teeth into a fresh date, catching the juice before it slipped past his lips. Just hours before, the hall was filled to the brim with man and beast alike, celebrating the latest marriage of the giant king and his newest bride. But now, in what little light the new dawn provided, the place was empty, except for the king's servant tucked quietly away within the shadows; always awaiting his beck and call.

The northern king displayed himself without a care in the world, welcoming any challenge that presented itself. And the celebrations of the night before might as well have been for Ceolfrid himself if not for Nurrock's wedding. If the giant weren't so simple-minded, then perhaps he'd find reason enough to be angered by it all, or perhaps, it was his naivety which served to his benefit. Being Ceolfrid's pet may well have been the best thing which had ever happened to the brute.

But there Ceolfrid stood, at the center of the barbaric hall, claiming it for himself. Sidonis approached the king and took a small piece of fruit from the tray beside him, mimicking the man's nonchalant disposition.

"If I'd have known that you held such parties as this, then I would've come sooner."

"And I'm certain that I'd have thrown you to the streets." Sidonis chuckled aloud at the king's response. "You are no friend of mine, Sidonis. Do not forget it."

"Of course not," he replied. He could feel the king's eye scanning him over from head to toe, searching for weakness however great or small.

"Winter shall be upon us shortly. And when the snow begins to stick, then it will only be a matter of time before the Dolam pass can no longer be crossed. My supply lines will be cut off, and my armies will be left to fend for themselves. But your offer to give me Faermire could not have come at a more opportune time. With your land and your armies, then I can march into the streets of Mistelfeld before the first of spring."

"With my help of course..." Sidonis was careful to remind the king of his place within their agreement.

"You will have your army, Sidonis. But hear me now; you will not fail to kill Ludica. For death will be far too sweet a mercy for what I shall do to you, if he lives."

He could hear the tone in Ceolfrid's voice shift. And for the first time, the man displayed an ounce of emotion toward him which carried the weight of his sincerity. Ceolfrid meant every word he spoke to Sidonis, and it showed just how much the king now had control over him.

Though still he carried on, discussing the plans for which they would employ once they marched on to meet their rivals. And what little Sidonis could offer, the king took to hesitant consideration. But for him, it was enough. The plan was sound, and the reward was great. Yet still, there lingered the looming sense of such an outcome where perhaps Sidonis would indeed fail.

For whatever alliance Sidonis thought he offered, Ceolfrid took that, and much more. And it was then, that he realized how much lesser of an ally he could ever be to the man before him. For it would have been better instead, to be considered his pet, than as the scum which Ceolfrid saw. For to the king of Abensloh, Sidonis was nothing more than a tool to be used in a far grander scheme than ever before.

# Elsterheim, Kingdom of Faermire

Days had passed, and Ludica watched from atop the wall as the elders from throughout land gradually arrived with their armies. Numerous blue flags stitched with the king's crest dotted the landscape near the camps as they separated according to their region.

It had been a long time since he had seen such great numbers as this, and there was still more to come, but the sense of dread would not appease itself within him. He had hoped that he would never have to face war again for the rest of his days. Though it found its way to his gates once more.

His children had yet to be born when last he fought, and they were all that he could seem to think upon in that moment. In his youth, he was audacious, willing to thrust himself into the heat of battle without care or worry for anything. And yet now, his youth had long since abandoned him, as did his recklessness. He dreaded the thought of it all.

All the while, his own daughter narrowly escaped the throws of death at the hand of his treacherous brother, and his youngest's life still hung in the balance. What thoughts he once held for the legacy of his kingdom had long since passed, as now he struggled to merely preserve it.

No matter which direction he looked, war stood around him and the gods reveled in it. He questioned for a moment what he had done to warrant such action against him or that perhaps the fault simply lay within himself. Whether he failed with his children, his inaction against Graefeld, or tolerating his brother's treachery, there was fault in everything he could see. Even as that same treachery slipped in within his own bed.

His own wife entangled herself with Sidonis' plot and should've been the first to serve as an example for those who sought to usurp his throne. And he had nearly done just that but spared the wretch's lift because of his daughter's mercy. He most likely would've carried on with the execution however, despite Estrith's intervention. But it was her face which stopped him; that same face her mother held.

Emelyn appeared to him in an instant, and her soft expression clung to him just as he remembered it. She was beautiful and captivated him with everything she possessed. And it was that same woman who threw herself before him, pleading to spare the life of the one who had taken her place.

Through the years, Estrith had grown to fill the void which he so longed for and found himself subject to the hand of her mercy. The woman, though so young, had such a grip on the king that he dared not let her see it, for fear that she could exploit him. Though it was also through her mercy that he could glean further knowledge from Richessa which would've otherwise been lost, had she not stopped his hand. And it was time he felt, that he needed to revisit that subject with his former wife.

He spoke with Eohric a moment longer atop the city's wall and made his way down into the dungeon where Richessa had been imprisoned. The light soon disappeared through the damp halls made of stone and the guards quickly rose to their feet as the king appeared, curiously watching as he passed them by.

He reached for a torch to light his way and fought to restrain himself against the horrid stench which permeated the air. Only a few cells were occupied by those who had long since been forgotten, and at the very end was where his wife awaited him. The occasional screech of rats echoed throughout, and few were brave enough to enter the depths of such a tomb as this.

But beyond the iron grid, a small figure clung to the corner, cradling herself from the cold. Her regal clothes were stained with dirt and grime as her hair was left wild and unkempt, forming mats within itself. She quivered silently and drew her knees closer within her body as the king approached.

Ludica affixed the torch into its place on the wall and the two waited in silence together. The king studied the woman before him and abhorred the very sight of her. Though finally, he found reason enough to speak.

"By my daughter's mercy alone you have been spared. Though, you will find none with me. So, speak plainly of your entanglement with my brother and I shall let you live."

The chains around her feet crackled as they slithered after her every move.

"There is nothing to say. Only that I sit here to rot, and he does not."

"He will soon enough," Ludica curtly replied. "He killed Rodmar to send me a message and you welcomed that message into my home. Do not take me for a fool, Richessa."

"Then you know all there is to know, lord King. What knowledge there is left to glean of

She scoffed aloud and brought herself onto a single stool which remained for her sit upon. He watched as she lifted her eyes to meet his own and gently pushed the matted curls out of her muddied face.

"Whether you take my life or not, husband, I have already been sentenced to death. So, if you wish to hear the truth, then I shall tell you the whole of it." Her expression changed before the man who stood behind the iron bars. That same arrogance he had always known of her had managed to find its way back as she lifted her head and pulled her shoulders back.

"I have hated you from the moment you took me as your wife. You've taken everything from me and have only ever demanded more. There was a time when I was happy... when I was betrothed to your brother..."

"I wanted it no more than you, Richessa," he replied.

"Yet, you did nothing to stop it! Not only did you take the crown for yourself, but you took me for your wife after your own had passed. My father was cunning enough to arrange the marriage, but you did well enough to see that nothing would come of it."

"I thought that perhaps, there might be a chance that I could love you, or that I could be your queen, but you would not allow it. I was queen by title alone, reduced solely to provide another heir, and what's more, is that after so many years, I still fell second to that bitch!" Richessa paused to steady the rage which boiled deep within her.

"Your bed was as cold as your love for me, and so I found the warmth I longed for, elsewhere. Your children also bear the very sight of your face and so I hated them more. The only solace I have gained in my marriage to you, was a child of my own, and one that was not from you..."

The expression on Ludica's face shifted suddenly in response to the words she spoke, and it was all to her delight. The more she spoke, the more she fueled his rage, and it greatly pleased the woman. And Ludica could do nothing but listen further as the words spilled from her lips.

"Your brother has laid with me for years. And it was in your very bed, Ludica, where we conceived our son. Have you not seen that the boy bears no resemblance to you or to your children? Only that he resembles his true father while he lives yet, under your own roof."

The king remained silent, for he knew that her only intent, was to drive a knife deep into his heart where she physically could not. But the news of his son stood alone against all that she continued to say. Richessa carried on, speaking with a tone that seized her further pride. And all that remained for Ludica was the encroaching silence that drowned her out. Meanwhile, the image of Siged's face appeared slowly before him, engrossing his mind completely.

She droned on for a time, spouting further insults at the king, until there was finally nothing left for her to say. And as she brought herself to silence once more, he looked to her while she awaited his response. He could see the bitter twinkle in her eyes, even against the darkness which surrounded them. It was for her a final blow, and one which could grant the satisfaction of pain to the man she hated most. Though as the silence continued, her satisfaction waned.

Ludica refused to grant the woman the pleasure that she so desperately sought, and instead, turned himself away without a single word. He then called for the guard before he departed and took the torch from the wall once more.

"Give her rations to the other prisoners. Their mouths are better left to feed. And when she dies, throw her body in the street for the dogs to glean what is left."

The guard quickly lowered his head to acknowledge the king's command and waited to lift it once more before he finally left their presence.

As he rounded the corner before the stairs, he rested his hand against the wall beside him. His knees had suddenly grown weak, and he stood alone as he lifted his head to the light which peered down into the tunnel. For as hard as he tried to mask the utter consternation which overwhelmed him, the king stood powerless against the revelation of Richessa's words. In the end, she had succeeded. And he was left alone, drowning in the turmoil of his own thoughts. For there, he struggled to find his way back into reason. For Siged was his son, and he loved the boy dearly. But that same child stood as reminder of the treachery within his own home and so too, was the prospect of his inheritance torn away.

The king grieved the boy's condition as he was reminded of Siged's plight. But as his son's life was nearly taken from the king, his wife only further served to rip him from his very hands. Ludica stood silent and struggled to maintain his composure. For in the blink of an eye, the king was losing his grip on what little he seemed to control and there was nothing which could be done about it. But as he remained, he took a deep and labored breath, as he fought to steady his mind.

After a moment longer, he lowered his arm and straightened himself, before finally taking the steps back toward the surface above. As the king reached the top, he looked to the world around him as they carried on with purpose. All was silent again for Ludica, and he struggled to find the purpose he once had, only moments before.

Eventually, he found himself walking through the castle halls and stopped to face the door of Siged's room. He slowly lifted his handle to push it open and made his way toward the bed. The room was empty aside from the boy who lay quietly asleep, unaware of the world around him. Ludica stepped closer and watched as the young boy's chest peacefully rose up and down, over and over again. Each steady breath was yet another reminder of the betrayal that had been revealed.

Though the king, likewise, remained still, and could not bring himself to move. Instead, all that remained for him was to watch over the young boy as his mind went blank.

# CHAPTER 14

ESTRITH OPENED THE DOOR TO find her father standing over Siged's bed, silent and unmoving. She slowly approached the king and greeted him with caution.

"He is improving father. Slowly, but surely."

He neither responded, nor acknowledged her, but simply turned and left the room, where she remained. She wondered if perhaps he was growing concerned with her brother's recovery and thought that it had proven to take a greater toll on him than she initially assumed. She thought about it a moment longer, but soon brushed the thought aside as she refocused her attention on the task at hand. She carried with her a bowl of porridge for Siged and fresh linens for the wound upon his head.

After greeting him with enthusiasm, she could see his eyes begin to flutter in her presence. There was nothing so gratifying for her to see than to watch his eyes open to the world around him, and she called for the servant to help her lift him up. As they removed the old bandages from his head, she observed the wound and noted its unusually swift rate of healing. Either way, it was progress. And that was all she needed to see.

Words of encouragement for her brother were followed by the mundane happenings of each day and she continued as though Siged was equally involved in the conversation along with her. As she wrapped the final cloth around and tucked it in, she looked into his eyes and paused to catch herself.

Though his eyes were open, they did little to acknowledge her presence nor move with a sense of purpose. He was there with her physically, but otherwise absent from her presence. She couldn't help but think back to the days before when he pestered her incessantly and she found herself filled with nothing but guilt and sadness for his current state.

The gods had saved him from certain death, of that there was no doubt in her mind. But to see him in such a state as this caused her to wonder if death would not have been better for her brother in the end.

The healers and priests alike were useless to explain his condition to her or her family and it vexed her to no end.

Though Beowyn refused to tell her what was required of him to heal their brother, it was apparent to her that it took a significant toll on him as well. He would often come to check on Siged throughout the days, but remained silent, never leaving the threshold from where he stood. The worry in his eyes was just the same as what she felt within herself, but neither of them could bring themselves to say it aloud, let alone to each other. But at the end of the day, it was Estrith who always remained by the young boy's side. She lifted the bowl of porridge which had begun to cool and dipped the spoon in to stir it about.

"I made this myself you know," she uttered with a smile upon her face.

"Father would be furious to know that I had been cooking in the kitchen, but I wanted to make certain that it was made by my hand alone. The servants helped me of course, but we'll just leave that part out."

She lifted the spoon to his lips where they remained slightly open but offered no response to accept the food.

"Just try a little Siged, it's really quite delicious."

Still, he remained distant from her, and she simply poured the meal into his mouth bit by bit. But with no attempts to even swallow it, she soon relented, and set the bowl aside.

The next day was the same, and so she remained by his side, choosing to read for him instead. Before long, he had eventually fallen back to sleep, and she watched him in silence while he fell deeper into his slumber.

Watching him there, she caressed his soft brown hair to comfort him from the dreams which seemed to haunt him as he slept. It was the same dreams that no doubt besieged her sleepless nights since the attack. He whimpered and winced but ignored her presence and all she could seem to feel was the deepening pangs of guilt that grew each day.

Though for a moment, she found herself relieved from the torment of it all as Qereth entered the room. His presence was comforting enough for her, but he greeted her still with a gentle smile upon his face. He carefully made his way to her side and set a plate of food on the table beside her.

"He will not eat it." The disappointment was evident in her voice.

"I know," Qereth replied. "It's for you." She glanced up to meet his gaze and caught the same lingering smile upon his face. The warmth in his eyes brought a sudden ease to the cold air around them and she could do nothing but smile at him in return.

"If Siged is to fare well, then it will most certainly be on your account. So, you need your strength now, more than ever."

"Thank you Qereth." He pulled a seat beside her, and she watched as he carefully adjusted the blanket over her brother's frail body.

"How is he?"

"Physically he seems to be improving, but his spirit still seems lost. I do not know what to do."

"Just give it time," Qereth calmly replied. "Soon he will be clinging to your side and speaking so much that you will have regretted he had been healed so quickly."

She chuckled slightly and glanced up at him once more.

"Yes, I suppose you are right. But I do miss the incessant talking. No matter how he annoyed me so."

She looked at Qereth, hesitant to ask him about their journey through the Donnorath Wood. But the question had lingered on in her mind since she saw Beowyn upon their return. Something had changed in her brother, that much was clear. And the fact that he would always redirect the conversation whenever she would bring it up, only made her worry for him that much more.

But since Qereth knew firsthand of the ordeal, then he could be the one to ease her mind as well.

"What happened out there? In the forest..." She could tell that the question alone was enough to make him stir in his seat. But he looked at her and back to the floor once more as he hesitated to answer her.

"Qereth, please... I have seen it in Beowyn's eyes that it troubles him so. And he appears...—"

"Older."

"Yes. Almost as if he has aged years since you both left the city."

"Because, I believe he has..." Qereth sighed aloud as he finally gave in to her plea. "We did find the seer in the wood. But the old man said that Beowyn needed to make a sacrifice; 'A life for a life' as he put it. Beowyn agreed and took the drink that was offered.

I thought surely, he had given up the ghost as the sorcerer's power consumed him with magic. But instead, with what little life there is in young Siged, that much was taken from Beowyn. So, I suppose that if the boy were any older, then his brother would surely be dead this day."

As he retold the story, she could further understand that look she had seen in her brother's eyes. But it made her sadness on his behalf grow even stronger. She was glad to have known, but she understood then why he chose not to speak on the matter. She'd have done the same if it were her place instead.

So much had happened in those recent days and there was still so much more to come as she saw it. Part of her wanted nothing more than to go back to the way things were, before her brother was hurt and her life turned upside down. But then, it also meant that she would still be lost, oblivious to the truth of everything which hid beneath the surface. And so, she had to contend with what she preferred in life, whether it was to be satisfied, yet lost within her ignorance, or suffer with the truth of what she had come to know. Though, it was with that truth that it granted her freedom, and the distant hope that things could always change for the better.

And having her friend there with her was proof of that. Though having to retell the story of all that happened made him visibly uncomfortable and she regretted her desire to ask him. The two sat in silence for a while longer before Qereth was the one to break the awkwardness of it all.

"With all that has happened, I haven't been able to wish you well. And for that, I am sorry."

She noted that he had suddenly become flustered and struggled to look back into her eyes.

"There is nothing for which you need to be sorry, Qereth. You have done far more for my family than I could ever hope to thank you for. Even now, Siged has a chance at life because of you."

As she spoke, he lowered his head, nodding to acknowledge her words.

"Well, I certainly don't do it all for Beowyn's sake. I mean, as much as I think highly of your brother, I'd much rather see a smile on your face than his. Not that he smiles much on my account anyways." She could see that he had mustered enough confidence to present a playful grin in her direction, and for once, she found herself distracted from the dread which laid so heavily over her these days past.

He had always been good at bringing a smile to her face. Even a passing glance was enough to warrant the comfort she needed when she least expected it. And throughout the years, though their lives took different paths, she always found herself cherishing the moments they had together as children. The truest friend in every sense of the word, and that was the one thing that never changed in him.

Though sitting together in that moment, she couldn't help but feel something a little bit more than what she had in the past. His deep blue eyes offered her a gentle solace which she had so longed for in all that had happened. And staring up at him, she quickly realized how desperately she needed the comfort which he provided, even when no words were spoken between them. Until that moment, she had never felt so alone. But sitting there beside her now, was the one person who had offered her such a gift, and never asked for anything in return.

Eventually, Qereth found his stride once more, and carried on, talking about matters that were both irrelevant and useless to anyone with sense. Yet even then, he still found a way to spin the nonsense into funny quips and ridiculous jokes that were more suited for a boy than for a man. But for Estrith, it was more than a welcome distraction. It was the one thing she didn't even know that she needed. And soon she was laughing. For the first time in so long, she laughed aloud, but caught herself in the midst of it.

She took notice of young Siged lying peacefully in his sleep and was reminded once more of her guilt. Though it was plain to see, and Qereth was quick to take notice.

"You know, you're right. A pregnant sow can tend to be a bit of a touchy subject at times."

"Oh no, it's not that, I—"

"You needn't say it, Estrith. I know... But you are alive, and so is your brother."

He was right of course, but it didn't do much to satiate the feeling which overcame her each day. And it was clear that she wasn't masking it well. Though his attempt at consoling her through humor worked for a time. But now, the veil had been lifted, and he stared deeply at her while she hoped to avoid his gaze. It was that same look that she had seen from time to time over the years and it pulled at her in such a way that she could never quite understand. This time, however, it brought a certain feeling that made her want to give in to it entirely.

He paused briefly, struggling to utter the words caged beneath his chest.

"What happened that day, was not your fault. For what could have happened, was stopped by your hand, and that is all that matters in the end. You are far stronger than you realize, Estrith. I only wish that you could see that for yourself."

His words sunk deeply into her heart so that all she could feel was a wrenching pit welling up inside of her. And even then, he offered a certain longing in his eyes for her that she couldn't help but feel for him in return. She had never allowed herself to be so close to a man in such a way, let alone with the one whom she had long considered her friend. But to see him then, in that moment, he carried with him a feeling which she had never known. She contended with the possibility that what she saw in him was merely out of her own desperation, entangled deep within her vulnerability. But then he reached for her hand, if ever so gently.

The warmth of his touch captivated her entirely, forcing her to avert her gaze, so as not to let him see how much more she wanted of it. Though despite her efforts, she craved him further, unwittingly drawing herself closer toward him, as he did likewise. And one desire led her to the next. When first she was consumed by the feeling of his hand around her own, she now longed to be held in his embrace. And with that embrace, she would want nothing more than to feel his lips caress her own.

More and more, she was engrossed by the craving she felt for him, and soon the two began to draw themselves closer to one another, as he spoke her name aloud.

"Estrith..."

As Qereth uttered her name, he leaned himself further, drawing his lips closer to hers until she could feel the warmth of his breath against them. The world around them disappeared, and the two were left alone to find themselves lost in their longing for each other.

Though suddenly, she could hear the faint creak of the door as it was pushed open, and she stopped. Pulling herself back into reality, she turned to see who had entered the room. And out of the corner of her eye, Qereth had lowered his head as he cleared his throat, then joined her focus toward their visitor. Beowyn had appeared through the door and carried a look of shock upon his face at the sight of them so close together.

"Am I interrupting something?"

"No." Estrith was quick to interject on both their behalf as she pulled herself back together again. "Qereth and I were just—"

"I was just on my way out. My father, I'm sure, is waiting for me within the camps, and I mustn't keep him waiting."

Estrith's gaze followed him as he rose from his chair and passed a quick glance back in her direction before finally leaving the room.

"If ever you should need me, you know where to find me. . ." he said at last.

"Thank you, Qereth." She couldn't help but feel as though she somehow played a part in the interruption by her brother, but the thought of what had almost happened between them had made her blush entirely. And it was clear that she did poorly to hide her embarrassment from Beowyn as he rolled his eyes at her.

"I suppose this seat is free to be taken then." He casually took his place beside her, and briefly kept his eyes fixed upon her, before refocusing his attention to Siged, as he lay asleep in his bed.

"Beowyn. . ."

"Forget it." He promptly lifted his hand to silence any attempts she could make at conjuring up an excuse for what he had seen.

"Whatever it is you've got going on between the two of you, I'd rather not care to know, if it's all the same."

The silence that followed came naturally but hung if ever so awkwardly between them before he spoke again.

"Though next time, you might want to choose some place other than at our brother's bedside. I'd certainly not appreciate my sister kissing a man at my bedside as I slept." He tossed a scornful look in her direction before reaching for the plate that Qereth had brought and helped himself to a healthy bite. Though she couldn't help but smile at his feeble attempts to deride her as their father could.

"You're right, Brother. Should I wait until you are awake then?" He scoffed aloud at her remark and shook his head from side to side.

"Better," he replied, and the two chuckled in unison. Though soon, the playful jabs between them subsided, and they were left staring down at Siged, once again reminded of his pain, and thus of theirs. The spark in Beowyn's eyes had once again faded, and she could see that his casual disposition was leaving him, so that all which remained was the sadness in his eyes.

But Estrith found herself curiously intrigued by Beowyn's presence at their brother's side. For in the days before, he had refused to cross over the threshold to his room, yet now, he was as close as he could possibly be. Something had sparked a change in him, but perhaps it didn't matter in the end. For now, he had finally brought himself to Siged's side and she was thankful for that.

Beowyn watched over his younger brother for some time, and she could tell that his thoughts had begun to weigh heavily on him once again.

"Forgive me, Estrith..."

She couldn't help but be taken aback by his words and looked to him with bewilderment in her eyes.

"You have been alone in all of this. Countless hours watching over him and praying to the gods, feeling helpless. I should have been here, with you. But in my weakness, I couldn't even bear to face him, or you for that matter..."

He dropped his head with shame which he had cast over himself, but she placed her hand gently over his back to ease him of the burden.

Reminded once more of the sacrifice which he had made, she couldn't help but feel as though a part of her had been taken along with him also.

"There is nothing to forgive, brother," she said as she struggled to hold back her tears. "I suppose that I have felt so helpless because the gods demand so much of my patience. But you have you given so much of yourself for the sake of Siged's life, that we have hope again once more. Because of you, Beowyn, our brother lives. And that is what I shall always cherish most of all."

What little strength he could muster to look back at her had quickly left him, and he turned himself away, withholding his own tears from her sight.

"My place will always be at Siged's side, just as it shall always be at yours," she continued.

He smiled up at her from where he sat, then lifted his hand and drew her in, as he gently kissed her head.

"And I would happily give my life for you, Sister. Always..."

The two sat quietly together for a moment longer before a knock could be heard at the door.

"Lord, Prince, the king wishes to speak with you." Beowyn's personal servant had emerged from the entrance, and humbly bowed himself before the siblings. They turned to each other, with a cautious apprehension, but Estrith squeezed her brother's hand to reassure him as he stood.

"Pray for me," he uttered, and turned, hoping to mask the nervousness in his voice. She could see the tension rising within his shoulders, but he continued, eventually leaving her alone with their brother once more.

# CHAPTER 15

AS BEOWYN ENTERED THE HALL with his servant, the man handed him a small noted from within his cloak.

"There is also the matter of a message, my Lord, from the lady Tanica."

"A message?" He pulled the letter from the man's grasp and promptly opened it to read of its contents alone. He could not decipher at once, however, whether he was elated or apprehensive by the prospect of the words which she had written to him. The words stretched across the page with the elegance of her penmanship, and he found himself relieved just at the sight of them alone.

It was nothing new for her to send him messages throughout their affair, and his servant did well to maintain their discretion, but though the marriage had been arranged, he had yet to hear from her since that night. He wanted nothing more than to know that she was well, and that she was safe. So, to have a letter which was written by her hand alone, gave him the solace he needed in that moment.

He took a deep breath, then began to silently read the words which had been written;

*Beowyn, My Beloved,*

*I cannot tell you the sorrow and the torment which I endured at the sight of your capture. I thought that surely, they would kill you at once, and that I would never see you or be held in your arms again. I was, at that very moment, prepared to die. For such a life, I could never live, if I knew that you were not in it.*

*It is your breath upon my neck that gives me life, and it is the warmth of your touch which gives me hope everlasting. So, when I heard that a marriage had been arranged for us, I thought that surely it could only be a dream. Yet here we are, and the news has been carried throughout our lands.*

*My heart is full, my love, and it overflows atop the brim. Meet me within a fortnight upon the Coventhon ridge, so that I may hold you, and know for once, that this is real.*

*Yours for eternity,*

*Tanica*

It was all he had ever wanted from the start; to finally love her freely as they so often dreamed. And to read her words upon the page, made it clear, that she felt just the same. Yet, as he stood there, he couldn't help but feel something different. And he hated himself for it. In a time when he should be just as elated as the woman he loved, he could not. Only, he found himself reminded of his father's words regarding the arrangement and the cost of that marriage.

At first, he felt nothing but betrayal from his father, and was only to be used as a pawn in the games of man, of kings. And so, at the first opportunity he found, he ran. With no clear goal in sight, it was all he could think to do, just to maintain his own sanity. But as he ran, he soon came to understand that the workings of things in secret had begun to reveal themselves, and that there was much more to the world than he knew. It was all tearing at the seams, and it was left to him, to help right the corruption which boiled beneath the surface.

Then came his brother's plight and the suffering which soon followed. One by one, the stones began to fall, and he was faced with having to pick up the pieces or abandon them forever. So much was demanded of him, and so much would be ruined because of him also.

As he held her letter in his hands, he tightly closed his eyes and lifted it up to kiss it. He wanted nothing more than to hold her in his arms, and to cling to her as the growing misery of the world fell away, lost entirely to their embrace. But soon, he opened his eyes and looked to the corridor, at the path which would lead him to his father's throne. He sighed aloud, and gently tucked the letter into his shirt, against his chest.

Beowyn then followed his servant through the halls and toward the court where his father awaited him. All that broke the silence of their journey was the constant echo of their footsteps upon the cold stone beneath their feet. His mind had raced with the countless thoughts that seeped in with each passing moment. One second, he was recounting the words which Tanica had written, and the next, he struggled to find the words which he would say upon meeting his father. But before he could devise any tactful responses, his servant had stopped him before the doors to the court.

He paused, delaying the inevitable, whatever that might be, and took a deep breath as he straightened his tunic. The grand wooden doors were all that remained as a barrier between him and the king. He desperately wished for them to remain closed, if only for a little while longer, but just as he had reconciled himself to the idea of it all, the doors began to open. Groaning and creaking like an aged man upon his bed, the wooden entrance expanded to reveal the court before him.

The prince's father sat heavily upon his throne, as though the life had been drained from his body and his hand did little to cover the dejection upon his face. In just a short time, his father had gone from the unwavering tower of strength to looking no more than a beaten and battered remnant of what once was. Beowyn at once, couldn't help but feel as though he had been the cause of such despair and it vexed him greatly.

The king did little to acknowledge his arrival and continued to sit in silence as he approached.

"Father," he uttered. The young prince shuffled nervously in his place before the king finally opened his mouth to speak.

"Eohric has told me that you journeyed to find a cure for your brother. What was it?"

"It was the sorcerer, Gorhan. I had heard that the man could offer the power to heal him."

"Gorhan..." His father kept his focus on the steps beneath him. Then fearing the response to be insufficient, Beowyn continued.

"When I came upon Siged, I could see that the life was draining from his body, and there was no time to spare, Father. I had to do something."

"Hm," was the king's only response before he continued, "And the price it seems, was a heavy one by the looks of you. You've aged son, I can see it on your face."

Beowyn lowered his head and lifted his hand to the side of his cheek. He couldn't bring himself to look upon his own reflection, as the dread for what he would see was too much to bear.

"I am still myself, Father."

"Perhaps. . ." He could feel his father's gaze still fixed up on him. The king looked at Beowyn for some time before he finally broke free of his gaze. "But whether Siged recovers, is for the gods to decide."

"He will, I have seen it."

"You would give so much of yourself, even as your fate remains tied to his?"

"He is still my brother, that much will never change."

"Much can change, Beowyn. Especially the bond which ties you to your brother."

He couldn't help but feel as though his father spoke of his own circumstances, projecting his own strife instead upon him. So, he remained silent, watching as the king wrestled within his own thoughts.

"Nevertheless, your uncle has brought a war to us all. And if you wish to run from your duties yet again, then I will not stop you, Beowyn. But know that this land, and our kingdom's fate now hinges fervently on the decisions we choose to make. The lives of our people here now face a greater threat than ever before. The hand of our enemies are upon us now, and how we fight will mark us for the rest of our days."

The king paused, as if the words he spoke aloud were directed at himself while he pondered them.

Beowyn could see the sadness rising within his father's eyes, though the man tried hard to conceal it. It was a look that he had never seen from him, only ever that of a stoic or calculated front. Though, more often than not, on account of the prince, it was anger which he saw. He couldn't help but feel, however, that the expression which his father held in that moment, was one which he was in part, responsible for.

He thought once more of the letter which rested against his chest and knew that his entanglement with the king of Valenmur only further exacerbated his father's plight. He wondered, however, if his brother would ever truly heal from his wounds enough to become king in his stead. And that perhaps, his father had wrestled with the same possibility.

But none of that mattered at present, if they could not even defend themselves against the impending war which stood upon the horizon. And until that time, Beowyn had resolved to stand with the king against the threat to their lands. Even if it meant that he would still lose it all, come the following spring. And that for once in his life, he and his father would fight a common enemy together.

As he stood, he replayed the death of lord Rodmar repeatedly in his mind. All while his uncle's face remained callous and emotionless, as he drove his blade deep into the man's gut. The sight of his own uncle's betrayal drove the knife deeper still, into the prince's heart.

Beowyn had often thought highly of Sidonis throughout his youth and admired the man for his confidence. Though his uncle often kept to himself, his arrival in the city always marked new tales of adventure and intrigue to the prince as a young boy. Tales of life out in the world brought about his own desire for something greater beyond the walls of Elsterheim. And so, he often looked to his uncle to feed his own hopeful ambitions.

Though, all of that had suddenly come to an abrupt conclusion that day at Taernsby. There, he saw a man whom he had never known before. And there before him, was not just a man, but a beast all in one.

But through it all, his father remained in midst, and for the first time, Beowyn no longer saw him as just a king alone, but that also of his father. A father at war within himself, and a father whose eyes were filled with sorrow.

And as he thought about those things, that same father spoke aloud while he stared intently at the prince.

"If Ceolfrid somehow agrees to an alliance with Sidonis, then we should expect something far more sinister at work within our own borders. Valenmur will be the least of our concerns."

Beowyn remained silent as his father gathered more words to speak.

"Time is short now," he continued. "The gods require much from me as they do from you. So, I ask you, Beowyn, where do your loyalties lie?"

He was taken aback by the question and could do nothing but let the words settle deeply within his gut. He could've taken the question at face value, but he knew instead, where his father had purposed. For it wasn't that the king distrusted him, as he would with anyone else, but that he was merely asking the question of his own intent.

His father had asked him then, the very question that he found to be asking himself. Was he motivated more by the love which he claimed for the princess of Valenmur? Or would he instead choose to serve the people who needed him most?

But before he could find the words to say, the door to the court began to open, and Sgell had appeared from behind it.

"My Lord, riders have approached the city, bearing a white flag in their midst."

"Riders, from where?" the king promptly asked.

"He calls himself Helgisson, the proclaimed leader of Graefeld."

Both Ludica and Beowyn looked to one another at once, carrying the same wary look in their eyes.

"It's a trap, Father. It must be."

"Perhaps..." the king replied. "What does he say?" he asked, addressing his servant once more.

"He will not say, my Lord. Only that he will speak to you, and no one else."

"Father—"

"Quiet." The king had stopped him before he could utter another word, and looked to Sgell, as he nodded his head in approval.

Both men stood in silence as Helgisson approached the throne. Beowyn himself, in disbelief at the pitiful sight which the man presented, though masked beneath the confidence which he toted upon his face. His clothes, though regal by nature, were worn and tattered. And his armor had begun to rust in places from the lack of care that was long overdue. His long hair hung in dreads upon his shoulders, and his beard was left to fend for itself.

His eyes scanned the room, observing the intricacies throughout with awe. The man himself, had never been given the pleasure of standing within the king's hall, and he envied the place upon which his rival stood. But at long last, he looked toward the king and bowed himself in their direction, if ever so slightly.

"I should like to think that you have good reason to ride upon my city, when I should have you seized for your crimes."

"I do," Helgisson replied with an unwarranted sense of confidence.

"Then speak." Beowyn could hear the shifting tone in his father's voice. The man had little patience for such impudence. Though the prince would have rather just forgone the pleasantries and arrested him where he stood. For there was no reason to trust such a man as this, who stood before them. Beowyn had seen what Sidonis and his men had done to the people of Taernsby, and all with the aid of this man, no doubt.

"I want assurances first." The king could finally stand the man no more and rose from his throne, with his fists clenched tightly at his side.

"You dare come before me, to demand assurances after what your people have done?" Finally, his father had found the sense enough to be rid of the scum once and for all. "Guards!" Immediately, the soldiers descended upon the so-called leader of Graefeld before he could utter another word. Though, as they locked him in their arms, he called out from within the mass.

"Your brother has sent word of an attack!"

And to much of his dismay, his father finally lifted his hand to stop them from carrying the man away.

"I know of your alliance with my brother. And as far as I'm concerned, you would only spit lies to lead me astray. So why should I ever believe you?"

The room fell silent as they awaited his response, and for once, Beowyn was just as eager to hear the answer. Though he paused, and lowered his eyes to the ground before him, as he stopped his struggle against the guards.

"Because. . . I hear that you are a man of honor, Ludica. And if I am to die, then I would rather it be by your hand, than by the hands of a scoundrel."

Finally, the king relented, and signaled for his men to release Helgisson so that he could plead his case. And what confidence he once presented had left him, so that only the truth could at last be seen within the emptiness of his eyes.

"My people are dying. They fight for the scraps of the earth like dogs, and what hope there was once for them, has all but gone on to the winds, lost forever... So, kill me, and attack the city if you wish, Ludica. For there is nothing left of our defenses, save the rotting stilts which prop them up."

"Why are you telling me this now?" Ludica asked.

"Because if I am to be remembered for anything in this life, then it should be that I died so that my people could live. For years, the men of Graefeld have fought and killed each other so that they could impose their own tyranny upon what little remained of our numbers. And now that they are gone, I am left alone, to be remembered for having done just the same. And because of that, there will be nothing left of us at all.

"In my folly, I had aligned myself with your brother, so that I could finally be rid of those who sought to tear us apart from within. But even, then he used me in his plot against you."

"You lie." Beowyn interjected. "I was there, I saw it for myself. All those bodies, piles of them were lined throughout the town, I even saw one of your own within my uncle's ranks as he rode on to Abensloh."

"Aye," Helgisson replied. "Anlaf rides with Sidonis, that much is true. But he does not see the world as I do. He is no man of mine. And if I were to carry on with our alliance, then I would suspect, that he would cut me down when the opportunity arises."

Beowyn could not bring himself to trust the words of the man who stood before them. But he could see that his father was beginning to think otherwise, and it troubled him. Though he remained silent, willing to listen still, as the man carried on.

"Your brother has been schemin' against you for some time, your majesty. And he used me to do it, that much I'll admit. But when he heard of Ascferth's death, he came to me once more, to use my people in a war which was to be fought alongside Abensloh. I thought the man was daft for something so far-fetched, but to my surprise, the bastard managed it, and now he sends words from within Ceolfrid's army."

"He means to do you in, Ludica. Once and for all."

The court fell silent once more, as the king mulled over Helgisson's words.

"And what is his plan?" Ludica asked.

"I will tell ye," the man replied. "All I ask is that you spare my people. Open up the trade so that they no longer starve. Then you will have yet another ally at your side, and one less enemy to contend with."

All eyes then looked to the king once more as he paused yet again to consider his words. Though to Beowyn's surprise, his father turned to face him directly. The king's eyes stared heavily into his own, so that he struggled to return his father's gaze. Confused, and bewildered by the act, he found himself at a loss for words to say. And even further still, he was astonished by the words which his father offered in response to the man.

"Alas, Helgisson, you present me with quite the conundrum. But the decision, I'm afraid, is not mine to make. That, I shall leave for my son to decide."

"What?" Both Beowyn and Helgisson replied in unison. Each man was dumbfounded by the king's words. For Beowyn, it meant that the fate of the war itself could depend on him alone. And for Helgisson, he was certain that the man felt utterly doomed to have their lives depend upon him, as the prince had made it abundantly clear where he stood on the matter.

But as much as he did distrust him, having to make the ultimate decision left him somewhat hesitant to be so quick with his answer. Beowyn looked at his father, and then to Helgisson once more. Both remained silent as they awaited his answer, but all he could seem to feel was the wrenching and writhing of his gut within.

His father had never allowed him to decide on behalf of the throne, let alone, one so great as this, and it terrified him to the very depths. Nor could he understand why his father would place such a decision upon him at such a time as this. For as far as they both were concerned, Beowyn would have no place upon the throne once his brother came of age. Even as the boy still struggled to survive.

Nevertheless, the power was thrust upon him in that moment, and it was left to him alone to decide. And for once, Beowyn made it a point to push his emotions aside, as he considered the paths which lay before him. Before, he hadn't considered the weight of such a choice, and the countless lives that would be affected by it. And now, the only thing he could think to do, was to pray to the gods as he opened his mouth to speak.

And as the words began to leave his lips, the fate of the world as he knew it was sealed.

"Your people will be spared."

He looked at once to see his father's response and could find the subtle approval deep within his gaze as he nodded and turned to face their guest. And to Helgisson also, the man remained silent for a time, taken aback by his words, albeit satisfied with the welcome response. He smiled with relief, then took a step closer toward the throne, as he proceeded to tell the men of Sidonis' plot.

# CHAPTER 16

THE SOUND OF IRON CLASHING rang aloud as the blacksmiths worked tirelessly to prepare the king's army. Newly forged weapons were thrown into carts to be wheeled out to the gathering encampments and distant shouts could be heard from where the king stood atop the city's walls. Flags representing the different clans dotted the landscape against the writhing skies above.

He scanned the fields where the armies had gathered and looked to the road which would lead them toward Mistelfeld. Scouts had brought word of Ceolfrid's army moving south, and that of recent attacks at Faermire's southern border once more. There was no doubt in his mind that his brother was the one to be leading those attacks. But all the same, Ludica's armies would march on to meet him there.

The recent discovery of Sidonis' schemes should not have come as a surprise to him, but the man was still his brother. His own flesh and blood had been driven mad with such greed, that there was no bond between them, which Sidonis would not so easily break. The man was a sycophant and a coward to the utmost degree. And as much as he hated the man for it all, he wrestled most with having let it all get this far. And that was perhaps where his own faults lay.

Ludica was blind to his brother's actions for far too long, and now he was forced to pay the price.

But as he stood there, Ludica swore to himself and to the gods that his brother would pay for his treachery. Whether it be on the battlefield or by his execution, the king would see to it with his own hands.

But soon he noticed that the air around him was getting colder, as the winter had finally drawn itself upon them. And each breath he took flowed visibly from his lips. The sun was lost yet again, and it would be gone from their sight for days at a time, hidden beneath the thickened clouds above. All hopes of warmth would disappear for the months to come. And from this moment on, they were left to fend for themselves.

All of it brought back the memories of those battles he had fought so many years ago. From the bitter cold to the hundreds which stood before him. The earth would soon be breaking beneath their boots as they would march along the surface, and those men would be fighting for their lives within the mud.

So much life would soon be lost, but Ludica swore to the gods that the enemy's numbers would be far greater than that of his own. And that blood which would soon be spilt, would be on his brother's head. But as much as he cherished the peace, the life of politics and of men, never suited the aging warrior. All he had ever known was the sword, and it was his curse. For he longed for a life in which his children would never have to know the brutality of war. And it was his hope that they could live out their days in prosperity because of the sacrifices he and his men had made so many years before.

What a waste of life, the schemes of man. For such death and toil are all that remain of those who seek to trample the world beneath their feet. And it would come to be, that the peace which

Ludica had fought so desperately for would be undone within a single fortnight. What a life indeed. He chuckled aloud to himself.

As he remained there atop the wall, he rested his hands upon stone and dropped his head below his shoulders, feeling the dread creeping up once more.

But in the midst of it all, he could hear a voice calling to him.

"My lord, your armies have gathered, and await your command."

Eohric stood patiently behind the king as he waited for a response. The man had served Ludica faithfully throughout the years, and the two had fought side by side for as long as he could remember. If ever there was man that he could trust aside from Sgell, it was the friend who stood now behind him. And it was Eohric who once again saved him at that moment.

"Thank you," Ludica replied.

"Shall I give the order to march, my Lord?"

"No. Have the elders gather at the court, so that they may give account."

The soldier quietly lowered his head to acknowledge the order and left his presence once more. And beyond the way, as he took to the stairs, his son appeared within his path.

The prince stood tall by the tower's entrance, but his expression remained cautious.

"I await your orders Father... My Lord," he muttered.

The king paused to consider his offer for a moment before continuing past the prince and back down the stairs.

"I have ordered the elders to gather in the court. You will join me there."

Beowyn's expression quickly shifted but was careful to mask it as best as he could. And for once, it seemed, that his eldest son, was eager to take part in the matters of state. Ludica could hear the prince's footsteps following closely behind his own as the two made their way into the palace. And in that moment, the king found comfort in Beowyn's presence.

It wasn't long before the last of the elders trickled into the king's court. The walls echoed with the jumbled voices of all the men who carried on in their conversations. The men, along with their sons, mingled throughout the court before the empty throne.

Each of them carried their weapons upon their waist, many of which had not been used for years. And their chests carried the crest of their clans from whence they came. The dark leather stood in contrast to the golden inlay within its stitches, and many stood with pride amongst their own. Their cloaks were each lined with furs, presenting them as large herds, gathered for a common cause.

But when the doors finally opened before them all, the king's servant announced his arrival, bringing silence to the hall at long last. The men parted themselves before Ludica and his son as they approached the crowd and made their way toward the throne. Beowyn searched the faces of all who stood present before his father and found that Qereth stood among them. His friend nodded with that ever-present hopefulness within his eyes but was quick to refocus his gaze back onto the king. And as Beowyn remained beneath the steps, he watched with the others, as his father ascended the throne.

"Let each elder along with his kin, give account of their clans." The king's command echoed throughout the room as his eyes scanned the numerous faces before him.

"Lord King, I and my son stand for Laeforath with our army to pledge our service to you." Edric was the first of the elders to approach the throne, followed closely by his eldest son. They each lowered themselves to one knee and bowed their heads as they offered up their swords to him.

Edric then carried on with the numbers of his men and the supplies that were brought along with them before they finally re-cused themselves from his presence, disappearing once more into the crowd.

Haemund came next, and was followed by another, until each of the clans had presented themselves before the king, offering their swords to him, as a symbol of their loyalty to his father. The call for battle was made, and all of them had come, ready to fight on behalf of their king and their lands.

And finally, Qereth's father, Aethelwyn approached the throne to offer his loyalty. Beowyn watched as Qereth, along with his brother both stood at their father's side, following the man as he bowed before the king. Such a moment of unity between the clans brought chills to his spine as he could see the true weight of his father's power throughout the kingdom.

So many times, before, he had only watched as the elders ar-gued amongst each other, seeming as though they were never able to find common ground. Yet here they stood, in solidarity for once, and all to grant fealty to his own father. And as he thought on the matter, he could suddenly feel that same rising pit within his gut once more and he grew anxious at the sight of all that had un-folded before him. For so many men were ready for battle, and they looked to the one man who could lead them all to victory.

He looked to his father once more, whose face remained stoic, just as he had so often seen. And he sat high upon his throne as he rested each hand loosely over the ornate stone. He was dressed for battle much like the others, but still wore the crown which branded him as their king and nodded with approval to each of the men who offered their allegiance to him.

But finally, the last of the leaders gave their pledge and rose to join the others, leaving the room silent to hear the king. And all at once, Beowyn was driven to follow in their footsteps.

Before his father could utter another word, the prince made his way toward the center of the room. He could feel that all eyes had suddenly been cast upon him, and it took everything within him to keep his knees from buckling beneath him. But he pressed on, looking back to where his father sat and he could see that the king had pulled himself forward ever so slightly, with an inquisitive look in his eyes.

He recalled the question his father had asked of him, and it rang out louder than ever before. But if there ever was a time for him to show his father the true intent of his heart, then it could only be in that moment. A surge of heaviness fell over him, and he lowered himself to one knee before the throne. All who stood within the court watched the scene with anticipation, and there was nothing but silence to fill the air.

"I am Beowyn, son of Ludica, and I will stand for my king. My sword is yours, Father, as is my life. Let me fight by your side and defend our lands and our people." He fought hard to keep the sting of his tears from welling up within his eyes, and he watched as the king rose slowly from his seat. His father then proceeded down the steps, and Beowyn lifted his eyes to meet his father's gaze. The man remained silent as he stopped before him, and lifted Beowyn by the shoulders, to his feet once more.

And for the first time the prince had seen something in his father's eyes that he couldn't quite place. There was a certain tenderness in the king's expression, and a wall had been broken between them. And for a moment, the two men stood alone, in the court as father and son. The king granted him a single nod as a smile emerged upon his face. Then, with his eyes still fixed upon his son, the king spoke aloud to address the men who had gathered before him.

"Today we march on to battle, and it is our sons who march with us for the first time. For years we have fought to defend our lands so that our children may live free. But now it is our sons who fight alongside us, so that they too may defend this land for the sake of their own children.

"Their blades have yet to know the taste of battle, but soon they shall be marked with the eternal stains of our enemies' blood. Today, gentlemen, our boys become men. So let us give them the fight that shall stand for all of time."

The crowd began to stir as the elders nodded their heads with approval. Men turned to their sons who smiled with pride and others began to cheer for the battle to come. Soon, the room was alive once more and the call for victory became their strength. No one could remain silent any longer, as the court filled with cries for battle. The older generations applauded each other for old times' sake, and the younger cheered for the rite of passage.

Beowyn could feel the hand of his father's grip tightly against his shoulder and he clung to the moment for as long as he could. There had never been such a time when he had felt the way as he did then, and it was the same feeling his father no doubt felt with him. Though no words were spoken between the two, he was content enough with that alone. And it was that desire that he craved all the more.

He watched as his father slowly disappeared within the crowd and began to mingle with the elders who had gathered around him. Several others approached the prince and applauded his deed before his friend finally emerged from within the crowd. He held a grin from ear to ear and patted him forcefully on the back.

"Well done, my friend. Though it'd have been just as well if you showed up at all."

The jab was a low one, but the prince brushed it off with a scoff and a forceful shove. Qereth laughed aloud, and it was clear that he relished the atmosphere around them. The two friends had yet to fight alongside each other, but the prospect was a welcome one. Beowyn reached and pulled his friend in close as he pressed his head against Qereth's.

"I shall look for you on the field my friend," the prince uttered.

"Well, you needn't look far, Beowyn, for I'll be there by your side."

The two smiled at one another before joining in with the others. It was a celebration which had come rather unexpectedly for the prince, but it was one that served to further fuel their drive to fight. Though eventually, as the energy had begun to calm itself within the great hall, the men began to filter back out into the cold. However, it was the bitter bite of the chilling winds which had brought each of them back to the realities of war as it lingered throughout. And soon, the world had pulled the idyllic veil from their eyes, as they went about their business.

The elders gathered with their men, and the drums of war began to pound through the air. The deep rumble of the thunderous tones echoed throughout the city, and all had begun to gather near the gates. The time had finally come, and yet Beowyn found himself, eagerly searching for his sister. For it was Estrith whom he sought to say his final farewell, yet she was nowhere to be found, and time was running short.

He called to one of the servants to locate the princess but was suddenly stopped by the call for his name. He quickly turned and was relieved to see Estrith approaching him from within the crowd. And though she tried to conceal it, he could still see the worry in her eyes. She tightly grasped her hands together and looked to him as she struggled to find the words to say.

But it was the very sight of her which had begun to tear at his heart. For there, was the only person who had always been at his side since the day that their lives began. She was alone in that moment, lost to find her words just as he struggled to do the same. And so, all that he could do was to pull her close and wrap his arms around her as she pulled herself in tighter.

"Come back to me brother, swear it."

"I swear," he tenderly replied. The two hugged once more before he kissed her on the head and pulled himself away. Though as their arms released their grasp, Qereth had appeared and was quick to offer his embrace instead.

"Would you spare your humble servant a warm embrace as well?" he asked with a grin.

"Gladly." Qereth's presence brought ease to the tension between them, and Beowyn was glad for that.

As the two spoke on for a moment longer, he quietly recused himself and made his way to the horse which awaited him. Though he still found himself glancing back toward his sister, hoping to capture her image in his mind one last time.

And as he watched Qereth depart from her as well, his father too, sought her out from within the crowd. Beowyn watched as their father held his sister gently by the arms and spoke softly to her as she lowered her head. Tears dripped swiftly from her face, and he was quick to wipe them away. But overcome with emotion, Estrith threw herself against their father's chest and waited as he finally brought his arms up to comfort her. Though before long, he offered his final farewell and left her alone once again in the street.

His father's face had changed as he approached the horses. And there once more, Beowyn could find nothing but sadness in his father's eyes.

He watched as the king pulled himself onto the horse and paused for a moment before going over to Beowyn.

"This is what we fight for..." his father uttered. Then took a final glance at Estrith who remained, wiping the sullen tears from her face. And with a final nudge, the king ushered his horse along as he led the line toward the road.

Beyond the walls, Beowyn was taken aback at the sight before him. The field had been covered, like a sea of men ready for battle and stood at arms, as they waited for the king's arrival. All eyes were upon them as they approached the ranks, and only the sound of flags whipping the wind stood out amongst the silence before them.

He watched as his father scanned the lines and directed his gaze to the road which led them south. Their land against Mistelfeld awaited the armies of Faermire, and everyone present looked to his father alone to lead them there. As he and the king approached the front, distant shouts from their leaders called out to the soldiers to march. Then like an endless serpent, the formation slithered along the ground as they all moved as one. The ground began to rumble from the weight of their feet and the ram horns were lifted into the air as they cried out through the distant beating of the drums.

To Beowyn, it was as if it were all just a fleeting dream to which there was no end. And before he knew it, his blade would soon be dripping with the blood of his enemies.

Estrith found herself a place at the top of the city's wall to watch as her father led his armies on. She pulled her cloak tighter around her waist to fend off the cold that clung to her. And before long, the sound of their beating drums had long since vanished, along with the men who carried up the rear. Soon, all that remained was the muddied path that showed the remnants of their presence, and she was alone once more.

The remaining guards along with the commoners had long since returned to their lives and duties, but all that she could bring herself to do was search the horizon for just one last glimpse of them.

It was the first time that she had ever witnessed such a mass migration off to war. A true sight to see for those young enough to bask in its grandeur. But for her, it only signaled the impending dread that would remain upon her until she saw them return.

Though finally, the sound of her father's servant called to her and broke the trance which had ensnared her.

"My lady, perhaps it is best to remove yourself from this cold and retire within the palace."

Sgell waited patiently behind her, standing tall just as he always did. The man had always provided a calming presence, no matter where his duties led him.

"Why did my father leave his own servant here in Elsterheim, when he needed you most?" she asked, while her gaze remained fixed upon the horizon.

"The king thought it best to tend to the ones he left behind. This is the place where he felt that there remained the greatest need."

After some time, she finally relented to the reality which had set upon her and made her way back down the steps as Sgell followed her at a distance. Along the way, she caught sight of the guards who stood at the entrance which led down into the dungeon.

The door was dark and lined with iron. It held a small opening barred by rods, which left a small window into the darkness beyond it. Suddenly, she was reminded of who it was that dwelt within its tomb. She stopped, enthralled by its intrigue. The dark tunnels where Richessa now lived seemed to call for her, and step by step she drew closer toward the prison.

"My lady, it unwise to go beyond that door."

Sgell was quick to interject, but his words went unheard. Estrith continued further, leading herself on, until she finally found herself ordering the guards to allow her passage.

They each looked at one another briefly with a cautious expression but acknowledged her command as one proceeded to pull the iron door open.

"Take me to Richessa," she ordered. The guard nodded, then grabbed a torch as he led her down the steps, treading further into the darkness.

She was greeted first, by the stench, and she fought to keep herself from cowering away from its sting. Next, she jumped at the sight of the countless rats which scurried across her path. From one squeal to the next, she desperately worked to steady her breath.

The guard stopped and waited for the princess to collect herself before carrying on.

"Do not fear the rats, my Lady, their appetites are more than satisfied in these parts. And besides, you lack the smell they crave."

Her face curled at the guard's remark, but she remained silent as she followed his lead. He took the princess to the end of the tunnel which faced a single cell and placed the torch against the wall before he left. She stood in silence for some time, staring deeper into the shadows where her father's wife supposedly remained.

"Come into the light," she ordered with a slight quiver in her voice. The damp coldness gripped her tightly, like the tendrils of a thorny vine. But before long, a chain had pulled itself further into the darkness, and all she could hear was the ever-familiar tone of Richessa's voice from within the corner.

"What a sight it is to see such a pretty little face in a place like this..."

"Come out into the light, Richessa." Estrith narrowed her eyes to better focus on the silhouette which slowly emerged from within the shadows. In such a short time, the woman appeared as though her life had been eaten away. The sight of her was difficult to bear, but the princess forced herself to remain still, and unmoved before her. The tight curls in Richessa's amber hair had begun to entangle themselves into thick mattes all throughout, and the bruises from her father's rage, revealed themselves effortlessly beneath the dirt upon her porcelain skin. Her dress had begun to tear near her feet, and the iron cuffs had branded their marks heavily around her ankles.

"Is this what you wanted to see? Tell me, Estrith, why is it that you've come here? As far as anyone is concerned, I am dead to the world."

The young princess pondered the very same words herself, as she entered the dungeon, but she couldn't find the answer she had hoped for. Perhaps, it was to see the state in which such a woman of stature had fallen, or perhaps, it was solely because of her son. Whether it was out of pity, or mere curiosity, she couldn't be sure.

But for whatever animosity there was between them, Richessa first and foremost, was still Siged's mother. It must have eaten away at her to be kept from his side in such a time of need, but the woman would never admit to such weakness as Estrith saw it.

For such disregard the woman held for their lives, Estrith couldn't seem to bring herself to hate the woman as she so greatly desired. All she could do in the end was to simply stand in that place, silent and watchful.

"This is what you wanted, wasn't it? To see me as I am, stripped of my place and of my power. And all the while, what threat there ever was for me, stands here now, to look upon me with pity."

"That is not why I've come," Estrith replied.

"Isn't it? After all, my son nearly died because of your stupidity, and it was because of your prying little eye that your father had me thrown in here."

Estrith stood in disbelief at the words Richessa spoke, twisting reality to suit her plight.

"I spared your life—"

"No, you doomed me to suffer death longer. I should've known that such a mischievous little whore would find a way to betray her queen. But I shall not make that mistake again."

"Surely, you shall not, Richessa. Whatever schemes brought you to this place was no one's fault, but your own. It was you, who slept with my uncle and plotted against my father. And it is you, who stands responsible for Siged's plight."

Richessa was taken aback for the first time, hearing the tone in Estrith's response, and remained quiet as she carried on.

"In my naiveté, I waited to tell the truth of your actions until it was too late, but I will not make that mistake again. Siged paid too great a price for your treachery and that is something that I will always have to live with. But if I am to speak the truth, as you desire, then I shall tell you that I came because by some ill-fated reason, I do pity you. Despite all that you've done, Richessa, I cannot bring myself to hate you, as much as I've tried. I cannot say that I would have spared your life however, if Siged had died. For then, I would have gladly let my father cut you down."

Estrith's voice began to break beneath the pain which had begun to resurface, but she stifled it as she met Richessa's eye. And only silence remained between them.

She had wondered for a moment, if what Richessa had told her about her marriage with Ealric was true. But as the woman was clearly driven mad by her own self-indulgence, it remained clear to her, that she was incapable of speaking the truth. Though finally, after some time, Richessa pulled herself closer toward the iron bars.

"How is he?" she finally asked.

But whatever desire there was to show her mercy, Estrith could suddenly find it no longer. She felt sick at the very sight of Richessa, and the words which left that woman's mouth only moments before. Richessa pulled herself closer toward the bars, tightly clasping her hands around them.

"Tell me," she demanded.

Estrith could see the rising desperation within her eyes but held her tongue and she took a step back. Richessa then threw her arm toward the princess hoping to gain a hold on her but fell short of her reach. She watched as the woman called out to her once more and continued to reach through the bar as she began to further demand a response from her.

And as Richessa writhed from within her prison, the proud facade that she so often held, had begun melt until there was nothing left but despair. Her eyes had grown wide, and the tone of her voice rose higher with each demanding call.

Though all that Estrith could find to do was to turn her back on the one who was once called Queen. She then lifted the torch from the wall to guide her path and began to walk away.

"You would deny me my right to know of my son's condition?! You owe that much!"

Estrith paused for a moment to consider the demand, but kept her eyes fixed toward the exit.

"I owe you nothing, Richessa..." The longer she tarried, she feared that she would regret her decision, so she left. And the woman began to cry out to her once more from the depths. She could hear Richessa fall to the floor and sob aloud for all to hear. The sound of her anguish echoed through the halls and each of her cries clawed at the princess, forcing her to quicken her steps.

The light from the door was all that she could see, and she brushed swiftly past the guards who rose to their feet. But the walls had begun to close in around her, and she clung to her chest to catch her breath with each passing step.

Finally, she reached the door and ordered the guards to open it, pulling herself back into the light once more. She flung herself out into the open, nearly bursting into tears as she caught herself in the midst.

And just beyond the way, Sgell remained there waiting, and offered his outstretched hand to her. All that was further granted from the man was his silence, but for her, it was more than enough.

She steadied herself from where she stood, and the man remained at her side. As she collected the pieces of herself, she thanked him and continued on toward the palace where Siged was waiting for her.

# CHAPTER 17

## HELMFIRTH, KINGDOM OF MISTELFELD

GWENORA STOOD, OVERLOOKING THE WATERS beyond her city from the balcony of her chambers. The winter sky hung heavily over the landscape, as the clouds sunk further over top of the land. But the waters of the Erythean sea were what always called to the queen. Despite the chaos which mankind was so eager to create, she always found her comfort in the stillness of the waters. For the sea was always her constant. Even if it often faced the wrath of a fearsome storm and its howling winds, it had always found its peace again at the very end. And for aging the woman, she had always turned to the sea as it beckoned her, now more so than ever before.

But for so many years, she had fought to mark her place amongst men, and stave off the ruin that her fool of a husband, was destined to bring upon her people. And for years, she was tormented by the blight which was left upon her name. She was free at last, but it came after the whole of her life had already been lived. For so long, she had waited for this moment, but as she stood there, she found that it was well worth the wait. The air was crisper, and the landscape, more beautiful than she had seen it so many times before.

For this was her home, and though she was alone in the midst of it, her heart was full.

"Soon, my friend," she said, looking out across the waters. She spoke to the sea as though it were the friend which had always remained so near to her. The years had sent so much life through its currents; from the travelers to the fisherman, and to the life which it carried within its depths. To the queen, it was the very essence of life itself. And she spoke aloud, making a promise to the sea, that she would at last, return to its shores one day. And by the stillness of the current, she would take that final journey, toward the everlasting. So that at long last, her dearest friend would guide her to the peace which she so desperately longed for.

But that time, would have to wait for just a little while longer. For as Gwenora saw it, there was still one last task at hand, until she could truly be free. It was a game that she had grown so weary of, but she had resolved to play it one last time, for the sake of her people. Countless wars had been fought throughout her life, and the ends never justified the means in her eyes.

So many kings, would use the gods as a means to push their own advances, while others truly believed that the gods demanded war from them. But she cursed the lot of them. For to her, they brought nothing but sorrow and havoc to those who served them. And for a time, she was their most faithful. But, no more. She soon came to realize that the gods' thirst for blood and greed, was no better than the men who served in their names. *So, to the unknown god, I shall pray.* She often thought to herself. *To the one who gives life, I shall offer mine.* But for the whole of Aecorath, the world as they knew it, none existed. Though she carried on with that hope and found herself delighting in the idea of meeting this god in the afterlife whenever that day should come.

And as she remained, gazing across the horizon, her servant approached her with a letter in hand. The man offered it to her, then waited for her in the distance as she took it. The message bore Ludica's seal across its seam in wax. When last she saw him, he had finally agreed to a treaty amongst their lands, but the news of his ailing son had pulled him away in such haste. And she worried if the truce would stand between them when she needed him most. So, she promptly broke the stamp to learn of its contents and scanned the lines, reading his words with a cautious intent.

He had spoken of the news regarding his brother, a man known as, Sidonis, and the plot against him with the king of Abensloh. But what had intrigued the queen most of all, were the words which pertained to the traitors within her ranks. Where he had gleaned such damning information was of little consequence to the queen, for if these words were true, then it meant that no war posed a greater threat to her, than from those who served her.

And in such trying times as these, one could never be too careful with whom they placed their trust, but for the queen of Mistelfeld, it was an alliance most favorable to have Ludica by her side. Already, the man had proven his worth to her, and the battle had yet to even begin. Or at least in terms of physical arms... For it seemed to her, that the battle had long been waged beneath her very roof, and it was time to finally bring it all to light.

And though the words which he had written were most distress-ing, it certainly came as no surprise to the queen. If anything, she alone was the one at fault for not having dealt with it long ago. But the time had finally come, and she was content with the prospect of it all. For at long last, she could deal with the traitors once and for all.

She signaled for the servant as she left the balcony and gently folded the letter back within her hands.

"Send for Aldred," she said.

The servant left her at once to fulfill her command, and she remained alone as she turned to warm herself against the fire. She watched as the logs crackled and popped within the flames, and it was a calming relief against the bitter cold which remained outside her room. But for her, the greatest comfort of all was knowing that the end was soon at hand.

And eventually, the soldier whom she had summoned arrived swiftly to her call as bowed his head to greet her.

"My Queen," he uttered, before raising himself up again. The man had served her well for many years and followed her closely wherever she went. In all the kingdom, he was her most faithful and loyal subject, and she trusted him most of all.

Even as her husband lived, Aldred remained loyal to Gwenora, and it was a sacrifice which she had never forgotten. A long scar had been carved within his arm in an attempt once to save her life, an attempt spurred on by her own husband no doubt. But it always remained true to her, that Aldred brought peace to her whenever he was near.

As he awaited her orders, she remained at her place by the fire, and gently tapped Ludica's letter against her hand as she pondered her course of action. The pieces had been laid out before her and now it was her turn to play the game.

"Have the scouts returned to give report of Ceolfrid's army?"

"They have, your majesty."

"What news do they bring?"

"They say that Ceolfrid's army marches west, toward Faermire."

Gwenora scoffed aloud at his words and looked upon the letter once more.

"Part of it, I'm sure. But not all... And these scouts, they report to Lord Ordric, no doubt?"

"They do, my Lady."

"Good," she replied. "Find a scout in whom you can trust, one who has not already gone to survey the lands. And have him report to you of his own findings with all haste."

"Yes, my Lady—"

"And Aldred..." Before the man could finish his acknowledgment, she looked at him once more. "I believe it goes without saying, that discretion is of the utmost importance."

"Of course, my Queen." And with that final word, the man crossed his arm over his chest and bowed to her again before leaving her presence.

But to hear the words uttered aloud, which confirmed the warning within Ludica's letter carried with it a feeling that she couldn't quite comprehend. Whether it was elation or apprehension she couldn't decide. Though perhaps, it was both. For the revelation of all that had come to pass meant that it only solidified the dread which she had long feared. But as the days drew near, so did her resolve. A battle was to be fought for the rights to her throne, and that battle came from both within and without her borders.

And although the letter didn't name a person directly upon whom she could pass her judgment, she only needed to confirm her suspicions once and for all. Lord Ordric was at the top of that list. For the man was loyal to only himself, and would bathe himself in the slop of pigs, if it meant that he could become king. Her husband was merely an obstacle of time, while she, on the other hand, posed a greater threat to his very pride. And that could never stand for such a man as he. For far be it, that a woman should hold a place greater than his. After her husband's death, he proved as much, taking so little time to gather what poison he needed to infect the minds of her subjects.

She did find it odd that the man's staunch objection to a war with Abensloh had suddenly fallen silent in the recent days. And now that the battle was soon upon them, Ordric stood amongst the council in favor of it.

But at last, she had the means to finally put him in the place which he so richly deserved.

Though as she remained within her chambers, there was a knock at the door.

"Enter," she said. And much to her delight, there appeared through the door, the personal servant to his lordship.

The servant humbly greeted the queen before announcing the reason for his arrival.

"My Lady, Lord Ordric wishes to hold a feast tonight in your honor. On this eve of battle."

"A feast?" She found herself taken aback by the gesture, but quickly found her wits again. "Well, isn't that delightful? The chief adviser would like to honor his queen with such a gallant tribute."

"Yes, my Lady. And he says that he would like to offer you the finest of his own livestock for the banquet."

She smiled, noting the irony of it all.

"Then you may tell him that I humbly accept his offer. What a pleasant surprise it is that Ordric should be so gracious at such a time as this."

It was clear that the servant missed the sarcasm in her tone, but quickly went about his business, taking her response back to his master. As he left the room, she couldn't help but sneer as she recalled the interaction just moments before. For such contempt that Ordric held for Gwenora, she was certain that the feast was by no means meant to honor her as his queen. If anything, his intent was to celebrate her untimely demise. And she would be the prized of his livestock to be served for all to eat.

It was to be the feast in which Ordric would celebrate the coming era, where he would finally be their king. And as the days carried on, it became clear that the man was growing more comfortable with his place upon a throne which he did not possess.

"So be it, Ordric," she muttered aloud and took one last glimpse of the sea from within her chambers, before readying herself for the night to come.

The festivities had carried on long before her arrival at the banquet hall, and the sounds of their celebration carried themselves beyond the doors to the place where she stood. For such a solemn occasion, the nobility of her ranks could not contain their merriment, and they drank to their hearts' delight. Meanwhile, the armies had gathered outside the city to prepare for a battle where countless lives were sure to be lost. And she was sickened by the whole of it.

But the fact remained that the game had to be played. And so, she would allow this move, for the next was hers to make. She finally stepped to approach the doors, and the servants promptly pulled them open. Inside, the tables had been filled with patrons hailing from all corners of the kingdom. Members of the council and every class of highest nobility were packed amongst the seats and Ordric sat at the very center of them all. But there next to him, was the single chair reserved for her majesty, their supposed guest of honor.

As she entered the hall, the room in its entirety fell silent, and all eyes went to the queen as they rose from their seats. The mood had suddenly shifted, and the patrons were reminded of whom the festivities were for. Or at least, what they were told of. And all but Ordric's expression had changed. For him, the man continued to carry a mischievous grin upon his face. It was for the queen, the subtle confirmation which she needed to feel content in her resolve.

"My Lords! And my ladies. . ." He proclaimed with a gentle raise of his chalice. "Your queen!"

The insolence of such a gesture further proved his contempt for her as she entered the hall. But all eyes remained fixed on the queen as she made her way toward her place and finally lowered herself within her chair.

"For an occasion to be held in my honor, Lord Ordric, it seems that you've found no trouble in starting without me."

"Only so that you could be welcomed with a ready heart, my Lady," he replied with a grin. "Would the queen like to say a word or two, before we resume?"

"The queen would not," she curtly replied.

"Very well." He then motioned toward the musicians to resume and lowered himself back into his seat. As the guests began to mingle once more, she scanned the room, taking note of all the faces that were present. Friends which had no doubt, been personally invited by the man himself. And had it been anyone else, she would have dealt with such treachery long ago, but as cunning as Ordric was, he made it a point to create friends in whatever places he could manage. Most of the people who had attended were either too foolish to know of his schemes or lay complicit in his ideals.

Those who were loyal to the crown and found honor amongst their people, though few there may have been, were coincidentally absent from the banquet. And so it was, that she was dining within a pit of snakes. The *prized meal* of Ordric's livestock happened to be nothing more than the venison which he no doubt commissioned his servants to hunt within her lands. It was yet another insult added to the list of many.

But she remained quiet, watching those around her take part in the celebration of the war which was to come. The happiest among them was the traitor who sat proudly beside her. He conversed with those around him without a care in the world and drank with a glimmer of delight within his eyes.

*Such hubris...* she thought to herself, as she sat amongst his acolytes. The jumbled voices echoed throughout the hall as the minstrels carried their sound within the midst. And the longer she sat there, the more deafening it became. But finally, a young servant arrived at her side and presented her with a cup filled with wine.

She studied it for a time as it sat before her and watched as the light from the torches bounced against the sheen of its surface. The deep red elixir rested within the chalice like a warm delectation which called to its bearer. She hardly found the satisfaction within its pleasures that so many often claimed, but on a night like this, it beckoned her with such a sweetness she had rarely known.

But then, it struck her. She gently lifted the cup within her hand and caressed its rim, running her finger over its smooth perimeter. She hardly doubted that Ordric would be capable of something so bold as to poison her drink. But then again, the man was far more capable of things than she had previously thought otherwise. Even still, the man went as far as hosting a banquet so that he could parade her like his personal trophy. He brought her solely to send her a message, and it was time at last that she offered one back.

"I think perhaps, I would like to say a word after all."

Ordric looked at her with curiosity in his eyes as she rose from her chair, silencing the room once more.

"Our people have endured such tribulation throughout the years but have remained resilient despite it all. Years of war and politics have ravaged our lands, and all at the hands of those who wield such power. I, being chief amongst them."

She could see the guests' eyes begin to wander with a hint of bewilderment throughout. But she continued.

"For far too long, there has been disunity amongst our ranks, and I have only served to further the divide between us all. It should come as no surprise that lord Ordric and I have not seen eye to eye on most things regarding matters of state." She feigned a smile to lighten the mood. Ordric chuckled, prompting the others to do the same and she carried on. "But no more... On the eve of battle, I should like to think that for once, we may at last become a united people. So let it be, that from this moment forward, there be peace between us Ordric."

"Here, here," he replied with a renewed sense of amusement. But his face quickly soured as she lowered her cup before him.

"Then drink of my cup," she calmly uttered. "Drink, so that all may know that we stand together. United at last for a cause which is greater than us all."

The man's eyes shifted from the cup in her hand, to face her directly with a glare so sharp, she could nearly feel the sting of it upon her face. He knew very well at that moment, where her message fell between the lines and hated her more than ever because of it. And all at once, his cheeks we flushed with ire.

The silence grew ever more oppressive within the hall as they waited for him to finally respond. And at last, he carefully removed the cup from within her hand as he studied its contents. She smiled down at him from where she stood, but he returned her gesture with the same piercing glare as he did before. Slowly, he raised the cup to his lips and remained staring into her eyes as he swallowed the wine. He drank of its entirety so that all could see that there was none to spare.

She watched as the liquid dripped from his lips like blood and gently received the cup which he had offered in return. And amid the silence, the queen and Ordric remained staring at one another without so much as a single word between them. Until finally, the decrepit elder, Burgred, raised his glass to the pair, as his quivering voice pierced the stillness around them.

"Here, here," he said. Then took a sip from his glass, unamused by the tension which had filled the room. Gwenora smiled, then lowered herself back into her seat as she saluted the old man. He was so far into his years, she was amazed that he still managed to carry enough stamina to participate in political matters. And the only reason that perhaps Ordric had even invited the man was simply because his mind was never present enough to even care what happened one way or the other. She nearly lost him amongst the crowd until he finally made his presence known. But he was certainly a welcome sight for the lonesome queen.

Out of everyone in attendance that night, Burgred was perhaps the only one who didn't wish for her death, and the feeling was mutual. But it was just as well, for then she knew who was loyal to her and who was not.

When the day had finally arrived, the armies of Mistelfeld stood ready to march upon the Queen's order. But as her scouts returned with news from the front, she called for all the members of her leadership to gather within the court. And the collective voices of all who had come carried the same question from within the crowd as to why the queen should require their presence so close to the armies' departure. For on the advice of her counsel, Gwenora had agreed to send them off toward the borders of Faermire, where Ceolfrid's army was spotted.

As she entered, Ordric was quick to voice his frustration for the prolonged delay.

"My Lady," he said. "The army of Abensloh marches west as we speak, and yet you delay the orders to send ours on?"

The irritable tone in his voice gave way to the confirmation she needed to carry on.

"In due time, Lord Ordric, in due time..." Her placid demeanor only further served to offend the man as he watched her calmly take her place upon the throne. She waited despite the contentious silence around her, and scanned the faces, taking note of those who attended Ordric's banquet. The others, who were not, seemed more perplexed by the ordeal than anything else.

"Our scouts first reported that the armies of Abensloh were spotted driving west. We were told that Ceolfrid has amassed his armies near the border where our lands meet Faermire. But I will tell you now, that this is not so..."

She could hear the voices among the room begin to stir, and took particular interest in Ordric's expression, as it changed, if ever so slightly. She watched as the man let slip the tiniest hint of distress in his eyes. He quickly scoured the room, and then looked to the queen, whose sole attention remained fixed on her chief adviser.

For it was by his words, that the whereabouts of Ceolfrid's armies were reported, and it was Ordric whose pockets were thicker than his own spine. For the man had paid each of them to say the words which he had devised from the schemes of his plot with the Northern King. And it would be by his words, that Gwenora would order her own armies away, leaving the city defenseless against Ceolfrid's attack.

But as the queen continued to look upon the man, she spoke further,

"Bring the scouts forward. Let them give account on their own accord," she ordered.

And upon her command, Aldred escorted all the scouts into the court. Several of the men began to shift nervously in their place as the queen watched them from her place upon the throne.

"You," she said, addressing the first within the line, "Tell us now, what you saw of the armies of Abensloh."

She could see the man's eyes shift toward Ordric if only for a split second before looking back at the queen as he straightened his posture. Meanwhile, the chief adviser refused to look away from the scout, furrowing his brow with each passing moment.

"They travel west, my Queen, toward our border with Faermire." The tension in Ordric's face eased, and he looked to Gwenora with a renewed sense of confidence.

"And you?" She looked to the next scout down the line. His response came just the same as the first, confirming Ordric's resolve. But she continued still. And then to the next, the answer fell just the same. Each of the men, reported the words that Ordric had devised, and he raised both his arms into the air hoping to stop her from carrying on.

"My queen! You would dispute the very words of your own scouts? Surely this is madness!" He turned to the crowd, instigating talk among his constituents, but the queen remained stoic.

"I am not finished, Ordric," she said tersely. "And you would do well, to hold your tongue unless spoken to." She nudged her head toward the next scout, prompting him to speak of his own account. But the man continued to shift nervously in his place as he looked toward Ordric and to the others, who all glanced at him from where they stood. It was clear that the pressure weighed heavily over the young scout, from both sides of the line, but he returned his gaze toward the queen as she nodded, prompting him to speak.

"Only some of the armies of Abensloh march west, my Queen. But there are far greater numbers waiting within the Dolam Pass, to the north..."

Ordric's eyes widened with angst and fury at the words which were spoken aloud, and the man could no longer contain himself,

"Lies!" he shouted and pointed his finger at the scoundrel he suddenly saw before him. Those present within the court began to speak amongst themselves once more, and the queen merely watched the scene from within her seat. All at once, the young scout became the target of blame and hatred from Ordric and the others beside him as their collective story began to crumble.

For though he had been paid by Ordric, like the others, the young man broke beneath the pressure of Aldred's prodding and spoke at last, the truth which would ultimately save his own life.

Gwenora looked to him with a glint in her eye before moving on to the last of the men, the one whom Aldred, himself, had commissioned to scour the lands. And the queen gently raised her hand to silence the lot, as she waited until the room fell quiet once more.

"Go on," she said, and the man began to speak.

"The lad speaks true, my Queen. Ceolfrid's army awaits us within the Dolam pass. I have seen it with my own eyes. He hopes that our armies will march on toward our border with Faermire, leaving Helmfirth defenseless against his advance."

"Very good, thank you," she replied, looking back at Ordric once more. "Let this be a reminder to those who wish to betray their own. For such is a penalty that shall not go unpunished."

She then looked to Aldred who ordered his guards forward. And all at once, the scouts were executed where stood, sparing only the two who had spoken truth to the queen. One by one, the guards had run their blades deep into the flesh of the men who stood before them. All were thrust so deep that their swords broke through to the other side, letting the blood spill freely onto the ground around their feet. The cold steel of their weapons glistened with the color red against the light, and all who were present gasped with horror. Ordric, being chief amongst them all, began to recoil within his shock.

"What have you done?!" he cried aloud, but his words fell silent against the queen as she carried on.

"Seize him!" she ordered, prompting the guards to surround the man. The court suddenly erupted into chaos, and the voices of those present created a deafening tone throughout the hall. But Gwenora finally rose from her seat as some began to shout from within the crowd.

"Ordric has aligned himself with Ceolfrid and has spread nothing but lies within our ranks. He has paid these men who lay dead here before you now, to leave our city defenseless. And this gentlemen, is your proof!" She raised the letter from Ludica in the air, for all to see and displayed his seal before the crowd.

"Faermire has sent us word of traitors within our midst, bearing witness to Ceolfrid's plot from among our own. And lord Ordric, has positioned himself to usurp my throne with our enemy's help!"

Once again, the crowd began to stir at the revelation which she had presented to them. Though many were quick to voice their opposition to the words she spoke.

"If any man wishes to dispute my claim, then speak now! So that I can see your faces plainly!" Her fierce gaze darted to those who were present at Ordric's banquet, and their lips were the first to fall silent amidst the disorder. Then, one by one, the voices died down as they all watched Ordric continue to wrestle against the grasp of his captors. He began to shout his pleas toward the crowd as his desperation grew by the minute.

"She spouts nothing but lies! And she will lead our men to their deaths, you will see!"

But as he spoke, Gwenora ordered him out of her presence and stood tall upon her place at the throne.

"Rest assured, Ordric, you will be held accountable for all your crimes against your people. And as for those who still doubt me, you need only to remain patient. For then we shall see whose truth we can believe."

Within a moment's notice, Gwenora had positioned herself upon her own blade, and the fates would decide if she should thrust herself upon it. But at least, if she would have to die, then she would do it on her terms alone. So, finally, she made the order. and the armies of Mistelfeld would remain, save for the smaller contingent which had been sent to help their new-found allies.

# CHAPTER 18

## KINGDOM OF FAERMIRE

AS THEY MARCHED DEEPER INTO the fog, Ludica narrowed his eyes, hoping to see past the mist which was growing thicker by the minute. Soon, he could hardly make out the men who marched beside him, and those who followed closely behind. The veil lay heavily over the earth around them all, so that they could no longer tell if their path led them straight any longer.

He looked to Beowyn, who fought hard to maintain his composure, giving way to the uneasiness within his eyes. But the king applauded his son for the effort, as he also struggled to keep his own fears at bay. For with the thickening mist, there came also the silence beneath its shroud. It acted as though it carried a mind of its own, blotting out the sound of their feet, even as they marched on. And soon, they would be lost, caught within the prison of their own dissolution.

But as they carried on, Ludica looked to the ground below, taking note of the blackened earth that had been charred by fire. And at long last, he could see signs of civilization appear from within the fog. The silhouette of a large building emerged into sight, but as they drew near, his heart sank. With each passing moment, he could at last, make out the remains of what it once was, standing now only as an empty shell which had been razed with the same fire that had blackened the earth around it.

And within the ashes, there lay the bodies, so many in number that he could no longer tell where one started and another began. Their limbs had been mangled beneath the flames of their demise, and some reached their hands toward the heavens as their final plea to gods. But even as the billowing smoke carried their spirits into the afterlife, those countless lives before them all, stood as a sign, a message for Ludica alone, and it grieved him to his core.

For this was his brother's doing, of that he had no doubt. And what little there was that remained of the man he once knew, had been lost forever. For the one who could do such an evil as this, was not a man any longer. Even the gods could not possibly find favor in such an act as this...

As more evidence of his brother's presence emerged from within the fog, Ludica made sure to keep himself from turning his eyes away. The town had been razed, and all the people within it, his own people. And for each of the lives lost, Sidonis would pay for it sevenfold.

But the further they marched, the more he came to realize that his army was left exposed. And soon he heard nothing aside from the feet of his soldiers upon the ground. He then signaled to his officers, ordering the march to a halt.

As he scanned the gray mist before him, he listened for the sound of anything beyond the silence, but there was nothing. Even the crows did not squawk for the dead overhead, and the wind dared not to even make a sound as it drifted beneath the clouds.

Suddenly, Ludica and his armies were stranded amongst the remains of those who had been killed. And even the dead could not mourn for themselves within the breeze. But as he remained, a soldier approached him from within their ranks, offering the king news from the front.

"My Lord, two of our scouts have not returned. And those who have, cannot see beyond the mist."

"They aim to entrap us here," Beowyn interjected.

"Yes. . ." Ludica replied.

It was clear that they had come upon the place where Sidonis and his forces were reported last seen. But where they stood was so void of life, that even his brother couldn't have planned it so that the gods too, had chosen to abandon it.

And had the fog not settled so heavily, they would have been able to keep their distance from the trap that they happened upon. But the lots had been cast, and this would have to be the place where they would make their stand.

"Have the line divide and send a portion of our arms to the flanks. Gather the rest and form a circle. We are too exposed here— "

"Wait, do you hear that?" Beowyn asked.

Before the king could finish his words, they each paused to focus their attention on the stillness around them. At first, he could hear nothing. And all that remained was the shroud of gray in every direction his head had turned. But just as he had nearly given up his search, there it was.

A distant rumble echoed throughout the land and its cadence rose with each passing moment. Soon, the cries of battle came from within the thunder, and they looked all around them, hoping to find where it was coming from.

"Do you see them?!" Beowyn shouted. Even their horses began to stir beneath them as the encroaching tremors grew stronger.

Ludica gripped the reigns tightly within his hands and fought to steady the animal which carried him.

"Shields!" Ludica cried, and the order was carried swiftly down the line. But the men had hardly the time to form the barricade before hundreds of figures emerged from within the fog, throwing themselves into his army like ravenous wolves. And in the blink of an eye, the battle had already begun.

The clashing of metal rang out into the sky, and the screams of death followed shortly after. Ludica searched the field before him, and at last, he found his son amid the fight. Swords flew through the air in a rage so violent that sparks emerged from within the field and one by one, bodies began to fall all around him.

"Beowyn!" Ludica shouted, but his cries were lost within the chaos. And just as he began to lower himself down from his saddle, a large spear had been thrust deeply into his horse's chest. The animal writhed and brayed in pain as reared itself up before falling back on the ground, tossing the king into the mud below.

A loud cry approached, and a man clad in black armor lifted his weapon to strike him down. But with what little time he had spare, Ludica pulled his blade from its sheath, and blocked the killing blow from within an inch of his life. And with a swift retaliation, the man was struck down from where the king lay within the mud.

As he pulled himself up, he wiped the dirt from his eyes and searched the field once more for his son, whom he had lost against the heat of battle. Enemy soldiers rushed toward him in droves, hoping to be the one to slay the king, but one by one, Ludica had proven his worth and struck them down. Even as the sun had yet to reach its peak in the day.

When at last he could catch his breath, Ludica scoured the field with what little visibility the fog would offer him, hoping to find his son again. but at last, Beowyn gripped the king by the shoulder, and he sighed sharply with relief at the sight of his face.

Though spatters of blood and dirt were caked upon his son's face, he delighted still in the confidence of the boy's fortitude, shattering the fears he carried with him throughout their march into battle. Before, he never had cause to worry so greatly for another man upon the field of battle, and for the first time in all his years, this was the first. For it was his son, his blood which would be tested against their enemy's rage. And it was for Beowyn alone, that Ludica sought so desperately to protect.

He looked to his son, eyes widened against the raging boil beneath his skin and his blade trembled within the impenetrable grip of his hands. It was that same look that the king had seen so many times before. And those who carried it were lost forever to the innocence they once knew. Never to behold it ever again. It was that look, that he hoped he would never have to see upon his own son, for then Beowyn would know firsthand the torment that came along with it.

But as he stood amid the storm, the enduring cries of those around him crept up once more, and soon the king was reminded of the task at hand. He realized at once that Beowyn was shouting at him, pointing to the lines which were beginning to break.

Though they carried with them the greater numbers upon the field, Ludica's armies became like a weakened snake, stretched the brink. The enemy was unrelenting in their attack against Faermire's defending stance, but the more they withstood them, the harder their enemy aimed to cut off their head where they remained.

"Find Aethelwyn and gather his men to defend our flank!" Ludica shouted, pointing toward an opening that had begun to emerge from within the line. It would only be a matter of time before they were surrounded, and by then, all would be lost.

His son quickly acknowledged the command and disappeared once more into the sea of warriors, dueling to the death. And at long last, those who could relay his orders appeared from within the chaos, offering news of their status upon the field. To his relief, several enclaves had begun to form despite their enemy's efforts, and the testament to Faermire's veterans of war, stood out from among those who were crushed beneath the opposition's heel. They were caught in a moment of blind weakness, of that there was no doubt, but hope still remained for the king, even against the odds which had been stacked against him.

And as he returned to the fight once more, Ludica had nearly forgotten the one whom he had vowed to kill at its very inception. Sidonis was nowhere to be found within the sea of Ceolfrid's army and it enraged the king to his core. For what sort of man was this, who could dare beguile his way into a scheme so grand yet refuse to show his face when it mattered most. Such a coward could not share the same blood as he, for then it would mean that he too was capable of such vile depravity. But if that was indeed his brother's resolve, then the opportunity to kill the bastard, would be left to cherish until another time.

So, he carried on, pressing hard against the lines that sought to drive them back. And as he delivered further orders to his men, his hope grew still as the battle waged on.

Yet there in the distance, a figure caught his eye. A silhouette emerged deep within the tangled mass of iron and blood, and in the corner of his sight, there appeared the very man whom he had vowed to slay upon the field that day.

Sidonis stood out amongst the scene as though the battle was simply unaware of his existence. He remained still, standing unabated by the rising havoc around him. And his sword rested loosely within the passive grip of his hand. But his brother's eyes peered deeply into the king, as though he had been entranced by something unnatural. All that remained in the darkness of Sidonis' eyes was the unquenchable desire to gut him where he stood.

And there, across the field, was a man no more. But simply a pawn, consumed by the cause which had driven him mad. It was his brother no longer, and that would suffice him reason enough to thrust his blade even deeper into his heart.

"Sidonis!" He cried with all his might. And all that he could see was the gentle glint of smile emerge upon his brother's face.

Beowyn fought and shoved his way through the masses, searching desperately for the man whom his father had demanded. He knew that Aethelwyn had to have been nearby, as the elder along with sons and clansmen rode only a short distance behind them moments ago. And just as he had eagerly hoped, Qereth appeared beyond the way, fighting alongside his own father.

He called out to the men as he made his agonizing journey across the field. All around him, weapons clashed, and men wrestled to no end until their final breath was drawn. And the earth upon which their bodies lay carried layers of mud which had been soaked with their blood. Both the flesh of men and the fragments of their armor littered the fields upon which they stood.

And the faster he raced toward his friend, the more he stumbled and tripped over the dead and wounded. Though he carried on, trudging through the masses, and wielding his sword against those who charged him.

The armies of Abensloh were unlike any he had seen before. For their soldiers had covered themselves in steel from head to toe. And the metal they wore was black as coal, hiding their eyes beneath the jagged contours of their helmets.

They were to him, like spirits of the dead, fighting as though they were men. But beyond what was hidden beneath the fog, the men of Faermire, faced the grueling constraint of fighting a force which held no face. For while his people fought as though this was their moment of glory, they still bore that same trepidation which he carried within himself. To face such an enemy whose eyes they could not see, brought forth a certain unrest within his soul that he struggled to understand it.

Most of those who fought for Faermire, were clad in little more than layers of leather and parcels of chainmail throughout. Few of them actually bore helmets upon their heads, and those who did brandished the ferocity in their eyes for all to see. Even his father, the king, chose to forgo the completion of his armor, by abandoning his own helmet long ago and Beowyn did just the same.

But the more he searched the fields around him, the more he could see the blackened steel of his enemies begin to blot out their existence upon the earth. And before long, he could feel the overwhelming sense that the world had begun to close in around him.

His racing breaths quickened all the more, and his chest became tight within his armor. He reached for the cold links of steel which clung to his body and tugged stiffly at his collar, hoping to gain more air to breathe. But as he nearly dropped his guard, that same menacing shadow of steel approached him from within the battle, and raised its sword high into the air, hoping to strike him down.

He pulled himself back and leapt from its path just in time to wield his sword in return. Suddenly, his blade had lost its weight, and his tightened grip drew it back, before at last, he swung it at the spirit with all that he possessed. But within an instant, the spirit's helmet was thrown to the ground and a man's head appeared from beneath it. The man's eyes were wide with terror, and his mouth hung open as blood began to trickle from his lips.

Beowyn stared for a moment at the head which lay opposite its owner's body and at long last, the prince was reminded that his enemy could die just the same as he. So, with a renewed sense of confidence, he turned from that place and looked once more toward the targets of his father's command.

The journey felt as though it had taken years for him to make, but at last, he called out to his friend, and Qereth turned with an elated smile upon his face. The two friends approached one another, and Beowyn relayed to his friend, the task at hand, ordering the men to gather.

The prince directed Qereth toward a point within their lines, displaying the weakness which had been left exposed. Qereth nodded with affirmation and relayed the information to his father and those around him.

The group soon rallied, and Beowyn joined them amongst their ranks. They shouted to one another, forming a cohesive band within the battle and soon forged a path together further down the line.

Inch by inch, they crept along until they had finally reached their destination. The patch within the dike was small, but it held strong against the forces which pressed heavily against it. And as their hopes began to rise, they could feel a distinct rumble against the ground from amongst the havoc. A rumble which felt different than all the rest.

Beowyn looked to see if any had noticed the same, and Qereth met his gaze with apprehension.

But before either could utter a single word, scorching flames erupted from behind the misty veil and the men before them were engulfed within a fiery blaze. Screams of terror filled the air around them, and the smell of burning flesh crept up, penetrating the draft which swept through the field.

Several more bursts of fire emerged from within the fog as they searched desperately for its source. But the panic in Aethelwyn's voice carried through, as he called for them all to fall back.

"Dragon!" he shouted as he pulled at the men around him. "It's the dragon!"

And just as he shouted the words, the creature appeared from within the haze and its jaw shuttered beneath its crushing bellow. Its short legs crawled swiftly over the earth, driving the beast forward like a slithering snake. And though it carried wings upon its back, the old wounds it bore, made them useless to fly. Like tattered sheets that hung from its frame, the skin of its wings began to shrivel against the wind.

But its wounds were of no consequence to the dragon, as it tugged fiercely against the chains which had been wrapped around its neck. It appeared to be the creature's own leash. And beyond the chains, there stood its master, the giant that they all called Nurrock.

Beowyn's eyes drifted up further into the sky until finally he could see Nurrock's full stature against those who battled upon the land, standing at the height of two men together. Strength abounded throughout the giant's frame, and not an ounce of fat could be found. The creature bore his chest openly to the world around him, donning only his trousers and the chains with which he used to control his equally enormous pet.

Nurrock carried with him the taste for blood as he shouted with eager delight. His dark eyes peered over the crowds who looked upon them with horror, and many had already begun their retreat.

The prince had only ever heard tales of giants in the world of Aecorath, but those who lived existed within the farthest reaches of the northern Skelleg lands. And within a single moment, Beowyn was faced with both a dragon and giant all at once.

His mouth dropped with awe, and his knees weakened by their very presence. He cursed aloud and looked to the men who remained beside him. But whether it was that they were frozen in fear, or driven to a fool's resolve, only a handful of them stood in their path and Qereth remained amongst them.

And as the prince struggled to make his move, another burst of flames spewed over the earth before him, carving a path to where he and the others remained. He turned and threw himself down into the mud, covering his head in a desperate attempt to shield himself from the blaze. But the scorching heat pressed deeply over his body, turning his armor hot against his flesh. He screamed. And he bore himself further into the mud, as far as he could possibly go, but still, the infernal torment would not relent.

The flames poured out of the dragon's mouth in an endless stream until finally, it stopped to catch its own breath. Beowyn at last, had come to realize that he still lived, even as his arm continued to feel the searing pain, rise up into his flesh. The pain, so agonizing he opened his eyes to find that his arm had been caught within the blaze. The flames engulfed the whole of his arm, as the burning remains of his clothing and armor clung to his flesh, melting within it to become as one.

His screams continued, and he frantically swatted at his arm, hoping to douse the fire which raged before him. And just as he nearly lost sight of the world around him, Qereth threw him down into the mud once more, as yet another wave of endless calamity spewed forth from the dragon's mouth. But as it passed them over, the two leapt to their feet, and ran for their lives.

The agonizing screams endured around them, and the two men continued to run, until at last the prince caught sight of a small formation of rocks just beyond the way. He quickly pulled his friend behind the barrier, and they hid themselves, clinging to what little remained of the air they breathed. But Qereth was the first to return his gaze upon the field and his screams joined along with those whose misery would find no end. He called out to his father and to his brother, for they had been lost beneath the flames. And he dropped down once more, burying his face into his hands as he sobbed aloud.

But as they remained, the giant and his beast continued their rampage upon the earth, and countless lives were being lost. Once more, the flames drew fiercely overhead, and the men cowered beneath what little protection the rocks had offered them. As it passed, they looked once more toward the giant and his beast, as their rampage endured.

"We have to run; it isn't safe here!" Beowyn shouted.

"It isn't safe anywhere! Look!" Qereth replied, pointing at the monstrous adversaries before them. "How are we to defeat them?! All who stand in their path are wiped from the earth! They're gone! All of them!"

Burning bodies littered the earth around them like torches amid the darkened skies, and death was encroaching upon them with an insatiable hunger.

It was clear that his friend was reeling from the deaths of his family and clansmen, but time was running out. For if they chose to wait any longer, then they too would be lost amongst the dead, and all would certainly be lost.

Beowyn looked upon the creatures once more and struggled to steady his racing thoughts. But at last, he stumbled upon a glimmer of hope, however impossible it might have been. He looked to Nurrock, who wrestled against the might of his beast. The chains curled tightly around the length of his arm, and he was at best, held to the mercy of where his dragon lurched.

"The giant," Beowyn uttered. "We must take down the giant!"

Qereth looked at him in disbelief. "You're mad! Beowyn we don't stand a chance—"

"We can if we strike him from behind. Qereth, we must do something! And I cannot do this alone. Please, my friend, I need your help!"

He could see his friend's eyes glance to the place where his father and brother's charred remains lay, then back toward creatures before them. He shook his head, mumbling words to himself and cursed, but looked to the prince once more as he finally relented.

"Alright," his friend replied. "Let's get this over with then."

Beowyn nodded and quickly relayed his plan to Qereth whom, to his surprise, did nothing to argue against his plans. He had hoped at least that his friend would provide some other means by which they could execute the attack, but the man remained silent, keeping his eyes focused instead, on the scene before him. And as they prepared to make their charge, the sound of horns rang out into the air. The deep drone of the ram's horns echoed throughout the land, and they all turned to find its source.

Beowyn sighed sharply with relief at the sight before him, and he turned toward his friend, with a smile upon his face. Numerous flags emerged within the distance, bearing the color green against the landscape, and hundreds of soldiers marched toward the battlefield, bringing with them the hope which they so desperately sought.

"Thank the gods," he uttered aloud before raising himself up again and his confidence restored once more. "It's Mistelfeld!" He cried aloud.

# CHAPTER 19

LUDICA WEAVED THROUGH THE FRENZY of fighting men before him, drawing himself closer toward his brother. Sidonis, likewise forced himself past those who fought for their lives. Both the king and his brother remained fixed upon one another, removing their gaze only as they encountered brief threats to their lives, though striking them down with ease.

The field was large where they stood, but the world around them drew close, tightening its grip upon them, so that only the two remained. But as they narrowed the gap, Ludica thrust his sword high into the air, bearing it down upon the blade which his brother used to block the blow. And one strike after the next, the two men exchanged their fury upon one another with no end.

But as Nurrock and his dragon made their entrance upon the field, spewing fire over all that stood in their path, Ludica paused, carrying a sudden upon terror within his gaze. Men were ignited into flames, and the screams of terror called out from amongst the dying.

He thought surely, they would have remained with Ceolfrid at the Dolam pass, but he cursed aloud, for as they scoured the land for whom they could devour, he realized how wrong he truly was.

Most of Gwenora's army would remain at Helmfirth upon his guidance, but in doing so, his own men were left exposed to Nurrock's unquenchable wrath. His plans had fallen short, and all at once, his men would pay the ultimate price for his failure.

Sidonis, however, smiled with delight and steadied himself to catch his breath.

"Tis a beautiful sight, is it not, Brother?"

The dragon still carried the scars which Ludica had left upon its back those many years ago, but its injuries did little to restrain the beast upon the field. Wave after wave, the dragon spit forth its fire and the giant swung his hammer upon the poor fools who remained within his reach.

As he watched, dozens had fallen within the blink of an eye, and there was nothing that the king could do to stop it. His army had been caught in such disarray, so that his orders could not be heard. And those who were still capable of holding the line, began to falter at the sight of Nurrock and his beast.

Ludica was helpless to stop the misery, and all that remained was the very face of the man who ushered them in. allip tightened further around his sword, and he lunged forward once more, driving his blade ahead with all of his might. His hands trembled with rage and his chest tightened within the confines of his armor, but he pressed on, striking again and again.

Sidonis did well to defend himself against his brother's fury but let slip a morsel of confidence in his guard. Ludica then forced him back and struck him with the hilt of his weapon as he fell into the mud. But before he could strike again, his brother lifted his sword to block another strike, giving him time enough to pick himself up again.

Blood began to trickle from the wound upon his head, and he struggled to wipe it from his eye.

"Look now upon the great king of Faermire," Sidonis muttered aloud as he gestured toward the chaos around them. "So many lives lost, Ludica. And there will only be more to come."

"Then let us be sure, Brother, that you find your place among them," Ludica replied, thrusting his blade forward once again. But as they carried on, they suddenly heard the call.

The sound of horns bellowed throughout the air, and they paused briefly to find its source. As the king caught sight of Mistelfeld's army, he smiled at last, for it was a welcome sight indeed.

And as Mistelfeld joined in amongst the fight, Ludica took solace in their presence upon the field.

He watched from a distance, as the calls were ordered, and the archers unleashed their reign of terror upon the enemy before them. Nurrock and the dragon turned to face the forces who had appeared behind them and again, the archers let loose a second barrage upon their enemy.

He could see, the confidence in Sidonis begin to waver, if ever so slightly, but the man pressed on, retaliating against the king. And before he could speak again, there came the arrival of those who were from Graefeld.

The barbaric forces raced into the heat of battle from the outskirts, driving another smile upon Sidonis' face. But as he watched them from afar, his expression quickly soured at the sight of his supposed ally, Helgisson, leading the charge against his own men and the creatures alike. The barbarians, though small in number, fought with such fury, against those in their wake. Perhaps, because it was that they had nothing left to lose, or that it was simply just their way, but they carried on, like crazed animals, searching for whom they could devour.

But the savages had betrayed the man, wielding their weapons instead, against the forces of Abensloh, and entrapped them all where they stood. His army was all at once surrounded upon the field, and what assurance he held in his plans began to crumble all around him. Soon, his army began to face the cold steel of slaughter amongst their ranks, and the grip of Faermire and its allies began to crush them in time.

"Tis a beautiful sight indeed, brother!" Ludica quipped. "Now you can watch as your own forces abandon you."

Sidonis scanned the field around him, taking notice of the truth in his brother's words and he cursed aloud, unleashing his wrath on any victim he could find within his reach. He drove his blade deep into the back of an unsuspecting man who fought another by the way and kicked his blade free from the depths of flesh which clung to its spine.

And as all hope was lost for the coward, he ran from his brother's presence, seeking out a horse upon which he could ride. Ludica, also, followed closely behind Sidonis, taking charge of another horse nearby and began his chase for the one he once called brother. They rode on, abandoning the battlefield and drove themselves deeper into the misty haze, until all that remained was the beating hooves of their horses upon the ground.

Beowyn and Qereth, both watched as Nurrock attempted to shield himself from the barrage of arrows which rained down from the sky. Meanwhile, his pet began to waver in its place, crying out in pain with each wave that poured over them. Soon, another horn blast echoed through the air, and the men of Mistelfeld commenced their charge.

Their cries rang out, bringing a chill to the prince's spine and he rallied himself with confidence once more.

"Now's our chance!" he shouted. Qereth too, was quick to join in the call to arms, and they both raced into the heat of battle once more. They soon took their place amongst the hordes which began to surround the giant and his dragon, and though many perished by their menacing reach, the waves continued to overwhelm them.

Nurrock struggled to swing his hammer against the masses as his pet whipped its tail and lurched against his reach. Fire continued to spew from its mouth, but as it shrieked in pain from the constant surge of attacks, its inferno breath was cut short, and it soon began to recoil itself against the multitude.

And for once, Beowyn could see that the giant who towered over his enemies, began to falter against their unified droves. Both the prince and his friend eventually managed to push their way through to the front, though quickly dodged another curve of the dragon's tail. They took cover just as its tail swept through the masses, hurling men into the air as though they were nothing.

But at last, the prince had seized his opportunity, and found his opening between the creatures as they remained distracted.

"Beowyn!" Qereth called out to him as he took his chance, weaving through the chaos and thrust his blade deep into Nurrock's thigh, clinging to the hilt which rested against his flesh. The giant cried aloud with a deafening tone as he looked down to meet the prince's petrified gaze. Nurrock released his grip from the dragon's chain and reached for Beowyn down below.

But just as he was certain that his life would meet its end, Qereth appeared beside him, driving his sword deep into the giant's leg as well. Again, the creature cried aloud, but his friend gripped him by the arm and pulled him away as Nurrock buckled beneath the pain and dropped to his knee.

The crowds at once pressed further in their advance but the dragon's roar made them cower from its piercing outcry. And just as it nearly made its escape, the giant grappled the trailing chain which scurried along the ground, forcing himself up again. He then heaved himself onto the creature's back and directed the beast away from the battle.

He violently swung his weapon from his perch and the dragon used what little remained of its stamina to blast a fiery path back toward their safety. But those that stood in their wake succumbed to the blaze of their escape and many had perished just as they nearly claimed their victory.

Beowyn looked for Qereth, only to find the man lost in his frenzy as he chased after the creatures along with many others. For this would be his chance to exact his revenge on them for having taken the lives of both his father and his brother that day. But as Beowyn watched them make their pursuit, they quickly lost their ground to the dragon's speed and were left standing in their trail.

The men around the prince soon began to cheer and raise their weapons high into the air, as many others drove the remaining soldiers of Abensloh further into the ground. And what little remained of their forces, quickly abandoned their place as they watched Nurrock sitting at a distance atop the ridge. For the giant knew that all had been lost, and he would not stand to witness their defeat any longer.

Whatever plans his uncle held for their demise was finally crushed, and the prince could see at last that the battle had been won. And had it not been for those who sought an alliance with his father, all would surely have been lost. But as it stood, Abensloh's defeat upon the field that day meant that his uncle had failed to secure his place as Ceolfrid's ally, and Faermire now stood stronger than ever before.

Overwhelmed by the sight before him, the prince soon joined in on the cries of victory and quickly searched his surroundings, hoping to find his father amongst those who celebrated their triumph. But as he surveyed the landscape, the king was nowhere to be found. And neither was his uncle for that matter.

Troubled by their absence, Beowyn could suddenly feel a rising pit within his stomach, and he began to scour the field in desperation.

"Where is the king?!" he shouted to those around him. And the longer he searched, the more distressed he became, as he grabbed at the bystanders, demanding that his father be found. But as time carried on, no one could account for the king's whereabouts until at last a soldier called out to the prince.

"He is not here, my Lord."

"What do you mean he isn't here? Where is he?!"

"His brother abandoned the fight, and the king made chase upon horseback. I seen them ride off that way, toward the ruins of Ballinon." The man pointed in the distance, opposite of where he stood. And though the fog still remained, it had begun to loosen its grip upon them as he could barely make out the landmark in the distance.

"How long ago was this?!"

"I cannot say, my Lord."

Beowyn then cursed aloud as he demanded a horse and rushed toward the place where he hoped his father would be.

Ludica brought his horse to a skidding halt as he approached the ruins. What remained of the ancient castle stretched high into mist, and the former shell of its glory stood as his brother's last stand. He could make out the tracks which Sidonis had left in the mud, and he cautiously followed them up into the remnants, carefully drawing his sword as he ascended the derelict steps.

The wind groaned against the aging stone, and the bitterness of the saturated air clung to his face as he narrowed his eyes against the cold. He held his sword tightly within his hands, searching in every corner and shadow that he could find, just waiting for his brother to jump out at him. But still, there remained only the misty fog as his companion, and he continued his trek further into the ruins.

Then he stopped. A faint sound caught his ear and he turned to find its source. Just further down the way, he heard the faint tapping of tiny stones dislodged from their place and fall toward the depths. So small they must have been, but they echoed loudly against the weathered stone to announce their final act. And at last, the king would root out the coward who hid.

He carefully placed his feet over the passageway which precariously stretched to the other side, and he took his initial steps. Then, one by one, he navigated his feet across the corridor which stood exposed to the elements.

And again, he heard the sound of tumbling gravel in the distance.

"Sidonis!" he shouted, as he grew tired of the chase. But there was no reply, much as he expected, and he carried on across the way. As he made it to the end, he rounded the corner and there emerged the menacing cry of his brother, as the man leapt from his hiding place and swung his blade down over the king. He blocked the strike in an instant, and threw himself against the wall, as he nearly lost his footing.

He looked to his brother who had unraveled at the seams and carried with him a certain madness which Ludica had never seen. And again, Sidonis flung his sword at him in a boiling rage which made his attacks turn sloppy.

The two men dueled once again atop the wreckage as they likewise struggled to keep themselves from falling to their death.

And as Sidonis slipped, Ludica swung his sword, striking the pillar which shielded his brother's life. The man backed swiftly away from the king and cowered further into the depths of the rubble as he disappeared once more behind the fog.

"Enough of this, Sidonis!" he cried. "Let us end this here and now. That is what you want isn't it?"

He scanned the misty veil and carefully followed his brother's trail.

"I want it more than anything, Brother." The man's voice echoed against the walls. "But you simply will not die," he continued.

"So, you choose instead, to play the cowards game... why am I not surprised?"

"I am no coward!" Sidonis cried aloud as he leapt from the shadows once more and engaged the king yet again. "It is you who are the coward, Ludica! You played the fool whilst men have been robbing you for years."

"You, being chief amongst them?!" Ludica replied as he returned a heavy strike.

"Hardly! This isn't first time men have sought to usurp your crown and it certainly won't be last. You are just too foolish to see that I was the one who spared you from their childish schemes. I was the one who protected our family from those who sought to overthrow us, and I was the one who shielded you from their wiles!"

"You cannot possibly believe the words which are coming out of your mouth, Brother! Truly, you have gone mad!"

"If I am mad, then it is because you have driven me so. We are more alike than you think, Brother. The only difference between us is that I am actually worthy of that crown upon your head. But mark my words, I shall cut it down this very day, whether I take the throne or not!"

Sidonis lifted his weapon high into the air once more, clashing it against Ludica's blade. But as the king braced himself against the impact, the ground beneath him began to shift. He stumbled and slipped against the loosened stone but caught himself from falling over the ledge.

As he pulled himself up, however, he could feel the cold steel of his brother's blade being driven deep into his chest. He froze in his place and looked down to see the widened edge of a sword wedged between the penetrated plates of his armor. He reached up to grab it, But Sidonis drove it further.

Ludica gasped. The wind was thrust from his lungs and his limbs grew numb, but he glanced up once more and stared deeply into his brother's eyes. The man's face had curled with rage and the king could no longer feel the grip of his hand upon his own sword any longer. His weapon then clanged and rattled as it landed upon the ground until all had finally gone quiet.

In such a brief moment, the king had let his guard down and fell victim to his brother's cowardice. But as he looked deeper into Sidonis' eyes, he knew that he would not let it stand to be his failure. So, he thrust himself farther along the man's sword until his brother was finally within his own reach. Sidonis' carried a sudden shock upon his countenance at the king's act and he stiffened his posture as Ludica approached.

But the king pushed himself again, and again, gasping with each pressing drive until his brother stood helpless and exposed against the ledge. Sidonis quickly began to panic at the realization of his predicament and reached for Ludica's shoulders, only to have the king commit himself further to his own resolve.

"Wait! Wait! Stop!" Sidonis scrambled against his brother's drive but remained helpless as he grabbed for anything he could find within his reach. But to his despair, his hands could find only the blade of which he had driven into Ludica's chest. And with one final push, Sidonis was thrust into the deep abyss of the misty haze just as he grabbed the hilt of his sword, ripping it free of the king's chest.

Ludica wheezed and his body was heaved forward as it was pulled from his flesh. The blood which had been trapped within its seal had also been set free, and it flowed like a stream from within his chest. But Sidonis' screams writhed in the air around him as he plunged to the earth below. Until finally, he could hear Sidonis no more, and the king rested himself heavily against a pillar nearby.

He struggled to catch his breath and he watched as his own blood began to ooze from his body as it pooled around his feet. But at last, he could no longer support his own weight and he slumped down against the stone as he lifted his head up toward the sky.

The world around him had begun to fade into darkness, but the king waited just a moment longer. He paused and listened against the silence as he took as deep a breath of the cold wintry air as he possibly could. For this would be the last, as he thought to himself. And as much as he so hated the cold, he suddenly found that it oddly brought him comfort in that moment. For in all his days, the cold was the only constant for the king. It was there at the very beginning of his life, and it was there now, waiting to embrace him in the afterlife. But even now, as he was ready to die, his thoughts began to wander and he could suddenly see the face of his beloved wife, Emelyn as she approached him from within the mist.

He smiled and lifted his hand so that he could finally touch her face. She was just as he remembered, and the years had lost their hold on her as her face had never aged. Her auburn hair fell loosely over her shoulders and the gentleness in her eyes greeted him along with that same smile which he had longed for all these years. Emelyn lowered herself to her knees and embraced the king, as he rested his head against her chest.

And for once, he was at peace.

"I'm so tired..." he uttered as she tenderly stroked his hair. He could hear the subtle beat of her heart against his ear and could feel the warmth of her body against his own. She was real. He couldn't understand it, but it didn't matter in the end. As long as she was there, he could see her one last time.

And as he looked up at her once more, she whispered his name aloud.

"Ludica..." And again, he could hear his name, but it came from someplace else. He looked to the side to see where it was coming from and then to another, hearing his name called over and over again. But as he turned toward his beloved once more, he found that she was gone.

And there, in his wife's place, sat his son. Beowyn cried, as he gently tapped the side of his face to keep him awake. The prince continued to call out for his father to remain, but as he slowly regained his consciousness, so too did the reality of his immanent death.

"Father! Father, stay with me please. I-I'll send for help. I just—"

His son was desperate, but Ludica was resolute in the knowledge of what would come to pass. For there, his wife awaited him, and he found comfort in the knowledge that he would not have to pass into the afterlife alone.

"Beowyn... stop..." But the prince continued to search his surroundings, as if by some means, he could find a way to get the help he needed for his father. But as nothing appeared for him, he quickly removed his gloves and firmly placed his hand beneath the king's armor, in a futile attempt to slow the bleeding. "Beowyn, please..." He gasped for his breath. "For once in your life, just listen to me."

At last, it took the boy for his father to be standing at death's door before he finally settled himself to heed the man's words. But the king continued. And it took everything within him to carry out the last of his commands, but his stubborn nature wouldn't allow him to pass before it was done.

"Gather what remains of our army and have the elders take account of all that remains... Send a party out to find any forces which remain." He gasped again, struggling to keep his head from falling forward and his son interjected once more.

"Father, please. Do not speak. . ." But Ludica ignored Beowyn's pleas as he continued. "Send word to Mistelfeld and grant them aid should they need it. And when you return to Elsterheim, Sgell will provide the means for you to take charge of the kingdom. He will guide you well—"

"I can't. . ." his son replied as his voiced cracked beneath his sorrow. "I cannot do this without you, Father. I— I am not worthy. . . I'm so sorry. . ."

Ludica watched as his son turned his face away in shame, but the king lifted his hand, draping it over Beowyn's arm.

"I am proud of the man you've become." His son could no longer contain his tears as they began to stream down his face, and he sat in silence as he looked toward his father once again. "Pursue honor. And defend those whom you love. . . Look after your sister. . . and your brother. . ."

His son nodded his head to acknowledge the king's words as he pulled him closer into his arms.

"I will," Beowyn replied. "I swear it."

Ludica smiled and turned to find his wife standing beside them both as she lowered herself to meet his gaze. She looked to her son also with a smile upon her face as Beowyn remained unaware of her presence. But Ludica found consolation in the knowledge that his time had finally come. And as he kept his eyes upon his beloved, the king breathed his last and final breath.

# CHAPTER 20

## ELSTERHEIM, KINGDOM OF FAERMIRE

ESTRITH LEAPT AT THE SOUND of the bells tolling in the distance.

"They're back!" she said as she stood by Siged's bed. The boy remained unaware of his surroundings, but she smiled down at him still, presenting her elated relief. "Siged, they're back!"

She promptly adjusted his covers over his chest and ran from the room as she hoped to watch their arrival. The days tarried far longer than they should have while they were gone, and she felt every minute of their absence. Just as she worried for Beowyn and Qereth when they left to find the seer, she worried more so than ever as they—along with her father— had gone off to battle.

She couldn't garner the appetite to eat, and what little she slept during that time, was fraught with endless nightmares of their demise. Aside from Siged, the three of them formed the crux of her world, and without them, her hope for the future dwindled.

For Beowyn, though boorish at times, always managed to bring her peace when he entered the room. And though the man still behaved as a child in her eyes, never caring for the affairs of anything other than himself, she still saw the good within him. Despite his many flaws, her brother cared deeply for those whom he loved. So much so, that he was willing to give his own life on their account without hesitation. And he had proven as much to her in those recent days.

As for Qereth, she smiled simply as she thought of him in that moment. The man's character had never changed since they played together when they were children. The only difference now was that he had grown taller and perhaps even more handsome. But the one thing which Estrith could always rely upon was the purity of his heart. For though he tried to mask it with his brutish exterior, Qereth was the most genuine of all whom she had known. And she was thankful for that. He was the truest of friends throughout her years and now, perhaps, maybe more than that.

But as she thought next to her father, she was reminded of the protection which he had always offered her. He was cold at times, and struggled to display his emotions when occasion called, but he always remained her fortress. And despite his calloused exterior, he shielded her from the world which seemed so ready to devour her. He showed her his love in the best way he knew how, and that was enough for her. But regardless of her father's rough facade, she would embrace him wholly upon his return and she would cherish every minute of it.

Though as she thought more upon her father, she couldn't help but feel a certain sadness fall over her. But she fought to brush it aside as she made her way through the palace and into the tower, hoping to find a better vantage. And if she could've had it her way, then the princess would have been the first to greet them in the fields where they marched. But for now, she was forced to wait, and lifted her hand into the air as she eagerly waved toward them.

As she remained atop the tower, she watched as her father's forces approached the city, growing in numbers from within the horizon. It was a sign for her, which meant that they were indeed victorious. But how could she have doubted such a thing? For none could stand against the might of her people and the sword of her father to lead them. It was foolish of her to worry as she did while they were gone, and she could see that now as they drew near. But the closer they came, the less she could wait for them any longer as she left her place from atop the tower, making her way down toward the city.

Sgell greeted her within the court, and she couldn't help but share her enthusiasm with the man who still managed to carry his placid disposition. And much to her delight, he had the forethought of preparing the horses for them to ride toward the gates. The distance was short, but he clearly understood her desire to make haste to greet the men as they arrived.

Out within the streets, the people had begun to gather with a sense of delight as the bells continued to toll, announcing the arrival of their army. But as they caught sight of the princess with Sgell and her guards in tow, they bowed in reverence to her, and she smiled down at them. Young children looked up to her with eagerness in their eyes and she couldn't help but share their sentiment.

And all once, there seemed to be a renewed sense of life within the air that she breathed and the world around her seemed just a little bit brighter in that moment. And the further her horse had carried her, the more she grew with anticipation.

The men who stood watch upon the walls of the gates quickly turned to face the princess as she approached, and they each bowed as she ascended the steps to catch a closer glimpse of the army.

Sgell, however, remained down below to send a rider on to greet their ranks, and to bring back their orders from the king.

She watched from up high as the man rode on toward the soldiers and wished more than anything in that moment that she could ride in his place. But the time of their arrival drew near, and she could soon make sense of the figures who marched within their ranks, first catching a glimpse of her brother, who rode at the front. She smiled in her elation and quickly searched the line to find her father and perhaps even, Qereth as well.

Much to her delight, Qereth appeared near her brother, as his horse followed closely behind. But she continued her search for her father, scanning the rows further and further down the line.

Surely, the king would not be lost amongst his own ranks, when he should be leading them in their victory... And the more she searched, the more her heart began to plunge with dread as her father was nowhere to be found. But as she looked to Beowyn once more, she finally took notice of the despondence which shrouded his face. And to Qereth next, she found the same.

She focused her gaze and eventually caught sight of the wagon which followed closely behind them. The priests had surrounded the cart, and all the elders of Faermire, were next in the line of the army's succession. All of them bearing a somber demeanor.

And as the rider approached the gates once more with word from within her father's army, she couldn't help but sense that thew news would bring her to despair.

She slowly turned and made her way down the steps to find Sgell speaking alone with the man who had just arrived. His head dropped. And for the first time, Estrith could see sadness within his eyes. He ushered the man along, then approached the princess as he placed his hands gently upon her shoulders.

The man could hardly look her in the eye as his struggled to collect his words, but she feared that she already knew what it was that he was going to say. She begged and pleaded in her mind that he wouldn't say them aloud, for then it would be true. For then, she would know that the man she wanted to embrace so tightly within her arms, would be dead.

"Sgell... please... " Her voice trembled beneath her sorrow and the man who stood beside her equally shared in her pain.

"I am sorry, my Lady, but the King— your father... is dead."

The words cut so deeply within her heart that she could no longer contain the tears which flowed freely from her eyes, and she crumbled to the ground.

"No... " she uttered, burying her face within her hands, as Sgell lowered himself to embrace her. "No, please, no... "

She recalled at that moment, her father's words to her that day. The day of their departure. In the chaos which surrounded them, she looked up to the man who gently held her arms within his hands and wished more than ever that he would remain. The one who was her fortress, was leaving her and she would again be left alone.

But as he stared down at her, the king smiled. And at last, it was meant for her alone. His hard exterior had been cast aside at that moment and he looked into her eyes with a love which she had never known. For it was pure, and it was honest. Her father looked at her in a way which she had always longed for, and she cherished every minute of it.

"When the skies are at their darkest, I find in you, Daughter, the light which gives me hope...

"I wish I were a better father to you. And I wish... I wish you knew... how much I truly love you."

It was the first that she had ever heard him utter the words aloud and to her despair it would also be the last.

As word had quickly spread throughout the city, the tolling bells of victory ceased around them as a new wind swept through the streets, carrying with it the mournful tone of emptiness. The world had fallen silent as it grieved for their king, and as Estrith grieved for her father.

Even as Sgell embraced her upon the ground, she felt more alone than ever before. Part of her had been ripped away, never to be seen again and she was lost. Her fortress was gone, and the world became like a barren wasteland all around her. And so, she continued to cry and mourn the loss of her father, for there was nothing else that she could think to do.

Eventually, the army had reached the city and Beowyn, approached the gates. He, along with the others in his party, did little to hide the forlorn expression upon their faces and Estrith rose to his meet his open embrace. She clung to him and buried her face deeply against his chest as he wrapped his arms tightly around her body.

"I'm sorry..." he whispered in her ear. "I'm so sorry..." He confessed the words to her as if he alone was responsible for their father's fate and it grieved her to the core. Qereth soon arrived at her side also, bearing a similar anguish within his eyes. She looked to the man and reached out her arm to him as she took him also within her grasp.

But eventually, the wagon which carried her father's body drew near, and she quickly cast her gaze aside, for she couldn't bear to look upon him. But as much as she couldn't stand the knowledge of what had come to pass, she needed to see it for herself. And she needed to know that her father was truly gone. So, she turned her eyes just enough to see him as they passed while still hiding herself beneath the comfort of Qereth's embrace. Meanwhile, Beowyn had left her side once more to join the procession as he led their father back toward the palace.

The priests had done as well as they could to adorn their king given the circumstances. And as pale as her father had become, he still bore the very same features which she knew and loved so deeply. But as she looked further upon him, the reality of his demise had begun to set in once again and her knees grew weak. For though it was her father laying still upon the wooden bed, all that remained was an empty shell of the man she once knew. His lips had turned blue against the cold, and she wished so desperately that she could warm his frigid body. But there was no blanket nor tender embrace which could bring her father back to life again. And she reached out to him as the cart slowly passed her by.

Beowyn rested against the wall within the shadows of the court as he stared at the throne which sat before him. Night had fallen over Elsterheim, and as the priests prepared for the funeral to come, he hid himself away, eventually finding himself in the very place where his father had spent so many countless days. He had been there for hours, and the court had long since been emptied. But there he remained, and even as the prospect of his kingship neared, he couldn't bring himself to even sit upon the throne on which his father sat.

But soon the doors groaned open, and the future king had been found. Behind them, appeared his father's personal aid, and the man remained quiet as he approached him within the shadows. Sgell fought hard to maintain his stoic disposition, but Beowyn could see that his shoulders drooped ever so slightly against the torches' light. The man's presence had always seemed to make the prince uneasy before. For he knew that the man always brought word from his father, and it was never to his benefit. But now, as Sgell stood before him, he felt at ease, as though a sudden weight had been lifted from his shoulders.

The man glanced at the throne briefly, before redirecting his gaze upon Beowyn before he finally bowed himself toward him. And with the vast emptiness of the court before them, Sgell's voice echoed throughout the hall.

"There is a place upon which you may sit, my Lord..."

Beowyn nodded in agreement but instead, leaned his head against the comfort of the wall behind him.

"It looms before me now, more so than it ever has before," the prince replied as he gestured toward the throne.

"Many would gladly take their place upon that chair. And many have tried."

"Yes, well I would've been among them not long ago. But even in my father's absence, I feel the weight of his charge over me. And I fear that I will never be able to escape it..."

Sgell nodded his head as he offered a faint grin of amusement.

The two remained in silence for a time, and it was clear that there was a purpose to the man's visit. But as he turned to face the throne, he finally offered the prince his words to break the stillness.

"Your father was a good man, my Lord. As are you... But even a good man can fall prey to the wolves which surround him."

Beowyn looked to find that Sgell had pulled a note from within the sleeve of his cloak and offered it to him from where he stood. In that moment, the prince couldn't help but feel once more the dread which had so often come with the arrival of the Sgell's presence. And he was reminded again of the reality which stood before him.

He then rose from his place of hiding and took the note from within the man's hand to read it.

"Your servant is not as discreet as he would like you to believe, my Lord."

Beowyn looked to the man with confusion in his eyes before finally lifting the parchment up to read it. And written upon the lines was a note from Tanica, requesting at once, to finally meet the prince upon the Coventhon Ridge which lay between the borders of Faermire and Valenmur.

"Your father's death will be welcome news for Elwin and his sons," Sgell interjected. But Beowyn remained silent, for he knew that there was truth to the man's words. And so, his aid continued.

"The young woman's love for you may be true, and her intent may be pure of heart. But I caution you, as a king, to be wary of whom you choose to align yourself with, my Lord. Elwin has betrayed your father once before and I am certain that he would gladly do so again."

The words he spoke drove themselves like a knife, deep into Beowyn's heart. And yet again, he could hear his father's voice ring out from among them. But this time, he did nothing to withstand the admonishment as he listened, and gently folded the paper up within his hands.

"Thank you, Sgell," he replied, and the man bowed toward the prince as he recused himself from his presence.

His journey toward the Coventhon Ridge was fraught with endless thoughts, and Beowyn struggled to think of what he would say to Tanica once he finally saw her. He wanted nothing more than to hold her in his arms once again and kiss her as she would happily return the favor. And he wanted to tell her about everything that happened so that she could tell him that it would all be alright. That in the end, it would have all been meant for good, and that time would prove to have made things right again.

But the closer his horse drew him near to his beloved, he couldn't seem to escape the overwhelming presage which lingered over him, and he nearly hesitated to finish the journey. Though, as she appeared atop the ridge, his heart began to race and before he knew it, she was already running to greet him.

His guards took it upon themselves to linger back at a distance as the prince carried on, and he hardly had time enough to lower himself from atop the saddle before Tanica had already leapt into his arms. The sweet smell of her hair against the wind drew his grip tighter around her waist and she lifted herself up to kiss him repeatedly. She smiled as tears equally rolled down her soft, porcelain cheeks and he brushed her golden locks aside, to catch a better glimpse of her soft hazel eyes. But as he looked at her once more, he couldn't help but pull her in for yet another kiss.

"Thank the gods, Beowyn! I truly thought that I would never see you again. But here you stand before me, and all has been made right once more." She could not contain the joy within as she caressed his face, making certain that he was real. But as she drew her hands down the length of his arms, she suddenly took notice of the large bandage which had been wrapped against his burns. The same wounds which would forever stand as a reminder of the day in which the world as he knew it, crumbled into pieces.

For countless lives had been lost, and the terror of what his eyes beheld would remain with him all the rest of his days. But the greatest reminder of them all stood to be the loss of his father, and the agonizing journey which brought him home again.

"Gods, what happened?" she asked with worry in her eyes.

"It's nothing," he replied as he pulled her in for another embrace. "Just let me hold you again…"

She happily obliged his request and leaned her head tenderly against his chest. But as the two remained in each other's arms, Beowyn caught sight of Tanica's brothers watching them from a distance. The men sat patiently upon their horses and each of their silhouettes hung against the horizon like the storm which lingered overhead. And as she took notice of his deepening gaze, she pulled his face away.

"Don't mind them," she uttered with a smile on her face. "They won't bother us, I promise."

But as he was once again reminded of the dread he felt, he lifted her hands, taking them each within the gentle grasp of his palms.

"Tanica, I—"

"And once spring comes to us at last, then all that we had been forced to endure will be but a distant memory. We will be married at last! Ah, just to say it aloud brings me such joy, Beowyn. The gods have truly favored us—"

"Tanica…" he struggled to say her name aloud as he could feel the rising guilt expand through the depths of chest. But she carried on, unaware of his drifting gaze, for he could no longer bear to look her in the eye.

"Word has spread quickly through Valenmur, and remarkably, Father has begun to speak favorably of our union. Never in my wildest dreams, could I have though such a thing were possible, but here we are." She snickered with amusement at the very thought of it all, but it stood only as confirmation to Beowyn, of the words his father spoke, and that of Sgell as well.

Then finally, he mustered the strength enough to stop her before she could carry on.

"I cannot marry you..." He lifted his eyes just enough to see the smile quickly fade from her blissful disposition.

"What?" She feigned a smile once more, and chuckled aloud, as though she thought that he meant it in jest.

"I'm sorry..." But as the reality of his words began to settle within her thoughts, she slowly pulled herself away.

"What— why are you saying this? What do you mean?" Panic began to fill the void which had been left by her enthusiasm and she struggled to find reason within his declaration. "I— I don't understand, Beowyn. Is this— is this because of your father? Surely—"

"My father is dead." Word had yet to spread of the king's death, but it would only be a matter of time. And it might as well have started with him.

"What?" Tanica was lost amid the shock and confusion of it all, and he grieved the state of her despondence. "Beowyn, tell me what is going on, please! Talk to me... We can make this right, but I must know what is going on."

"With all my heart, my love, I wish that I could. But things are not as they seem, you must understand." His voice cracked beneath the sorrow within his heart, and he reached his hand out toward her, but she swiftly pulled herself way.

"How am I to understand anything, Beowyn, when you will not speak to me?! Why are you doing this?!"

"Because Elwin intends to besiege Faermire's throne, and he will use our marriage to do it."

"You do not know this!"

"He has betrayed us once before—"

"And you betray me now..." The prince couldn't help but cast his eyes down at her words, for he couldn't help but feel that they were true. "You told me once that you wanted nothing to do with your fathers crown, but now that you have it, I can see that it suits you well. For you are indeed Ludica's son, and I curse you, Beowyn. With every fiber of my being, I curse you!"

Tanica buried her face into her hands as she began to sob aloud. She then lowered herself to the ground, for she could no longer bear the weight of her body against her feet. And her words gutted him as he stood helpless against her sorrow.

He fought hard to withstand his own tears as he bit his lip to draw the pain he felt so deeply. And as she sat alone on the ground, he drew himself forward, in a feeble attempt to comfort her. But as he laid his hands upon her body, she recoiled harshly against his touch and slapped him across the breadth of face.

"Do not touch me!" she shouted as she took a step back.

Suddenly he could see that her brothers had taken notice of their sister's plight and began to urge their horses forward. But still, he outstretched his arm toward her as she continued to back away.

"Leave me be, Beowyn. Please, just leave me be..."

At last, he could no longer contain his sorrow, and the tears began to well up within his eyes. Then came the call from one of his guards who swiftly approached the prince from behind.

"My lord, I fear we have overstayed our welcome." The man said as he gestured toward the sons of Valenmur. Tanica glanced back toward them as they rode in their direction, and she drew herself further away from the prince. She then wrapped her arms tightly within the comfort of her cloak and continued to stare back at him with each passing step. The wind, in its grandeur caught her golden hair, drawing it across her face, so that only her eyes remained peering back at him while she walked. She remained silent, and the sorrow was all that spoke to him in that moment as she abandoned the place where he stood.

"I'm so sorry..." he whispered against the wind and slowly turned to heed his guard's advice. His horse was then guided to where he stood, and within a moment's notice, the prince was carried away, drifting further and further from the woman whom he loved.

# CHAPTER 21

AS THE DAY OF HER FATHER'S funeral drew near, Estrith hoped to escape the stifling air within the palace and found her place atop the wall which overlooked the city as it stood against the river. It would have normally been far too cold for her to stand against the wind, but since their armies had returned with her father's body, she lost her ability to feel anything against the numbness which overwhelmed her. She had been utterly lost since the day of their return, and there was nothing by which she could find her solace.

The whole of Elsterheim had gone quiet, and the streets below seemed emptier than ever before. All had begun their process to mourn the loss of their king, and yet she struggled to find her will enough to simply rise from out of her bed in the mornings which followed.

The quiet air that surrounded her began to grow all the more deafening and she found once again that she could no longer escape the lingering the thoughts which vexed her to no end. But soon, she could hear footsteps approaching her place from the stairs below. Beowyn then appeared at her side, and he breathed a sharp stroke of the cold and bitter air, deep into his chest. He followed her gaze over the landscape before them and the two remained in silence for a time before he finally opened his mouth to speak.

"I figured you'd have been at Siged's side. But here, I find you alone with only your thoughts and the frigid winds to keep you company." He glanced down at her, as if he hoped to catch her gaze, but to no avail. "It's a dangerous game, Sister... I know because I endure the same. That is why I sought you out."

She was glad for his company, but still struggled to offer anything in response aside from her silence.

"Estrith—"

"I cannot do this, Beowyn..." she finally relented as she kept her focus upon the horizon. "Even now, they prepare to bury our father, and I cannot bring myself to stand within his presence. If I look upon his face, then I know that I shall crumble at the very sight of it." Finally, the tears began to stream from her eyes once more and she did little to fend them off any longer.

Meanwhile, her brother remained silent, casting his eyes instead upon the place of which she once stared. He was equally helpless against her anguish, but she eventually leaned herself against his shoulder, hoping to ease the weight of her suffering.

"I wish that I could offer the proper words in which to comfort you, Sister. But even I cannot find the means in which I might find any consolation. For there is nothing which can grant me the slightest comfort to mask the sorrow which I so deeply share with you."

Finally, he pulled her tightly against his chest as the siblings embraced one another where they stood.

"You have always been the one to grant me comfort in my hour in need, and for once, I would like to do the same for you. But

I fear that I simply don't know how," he said as he wrapped his armed further around her shoulders.

"This is enough..." she replied, taking a deep sigh of relief as she listened to the tender beats of his heart against her ear.

Both Estrith and her brother stood together, watching the sun slowly drift further onto the river. It was a rare moment to catch such a glimpse of its elusive beauty, but for once the sun had displayed the elegance of its vibrant colors against the sky and waters beneath it. The city then took its radiance upon itself, basking in the grasp of its rays.

She had hardly taken the time to embrace the grandeur which their kingdom beheld, choosing instead to spend her days within the palace, or sneaking throughout the city's walls. But now, as she remained, she was reminded once again of how much she had taken for granted. For what once stood as the pinnacle of perpetual ire within her life, it now stood as nothing against the misery which had come to take its place.

So much had happened in so little a time, and she was forced to face the realization that life would never again be the same. And not only for her, but for those who remained at her side as well.

"Qereth told me everything," she said. "I must come to terms with the death of my father alone, yet both of you must contend with the horrors of so much more."

She finally mustered the courage enough to look into her brother's eyes, taking notice of the redness which had engulfed them.

"I'm so sorry..." It had been the same words which she offered to Qereth as well, but it was all that she had enough to give. Beowyn remained silent, even as he listened to her speak, but she was glad for that. For even in his silence, he embraced her still.

And as she remained within his embrace, she suddenly took notice of several ships appearing against the horizon. Slowly, she pulled herself away, leaning her focus instead upon river beyond the way. Beowyn soon took notice of her movements and looked to find the target of her eye.

"Who is that?" she asked as she could feel brother's grasp loosen from her arms.

"I— I do not know," he replied.

The ships appeared from the south, bearing with them the insignia of Mistelfeld upon their flags. And as Beowyn made his way toward the docks, his sister followed closely behind. The two of them looked to one another with shock in their eyes and the men of Faermire's ranks scrambled to prepare for their ally's arrival.

Sgell had already made his way to the landing and greeted the siblings with a humble bow.

"What's going on?" Beowyn asked.

"I cannot say, my Lord. Only that our newest ally approaches as their queen stands among them."

"The queen?" Estrith asked.

"Yes, my Lady. It is Gwenora."

Beowyn had heard mention of the queen's name in their discourse with Helgisson days before the battle. But now, at last, he would get to meet the woman who, by the hand of troops, saved their lives upon the field that day. When all hope had nearly been extinguished, the welcome sight of their newest ally renewed their strength and resolve against their overwhelming odds once more.

And as the ornately curled head of their ships approached, he could see the elderly woman standing at the starboard side. Her eyes peered over the city as she remained wrapped within the comfort of her cloak. But upon taking notice of Beowyn and his sister, a smile suddenly emerged upon her face.

And as they finally landed at Elsterheim's shore, she gently took her servant's hand as he escorted her down the ramp. She was careful with her steps but carried herself with such confidence that the prince was taken slightly aback by the nature of her rather petite stature.

Though, as she met them, the prince and Estrith both bowed their heads to greet the queen. Beowyn, however, remained perplexed by the loving gaze in her eyes as she looked to him first and then to his sister.

"Lady," he said. Estrith then repeated the word as she too greeted the queen with due respect. But as his sister spoke, Gwenora couldn't help but keep her eyes from leaving her sight, making Estrith visibly confused by the encounter. But the queen finally caught herself in that moment and returned to greeting at hand.

"Please, forgive the intrusion, but when I received word of Ludica's death, I made haste in hopes that I might pay my respects."

Both siblings lowered their heads at the reminder of his passing, but the prince continued.

"We are honored by your presence, Lady Gwenora," he said.

"As I am by yours, Lord Beowyn... Lady Estrith... My, how you bear your father's resemblance," she said as she looked upon the prince, then back again toward his sister. "And you, your mother..."

The queen lifted her hand as though she sought to touch Estrith's face, but quickly stopped herself and returned her hand beneath the safety of her cloak.

"You knew our mother?" Estrith asked.

"Oh, yes," Gwenora replied as her eyes began to fill with tears. "She was very dear to me..."

"Would— would you perhaps tell me of her sometime?"

Their father never spoke of her to them. So, his sister had suddenly found herself intrigued by the prospect of the queen's professed acquaintance and let slip a glimmer of hope within her eyes.

"I should like that very much," Gwenora replied. "But first, let us retire to a place where an old woman might warm her ailing bones."

"Yes, of course," Beowyn gestured toward the palace and Sgell was quick to lead them on. She happily accepted the offer and rested her hand over her aid's provisioned arm.

"Thank you, Aldred," she said, and the man gently led her down the steps.

After they escorted her into the castle, the queen eased herself into her chair, sighing with relief as she rubbed both hands over her tender knees.

"Forgive the informality, but a person of my age can no longer tolerate a journey as I had before."

"There is nothing to forgive, Lady," Beowyn replied as he remained hesitant to sit upon his father's throne. Choosing instead, to remain standing beside it.

Estrith also chose to join in Gwenora's company as she found her place among the other seats opposite the queen. And for once, since his sister learned of their father's death, she almost seemed to have forgotten her grief as she remained captivated by Gwenora's presence.

"How is your brother? The young one. Siged, I believe? I was sorry to hear of his injuries."

"He has yet to fully wake, but his wounds are healing," Estrith answered.

"Good, good..." she replied with a smile. "I shall have to introduce myself to the boy when he is well. Which I am certain won't be long." She then passed a reassuring wink on to Estrith before she continued. "But onto other matters—"

"I should thank you, Lady," Beowyn interjected. "For the reinforcements you provided us... Without them, I fear that we may not have returned from battle that day." Beowyn looked at Gwenora as she brushed her hand through the air.

"If it weren't for your father, then fates far worse would lay in wait for us all."

"And what of the armies of Abensloh?" he asked.

"Ceolfrid has abandoned his campaign against my kingdom. For now, at least... He took a great risk in trusting your uncle, but it only contributed to our benefit in the end. With his armies divided and the giant gone from his side, he was forced to withhold his attack on Helmfirth. My men eventually spotted his retreat back toward the North, through the Dolam pass.

But with all thanks to your father, he sent me a letter warning me of certain traitors within our midst and laid out Ceolfrid's plan to lure my army away from the city. — Tell me, how did he come by his findings?"

"It was the leader of Graefeld. Helgisson is his name," the prince replied.

"Helgisson..." she narrowed her eyes as she thought upon the name. "Yes, I knew his father." She then chuckled as she began to recollect the connections within her own mind. "No matter. Carry on."

"He was in league with our uncle but betrayed him for an alliance with my father instead. Once he received word of Sidonis' plan, he brought them to us here, and that is when my father relayed it to you."

"Then it seems that I also owe a debt of gratitude to the barbarian as well. I shall also have to pay him a visit upon my return. Does he live?"

"He does, Lady," he replied.

"Very well." Gwenora continued to speak amongst the siblings as they mostly listened to her. She carried on with her recollections of the past and of their kingdom. But before long, Sgell had appeared before the group relaying the news that the hour of the king's funeral had finally come.

Suddenly the hall fell silent as each of them was faced with the reality of what was before them. But the queen was quick to interject on their behalf.

"Well, we mustn't keep your father waiting then," Gwenora added as she offered the siblings a reassuring smile. "Estrith, will you lend your hand to an old woman in need?"

"Yes, of course," she replied, making her way swiftly to the queen's side. Beowyn could see that Gwenora was quick to tend to Estrith's growing sadness and he was glad for that. And perhaps his sister could finally find her consolation in the woman's tender embrace. Offering Estrith something which no one else could give.

But as the two women lingered behind, Beowyn carried himself on toward the path which would lead him to face his father one last time.

The hall of kings had been filled to the brim with people who had arrived from throughout the realm. All, from Ludica's advisers and elders of the lands, to the lowest of classes had come to pay their respects to the man who had ruled them well. Gwenora watched as those who were present, looked to the king with a genuine sadness in their eyes and listened as the priests chanted in the language of old.

And though she too was grieved by the man's death, she couldn't help but envy the state of reverence which his subjects presented him with. For it was the greatest of offerings that a people could grant their ruler, she thought. To be so loved by one's own people is a rarity indeed. She then wondered if the same would be thought of her also upon her own passing, and if her own subjects would honor her as the people of Faermire honored their king now. How many would come to pay their respects for her?

But as she stood among them, she could suddenly feel the grip of Estrith's hands tightening around her arm. The poor girl was certain to have never known such a loss in her life, and sadly, there would only be more to come. Though still, Gwenora cherished the moment despite the circumstances. For never had she thought that she would finally be granted the opportunity to see her grandchildren. Let alone, be held so tightly as she did now. And she would remain for as long as her beloved would allow her to. If only so that she might be held as tightly as Estrith did once more.

But as they waited, the large gathering remained within the great hall itself and parted for the priests who made their way toward the king. Then finally, they all moved to unveil the king whose body lay beneath a decorative blue shroud which had been stitched with threads of gold. Below it, Ludica had been dressed in his armor which had been polished, reflecting the soft light of the torches against its sheen. And over his face, lay a mask made of gold. It matched the contours of his own resemblance and it had been carved with a delicate inlay that displayed the illustrated feats of his reign. The whole of his body had been covered so that none of his flesh could been seen. And all that lay before them was the enduring reminder of the man who once was.

In all its majesty, it was truly a sight to behold for the aging queen and she watched as Beowyn, approached his father, wielding the king's sword tenderly within his hands. The prince struggled to withhold his tears and gently placed the weapon between Ludica's hands as they rested upon his stomach. Then, after he whispered words known only to his father, Beowyn slowly left the king's side and returned to his place with those who mourned with him.

Finally, a large set of doors behind the king's body were pulled apart, revealing the ornate sarcophagus in which Ludica would forever reside. But as Gwenora looked within the room, she suddenly took notice of another coffin which lay beside it. And atop the stone which sealed the body within, rested the figure of her own daughter carved upon it. The glass dome overhead gave way to the gentle beams of light which rested over top the sepulcher and her beloved Emelyn lay peacefully beneath the sun's tender embrace.

Her knees grew weak, and the queen's lips began to quiver as tears began to run swiftly down her cheeks. For it was the first that she'd seen of her daughter after so many years. And at last, she had found favor enough in the unknown god, to be granted one last look upon the one whom she cherished most of all. But much to her dismay, Gwenora could no longer contain the sorrow and joy which overwhelmed her in that moment, and she gripped her own hands tighter against Estrith's. The young princess then leaned her head against the queen's and the two embraced each other as Ludica's body was lowered down beside his wife.

The ceremony continued, and the seal which carried the likeness of Ludica's body was carefully placed over his tomb, bringing it all to a lasting conclusion. But Gwenora could not keep her eyes from leaving the place on which her daughter rested. And as the people eventually began to filter out of the hall, the old woman slowly drew herself past the doors, into the room, and laid her hands over the likeness of her daughter's face.

She smiled, and gingerly caressed the woman's head as the stone was made wet by the tears which fell from her aged cheeks.

"Oh, Emelyn. . ." she uttered. "My sweet, my beautiful girl. How I have I missed you so. . ." Gwenora's hands began to tremble and at last, she could no longer contain herself at the sight of her daughter as she lay herself against the cold stone, sobbing aloud. And while she stood alone against her daughter's coffin, the queen then looked toward the seal which bore Ludica's face, and she thanked him for the love which he offered her daughter.

Their love was brief, but it stood the test of time. And finally, her daughter would no longer need to rest alone. She thanked him once more, then placed a tender kiss over Emelyn's face before she finally turned to leave the room. But as turned, there stood the princess with tears that equally trickled from her eyes.

"Tell me, Lady. How is it that you know my mother?" Estrith asked.

Gwenora then approached the young woman and as she gently laid her hand upon Estrith's face. And she replied with a tender smile.

"She was my daughter." Her words confirmed the realization in the young woman's eyes and the two embraced one another as they remained within the king's hall, crying yet comforting each other in their moment of greatest need.

# CHAPTER 22

ESTRITH LEFT YOUNG SIGED'S SIDE to prepare for Beowyn's coronation as the new king of Faermire. In the early morning hours, all was quiet in the city and within the palace. The cold winter air was a fresh reminder of the new dawn and what that would mean for their future. Beowyn had grown quiet in the recent days, and she worried for her brother. Whether it was for the loss of their father or the impending ceremony to come, it didn't matter. For in the end, all that remained was the struggle which she had seen within his eyes and all she could think to do was to be there for him in his solitude.

She walked through the corridor overlooking the courtyard below and found Beowyn standing in the center of it as Gwenora spoke quietly to him in the midst. But taking notice of them, she quietly tucked herself behind the pillar which formed a corner of the square. And unsure if they had seen her, she waited, feeling suddenly as though she had interrupted something important just by her presence alone.

Her brother remained quiet throughout most of their conversation, but their words were too quiet for her to make out anything substantial of the subject at hand. And after a little while longer, she could see the queen utter her last remarks as she then placed her hand gently over Beowyn's cheek before turning to leave his presence. But even as Gwenora left, his head remained low as he stood alone in the courtyard once more.

Taking her cue, Estrith then left her place of hiding to greet him down below. Upon noticing her, however, Beowyn's disposition suddenly shifted, and he smiled as she approached him.

"Good morning, Brother," she said.

"Sister," he replied.

"I saw you talking with Lady Gwenora and did not wish to interrupt. Is everything alright?" She was hoping to perhaps get his insight on their conversation just moments before, but to no avail.

"It is," he simply said.

"Very well then. How are you feeling?"

"Considering that I am to be crowned king today, I suppose that I should say that I am well."

"But you are not."

"I will be in time, I'm sure. Though since you are here, there is something I've been meaning to discuss with you. Once I am crowned, I should like to appoint you as an adviser to the throne."

"Me?"

"Do not tell me this surprises you, Sister," he said with a slight grin. "You have always been the voice of reason to me, the only problem was that I have failed to heed your counsel."

"That much is certain. . ." she replied while nodding her head.

"Indeed," he chuckled. The others may not approve of it, but I am their king. And they will come to accept it in time. I cannot do this without you, Estrith. And besides, you'll no longer have need to hide away in the shadows to learn of what transpires within these walls. As you've said it yourself, half the men around here spend more time wetting their cocks than making themselves of any real use to the throne."

Estrith laughed as she recounted his words and tears began to fill her eyes. Never would she have thought that such a thing would be possible for her. But by way of her own brother, she could see at last that there was hope for her future and she hugged him.

The two remained for a time and Beowyn eventually recused himself to prepare for the task at hand. Meanwhile, Estrith lingered within the courtyard as she thought on the prospect of it all and she couldn't help but smile as she did.

But eventually, she found herself wandering throughout the palace until she came to a place that offered her solitude. And as the hour drew near, she watched from a distance as people had begun to filter into the great hall. They mingled with one another as they greeted those who arrived shortly after and soon, a great multitude had gathered for procession. But as she watched, she suddenly heard a voice come from behind.

"I wondered where I might find you."

She then turned to see Qereth smiling at her by the steps which led him to where she stood. Estrith was elated at the sight of the man before her, and she embraced him deeply when he approached.

"I have missed you," she said as she leaned her head against his chest. Her words led him to grip her tighter within his arms and he rested his head against her own.

"I would've come sooner, but my duties have required much from me as of late."

"I understand. I'm just glad that you are here now... with me..."

Estrith turned to survey the court once more and Qereth soon followed her gaze.

"I can imagine how your brother must be feeling at present. I felt the same as I took my own father's place."

"And now?" Estrith asked.

"Now..." Qereth sighed as he pondered the question. "Now the weight still bears over me, but I can breathe just a little bit more.

"At first, I thought to abdicate my place to another, but as I looked at my sisters and at my mother, I soon realized how much more was required of me. As both a leader and as a man, I had to choose then, how I should live out the rest of my life.

"But at last, I'm glad that I chose this path. Just as I'm sure that Beowyn will feel the same in time. But until then, he is blessed to have you at his side..."

As he looked down at her, the bells began to toll in the distance, announcing to the city that the time had finally come. Estrith smiled up at him once more and turned toward the steps, but he lifted her hand and tenderly gripped it within his own.

"The future for us all remains uncertain. But despite wherever my duties shall take me, Estrith, you will never be far from my heart. And if you'll allow it, then I would like to finish what we started."

He suddenly looked at her in that moment the same as he did that night while they sat together by Siged's bed. It was that same longing in his eyes that he held for her then. And she was reminded all at once of the longing she equally felt for him.

And as she lifted her head up to meet his gaze, he lowered himself down and gently kissed her on her lips. She then placed her hands over his chest and drew herself further into his embrace as he cradled her head against the safety of his palm. And as they soon pulled themselves away, he kissed her once more on the hand before the two walked together toward the court.

The court was filled to the brim much like the hall had been on the day of his father's funeral. A knotted pit churned within his gut, and he struggled to keep his eyes from wandering to those who watched him. The formal tunic which Sgell had laid out for him began to tighten around his chest and the cloak around his shoulders felt heavier than ever before.

As Beowyn made his way down the aisle, he wanted nothing more than for it all to be over with. But the moment seemed to drag along as though an anchor had been tied to it, prolonging every bit of its agonizing existence.

The crowds watched him as he ascended the steps, but there before him remained the one thing which he feared most of all. The throne was the same as it had always been, but it presented itself as something else entirely on this day. It was for him, the seat which carried the weight of the world and the call of his father's words so many times before.

But the ceremony continued, and the priest approached him, bearing the crown within his hands. And before he knew it, the man gently placed the embodiment of his new power onto his head. Then, after several words and a blessing on behalf of the gods, the king of Faermire was announced before his subjects.

He hesitated to turn but relented at last and lowered himself onto the throne, overlooking the people before him. He took notice first of his sister, who stood at the front with a smile upon her face. And on either side of her was the queen of Mistelfeld and his friend, Qereth. Both carrying an equal look of approval within their expression.

But then came the call which echoed throughout the court.

"All hail the king!" A man shouted and the words were repeated by those who were present.

Beowyn watched as the gathering then bowed in unison toward his place upon the throne and all at once, his fate had been sealed.

After its conclusion, the day was lost in a haze to the new king. But he found comfort in the presence of those most dear to him. Many had come to offer their respects to Beowyn as he obliged their company, but at long last, the day would finally come to an end.

And as time had carried on, the city eventually resumed its customary routines, giving way to a temporary respite for the king. Gwenora eventually offered her farewells to the leaders of Faermire and more notably, to his sister. He watched as the two women held each other in a loving embrace before the queen finally departed over the river.

Qereth also bid the king well, and he hugged his closest friend before returning to his land as the newest elder of Caelfall. Then at last, there remained Estrith who offered him a reassuring smile before she returned to her place at Siged's side.

And as all had returned to their roles and to their lives, Beowyn was finally left alone to breathe a steady sigh of relief. The sun had nearly begun its descent upon the horizon, and he took the moment to bask in its glory.

So, he ascended the steps of the wall to overlook the vast expanse of the land before him and rested in the silence which surrounded him.

But there, in the corner of his eye, he caught a glimpse of something in the distance. He turned to focus his gaze and took notice of a figure which stood against the horizon. And there atop the ridge was a man who rested upon his horse. The figure remained for a time and watched as Beowyn equally returned his gaze.

But just as he appeared in the distance, the man vanished once more. Disappearing over the ridge and into the land of Valenmur.

# ABOUT THE AUTHOR

Tabitha Min has always found that the stories people tell, whether they be written or spoken, carry with them a certain quality and magic that can never be undone.

Those who choose to immerse themselves in such worlds can be captivated by its characters and be driven by the adventure that lies beyond.

Thus, it had always been her hope to one day bring such a story to the world. And that perhaps, you the reader, might find it worthy enough to turn the next page.

However, the story is far from over. So, to find out more about this series, visit her website at www.tabithamin.com.

# ACKNOWLEDGEMENTS

When that final sentence marks the end of a book, it's still far from being complete. The next stage comes into play and it's daunting, to say the least. But this book wouldn't exist without the help of those who were hard at work behind the scenes. Many thanks to Marnie MacRae, Rodrigo (aka khadarsensei), and Eve Hard for all that you've done. And to Jesse, Louise, and Jack, your input has been invaluable. Also, my gratitude goes to "Bob" Hunt for all your support and for keeping me grounded whenever I start to wander.

Thanks for reading! Please add a short review on Amazon and let me know what you thought of the story!

You can stay up to date on all of the latest news regarding The Siege of Aercorath series by signing up for the newsletter on my website at www.tabithamin.com. From time to time, I will offer special perks and deals for those who opt-in.

You can also find me on Instagram as AuthorTabithaMin